Marshall

The Rural Economy of Glocestershire

Including Its Dairy Together with the Dairy Management of North Wiltshire; and

the Management of Orchards and Fruit Liquor, in Herefordshire. By Mr. Marshall.

In Two Volumes. Vol. 1. 2. Vol. 1

Marshall

The Rural Economy of Glocestershire
Including Its Dairy Together with the Dairy Management of North Wiltshire; and the Management of Orchards and Fruit Liquor, in Herefordshire. By Mr. Marshall. In Two Volumes. Vol. 1. 2. Vol. 1

ISBN/EAN: 9783741182419

Manufactured in Europe, USA, Canada, Australia, Japa

Cover: Foto ©Andreas Hilbeck / pixelio.de

Manufactured and distributed by brebook publishing software (www.brebook.com)

Marshall

The Rural Economy of Glocestershire

THE

RURAL ECONOMY

OF

GLOCESTERSHIRE.

VOL I.

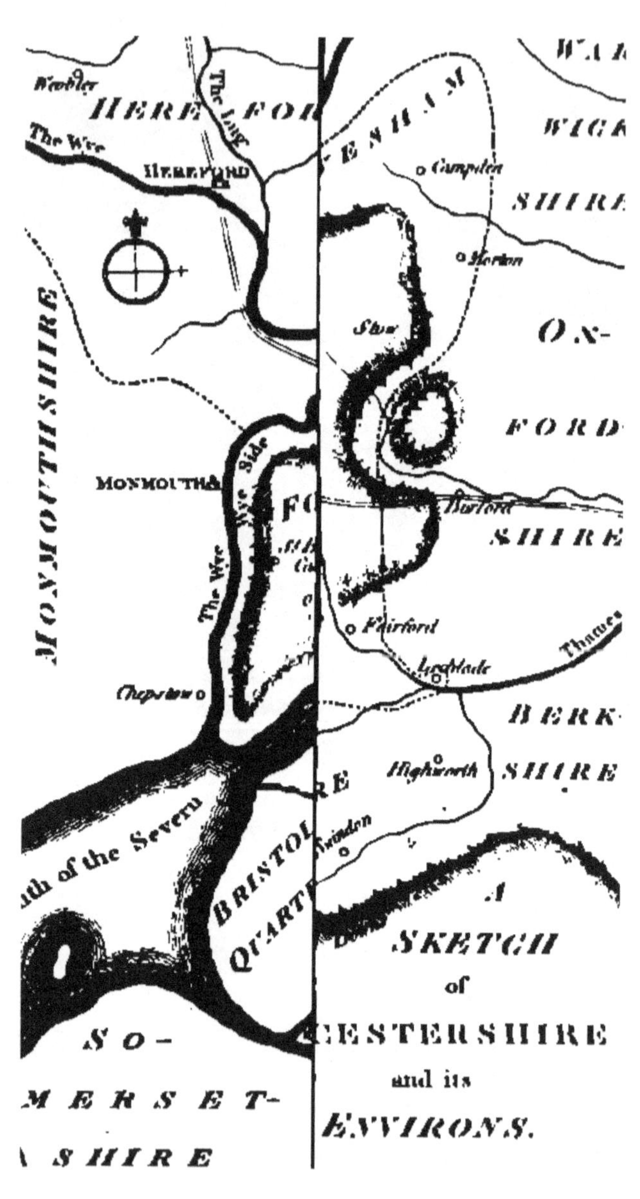

Newbler
HERE FOR
The Wye
The Lug
HEREFORD
ENHAM
Campden
WICK
WAR
SHIRE
Horton
Stow
OX-
MONMOUTHSHIRE
FORD
Wye Side
MONMOUTH
The Wye
FO
Burford
SHIRE
Fairford
Chepstow
Thames
Lechlade
BERK
SHIRE
RE
Highworth
th of the Severn
BRISTOL
Swindon
QUART
A
SKETCH
of
CESTERSHIRE
SO-
and its
MERSET-
ENVIRONS.
SHIRE

THE
RURAL ECONOMY
OF
GLOCESTERSHIRE;

INCLUDING ITS

D A I R Y:

TOGETHER WITH THE

DAIRY MANAGEMENT

OF

NORTH WILTSHIRE;

AND THE

M A N A G E M E N T

OF

ORCHARDS and FRUIT LIQUOR,

IN

HEREFORDSHIRE.

———

By Mr. MARSHALL.

———

IN TWO VOLUMES.
VOL. I.

———

GLOCESTER:
PRINTED BY R. RAIKES,
FOR G. NICOL, PALL-MALL, LONDON.
M. DCC. LXXXIX.

ADVERTISEMENT.

BY MY PRACTICE in SURREY, I became acquainted with the AGRICULTURE of the *southern* counties. By my residence in NORFOLK, that of the *eastern* quarter of the kingdom was rendered familiar. By passing in YORKSHIRE the early part of life, by visiting it repeatedly, and finally reviewing it analytically, that of the *northern* quarter became strongly impressed on my mind. But, when I left Yorkshire, in 1783 *, I was as much unacquainted with the practice of the *western* counties, as if I had been a stranger to the general subject.

Having, however, remarked, in the widely differing practices of the three distant

* See advertisement to RURAL ECON. of YORKSHIRE.

a 3

diſtant countries I had ſeen, the various means of obtaining the ſame objeƈt,
and the varying methods of conduƈting
the ſame operation, I was deſirous to
become acquainted with the praƈtice
of the fourth quarter.

I had other motives to it than curio-
ſity. For though I had yet no hope of
executing my plan on the broad baſis I
have ſince entered upon, I nevertheleſs
had my reaſons for wiſhing to be poſſeſſed of a general knowledge of the
Rural Economy of the kingdom at
large. Beſide, in Norfolk, I had made
an eſſay in the art of manufaƈturing
CHEESE, and was deſirous to become
maſter of it. The management of
FRUIT LIQUOR, too, was a ſubjeƈt,
which, being no where elſe to be ſtu-
died, was of courſe a farther induce-
ment to my viſiting the weſtern quarter.

GLOCESTERSHIRE I found to be the
only individual county, which could
furniſh me with the requiſite information. Therefore, in the wane of the
ſummer

fummer of 1783, I came into this county; and, agreeably to the plan originally propofed *, took up my refidence in a farm houfe;—near the center of the vale of Glocefter: where, and in the vale of Berkeley I remained, until I had exceeded my expectation, with refpect to the manufacturing of cheefe; and had obtained a general idea of the rural affairs of the diftrict, adequate to the purpofe I then had in view.

But my regifter, in this cafe, as in that of Yorkfhire, was not fufficiently finifhed, for public infpection. Nor was it, indeed, fufficiently full to bear the title I wifhed to give it. My obfervations had been confined to one feafon of the year : whereas to gain a complete knowledge of the rural economy of an extent of country, it is proper that its feveral departments fhould pafs under the eye in every feafon.

a 4   Therefore,

* See RURAL ECON. of NORFOLK. Addrefs, &c.

Therefore, in the beginning of April laſt, immediately on the publication of the RURAL ECONOMY OF YORKSHIRE, I returned, without loſs of time, into GLOCESTERSHIRE: where and in its neighbouring diſtricts, I have remained a further time of ſomewhat more than twelve months: a period which has been appropriated, ſolely, to the work which I am now offering to the public.

IN A PREFATORY ADDRESS, affixed to the RURAL ECONOMY OF NORFOLK, I endeavoured to explain the PLAN OF THE WORK I was then entering upon; and hoped that I had left no ground for miſapprehenſion. Indeed, it appeared, to my own mind, ſo ſimple and ſelfevident, as not to be eaſily miſunderſtood.

Nevertheleſs, from a general OBJEC-TION which, I underſtand has been made againſt it, there is ſome reaſon to ſuſpect that I have fallen ſhort in my explanation.

explanation. The objection held out is
—" that the fame fubjects are treated
of in YORKSHIRE as in NORFOLK."

To anfwer this as an *objection* is impoffible : for had it been put—" that
nearly the fame fubjects are treated of
in Yorkfhire as in Norfolk,"—the pofition would have been fully granted :
as being perfectly confonant with the
principle on which the plan is raifed.
It is indeed, one of the beft evidences
that can be offered in its favor : inas-
much as it fhows the PLAN OF THE
REGISTER to be fuch, as, in its full
extent, to admit under the feveral
heads, every idea relative to the fubject :
for, fimilar as the heads really are, in
the two fpecimens already given, I
found not, in either diftrict, a fact belonging to the whole circle of rural affairs which would not have fallen aptly
under them.

The OBJECTS and OPERATIONS of
HUSBANDRY, are, in *number* and *fpecies*,
the

the *same*, or *nearly the same*, in every quarter of the kingdom. But the methods of obtaining the objects, and of performing the operations, are infinitely various. To catch the VARIATIONS, whenever they are sufficiently marked, whether with excellency or defect, is one of the main objects of the part of the plan I am now executing. Another, to give practical descriptions of such PARTICULAR OBJECTS and OPERATIONS, as are confined to particular districts. And a third, to register the EXCELLENCIES and DEFECTS, in the practice of each district, relative to every other department of RURAL ECONOMY.

By thus adducing in each station (were it possible) every valuable idea it is possessed of on these subjects; and by arranging those of different stations in registers formed on the same, or nearly the same plan; the different modes of conducting any particular branch of management may be referred to, and

the

the feveral practices be compared. Confequently, in the completion of the
plan, may be feen the various practices
of the kingdom, relating to any individual fubject.

An art fo extenfive, and in many
things fo abftrufe, as that of AGRI-
CULTURE, muft remain in a ftate of
great imperfection, until the leading
facts belonging to it, which are already
known, be reduced to a ftate of refe-
rence. To raife fchemes of IMPROVE-
MENT, public or private, before this be
effected, muft be an act of improvi-
dence fimilar to that of fetting about
the ftudy of chemiftry, or any other
branch of philofophy, by experiment,
without having previoufly become acquainted with the facts that are already
afcertained. A man, thus employed,
might fpend a lifetime of ingenuity,
without bringing to light a fingle fact,
which was not intimately known before he began.

Such

Such is the LEADING PRINCIPLE, the MAIN OBJECT, the SUBSTANCE of the plan. But this, as other SUPERSTRUCTURES, requires a GROUNDWORK.—— Rural economics are founded in NATURE: much of the art depends upon climature, situation, soil, and a variety of natural circumstances. Hence, not only a GEOGRAPHICAL DESCRIPTION, of the district under survey, becomes requisite; but the THREE KINGDOMS OF NATURE, so far as they are intimately connected with the subject, require to be examined and described, with SCIENTIFIC ACCURACY.

Nor are these the only requisites. The work, before it be fit to meet the public eye, requires a degree of finish. It is necessary that every part should be conspicuous. The excellencies, not being sufficiently evident, perhaps, to common observation, may require to be *relieved*; and the defects to be *brought out*, and shown in their naked deformity;

mity; that their impreffions on the mind may be the ftronger and more lafting.

Nor does the labour end here. In carrying on a work of this nature, the reflection will be voluntarily employed, in drawing PRACTICAL INFERENCES; and in FILLING UP DEFICIENCIES; not altogether, perhaps, with felfevident or theoretic ideas, arifing out of the fub-ject in hand; but with PRACTICAL KNOWLEDGE, collected incidentally, not in any particular diftrict, but in every quarter of the kingdom, and which, being nowhere on record, might be loft to the general defign, if not laid up in this manner.*

If

---

* It may be proper to remark here, that, (through various motives) the rural economy of Yorkfhire contains a greater number of thefe FUGITIVE IDEAS, than either the Norfolk or the prefent volumes; which, neverthelefs, have their refpective fhares. They are frequently thrown into the *didactic* form; as being the moft concife, and the moft *practical*.

If the ideas thus offered by the reflection, do not appear to the judgement
fufficiently afcertained, to become evidently ufeful in promoting the general
intention of the work, they are, with
other unafcertained ideas, arifing to the
obfervation in the diftrict immediately
under furvey, either thrown out as
HINTS, and inferted with fuch marks
of *diffidence*, as cannot eafily be mifun-
derftood, for the ufe of thofe who are
in practice, and have leifure to afcertain
them; or, are ENTIRELY REJECTED.

The rural economy of Yorkfhire, if
duly examined, will be found to be executed on thefe principles. Thus,——
to fpeak in reply to the *objeFtion*, which
has given rife to thefe explanations,——
under fuch heads, whether they include
general operations, or ordinary objects
of culture, as were amply treated of in
Norfolk, DEVIATIONS only, whether
they arife from cuftom fituation or
foil, are brought forward. But, where
a crop

a crop, or an operation, not cultivated
or performed in Norfolk, arifes, it becomes a *frefh* fubject; and an additional
divifion or fubdivifion is, of courfe,
opened for its reception; and every
thing deemed ufeful, refpecting it, regiftered. Again, where a crop or an
operation common to Norfolk, is not
found in Yorkfhire, the head or com-
partment of the regifter, which received
it in the former, is, of courfe, dropped
in the later.

If, in the rural economy of Yorkfhire,
I had defcribed the dibbling of wheat,
for inftance, or the cultivation of buckweet; or, in the rural economy of Norfolk, the operation of planting potatoes
with the plow, or the cultivation of the
rape crop; or had even inftituted heads
for thefe fubjects; I fhould, indeed, have
rendered my work liable to objection.

But, becaufe I had defcribed the general management of foils and manures;
and the general operations of fowing,
weeding,

weeding, and harvesting; the cultivation of wheat and barley; and the management of cattle and sheep;——as practised in Norfolk;——— were these subjects to be passed without notice, in describing the practice of Yorkshire! Or, because a writer, on geography, has described the mountains and rivers of France, for instance, is he, in giving a description of Spain, to pass over the mountains and rivers unnoticed!

But ill founded as that objection (if it will bear the name) evidently is, the making of it implies a degree of dissatisfaction, or, if the word be applicable, a degree of disaffection toward the work.; and I am desirous to render it, were it possible, free from disapprobation.

Perhaps the objection arose in misapprehension. It may be conjectured, that my stations are unlimited, and my volumes, of course, unnumbered; especially as some insinuation of this nature

ture

ture was, I understand, tacked to the objection.

 Lest, therefore, some of my readers, whose approbation I am desirous of preserving entire, should have conceived the same idea, it becomes requisite to aprize them, that, unless I make a resurvey of the SOUTHERN COUNTIES (thereby completing the FIVE PRINCIPAL STATIONS I have been led to fix in) the rural economy of the MIDLAND COUNTIES (now preparing for the press) will close my SURVEY OF PROVINCIAL PRACTICE.

The completion of my plan extends no farther than to SEVEN STATIONS: adding, to the five MORE CENTRAL, one in the MORE WESTERN counties, of Somerset, Dorset, and Devon, and another in the MORE NORTHERN provinces; including Northumberland, and the LOWLANDS OF SCOTLAND.

At present, however, there is little probability of the survey being extended

b

to

to the two latter ſtations: and no degree of certainty of its being continued
to the ſouthern counties.

This in reply to VERBAL objections.

Under a deſire——a pardonable one
I truſt——of freeing the work, as far as
in the extenſiveneſs of its nature it is capable of being freed, from objections of
every kind; I think it prudent to take
notice, here, of ſome leſs general obſervations: made in a more liberal manner,
by a different order of men, and through
a different channel of communication,
the LITERARY JOURNALS.

But, in doing this, I muſt neceſſarily
place myſelf in a ſomewhat delicate ſituation. The flattering accounts, which
have been there given of the work (in
one inſtance flattering indeed!) may ſeem
to preclude every ſpecies of reply; as I
muſt, in making it, place an oppoſition
of ſentiment where gratitude, only, may
ſeem to have a right. But ſeeing the
very handſome manner, in which the

remarks

remarks are conveyed, I may with ſafety conclude, they riſe from a liberal ſource; and that *vindication* will not be miſtaken for *controverſy*. There are, indeed, only two which require the form of reply. One of them relating to a part of the plan of the work, the other to my own character as a public writer.*

The firſt relates to the botannical catalogues of plants given in the rural economy of Yorkſhire. But the remark, in this caſe, ariſes evidently through an omiſſion, or rather a misjudgement of my own. The objection made is, that no *proportion* of the number or quantity
which

---

* Some ſtrictures on the inſtance of the effect of whitening grounds ariſe, evidently, in miſconception: owing, probably, to a want of perſpicuity in the paſſage: no *concluſion* whatever was *intended* to be drawn.

And the *looſe bints* on curled topped potatoes, thrown together in a *note*, with (as I conceived) every mark of diffidence, which words and *printing* could give them, are not ſurely fair objects of criticiſm. *What motive* could induce ſo very able a pen to condeſcend to treat them as ſuch is to me altogether inexplicable.

b 2

which each species bears to the other
being given, the information becomes,
of course, vague and unsatisfactory.——
The two first lists were cautiously guarded in this respect, by saying that the
plants stood in them *agreeably to their
degrees of prevalency:* an explanation,
which I judged unnecessary to be affixed
to the other catalogues; from which
the observations alluded to have evidently
risen. In the present volumes, I have
been careful to guard each catalogue.

The other remark relates to river embankments. In speaking of the marshes
or fens, which now lie in an unproductive state, by the side of the river Der-
went, I have, it seems, proposed a method of draining, similar to " directions
given for the same purpose, in Anderson's essays relating to agriculture and
rural affairs, published about twelve
years ago."

I am happy to find that I have fallen
into the same train of thinking, upon
any

any occafion, with Dr. ANDERSON;
and am fingularly obliged to the ingenious writer who makes the obfervation:
not only on account of the very hand-
fome manner in which it is made; but
becaufe it gives me a fair opportunity of
explaining, ftill farther, the execution
of my plan.

The part, which I have hitherto been
executing, is drawn from PROVINCIAL
PRACTICE, and my OWN EXPERIENCE:
Or, in other words, is an accumulation
of facts arifing in NATURE, and PRAC-
TICE, or, of reflections aptly refulting
from thefe facts.

Excepting one inftance, that of IN-
CLOSURES, I cannot call to my mind
one deviation from this principle.* But
that appeared to me a fubject of fo much
importance, yet fo little underftood,
that, feeing the fairnefs of the opportunity, and the materials I was in poffeffion

---

* Unlefs the article ORCHARDS in thefe volumes may be
deemed fuch.

seffion of, it would have been wrong to have let flip, unneceffarily, one Seffion of Parliament, before I laid the materials I was poffeffed of, in the beft manner I was able, before the public.

In the inftance under reply, there is ample proof of the principle, on which the work is conducted. I refer, from the paffage itfelf, to an inftance, in which the moft material part of the practice I recommend is executed, on a large fcale, by raifing the water with draining engines, or marfh mills*. In the fame volume, only a few pages from the paffage, I give another inftance, on a fmaller fcale, in which the water is got rid of, by finking a counter ditch, only, without the help either of mill or floodgate †. And I knew, at the fame time, that the Severn is embanked, and its meadows kept dry, by floodgates, only: and moreover knew that, in this cafe, the

* See NORF: ECON: min: 118.
† See YORK: ECON: vol. i. p. 248.

the banks being placed at fome diftance from the river, their requifite height for the purpofe intended, is rendered inconfiderable ‡: and farther, that, between the Severn and its banks, ozier beds are frequent; and fhoot, in general, with uncommon luxuriance*. Poffeffed of thefe, and numerous other facts belonging to the fubject, I had no need of books to affift me in drawing the *fketch*, which is the fubject of this reply; and which I drew in Yorkfhire, becaufe I knew no inftance in the other diftricts I had · vifited, in which the practice was fo applicable, or where the art of draining in difficult cafes is lefs underftood.

Groundlefs, however, as the remark replied to moft affuredly is, I repeat my acknowledgements to the writer who brought it forward. Other readers,

equally

‡ See this volume p. 12. note.

* See PLANTING and ORN: GARD : (publifhed in 1785) P. 547.

equally unacquainted, of courfe with the fources of my information, may have feen the paffage alluded to in the fame point of view. Befide, it affords me an opportunity, which otherwife I might not have had, of faying ftill farther, that, from the commencement of the minutes of agriculture, in 1774, to the prefent time, I have read nothing on the fubject of rural affairs ; excepting fome few modern publications, which have fallen cafually under my eye* ; and excepting that, in the year 1780, I fpent fome weeks, or months, in the reading room of the Britifh Mufeum, looking over and forming a catalogue of books, formerly written on the fubject.

This

---

* And, among the reft, a book written by Mr. Anderfon ; but whether it contained obfervations on river embankments, I have not the fmalleft recollection. At the time I read it, river embankment was a fubject totally uninterefting to me ; and, fuppofing that I attended to the article, it is not probable, that any trace of it fhould remain on the mind ten or twelve years.

This difregard of modern books has not, of late years at leaft, rifen altogether through *neglect*. I have *defignedly* refrained from them; *left* I might catch ideas, imperceptibly,—and, by interweaving thofe of BOOKS with thofe of PROVINCIAL PRACTICE, blend the two parts of the general work, which I wifh to keep perfectly diftinct. And I have refrained more particularly from modern books, which have gained a degree of popularity; left I fhould be led, imperceptibly, into controverfies, public or *private*, which might fwerve me from my main defign.

The part of the plan which I have, hitherto, been executing has, in itfelf, been fufficient to engage every hour of my attention. I have purpofely fhut my eyes to every object not immediately connected with it; under a conviction, that the magnitude of the fubject is more than fufficient for any man's attention; and, of courfe, that whatever part of it

c   fhould

should be applied to other objects would be lost to the main pursuit.

My sources of information are ample; almost without limitation. The two wide fields of NATURE and SCIENCE, so far as they are connected with the subject under investigation; the ESTABLISHED PRACTICE of the KINGDOM at large, with respect to the three grand branches of RURAL ECONOMICS; the individual practice, and sometimes the individual opinion, of the SUPERIOR CLASS of PROFESSIONAL MEN; together with interesting incidents arising in my OWN PRACTICE, have, hitherto, been the objects of my attention.

C O N.

CONTENTS

TO THE

FIRST VOLUME.

	Page
THE SEVERN and its vale defcribed -	1
GLOCESTERSHIRE divided into diftricts -	6
THE VALES of GLOCESTER and EVESHAM diftinguifhed - - -	8

THE VALE OF GLOCESTER defcribed with refpect to its

Outline -	10	Subftrata -	13
Extent -	10	Roads - -	14
Climature -	10	Townfhips -	15
Surface -	11	Inclofures -	16
River, &c. -	12	Produce -	18
Soil -	13		

The RURAL ECONOMY of the VALE OF GLOCESTER regiftered, under

1. Eftates and Tenures - - -	19
2. Management of Eftates - -	20
3. Farm Buildings - -	30
4. Field Fences - -	40
5. Hedgrow Timber - -	42
6. Woodlands - - -	44
7. Planting - - -	46
8. Farms - - -	48
9. Farmers - -	50
10. Workmen	

		Page
10.	Workmen	51
11.	Beasts of Labour	54
12.	Implements	57
13.	Seasons	59
14.	General Management of Farms	62
15.	Course of Husbandry	64
16.	Soils and Tillage	66
17.	Manures	86
18.	Seed Process	90
19.	Corn Weeds	91
20.	Harvesting	101
21.	Farm Yard Management	103
22.	Markets	105
23.	Wheat	112
24.	Barley	132
25.	Oats	136
26.	Pulse	140
27.	Cultivated Grasses	154
28.	Natural Grasses	170
29.	Horses	207
30.	Sheep	208
31.	Cattle	211
	Cows	215
	Rearing cattle	234
	Fatting cattle	239
32.	Dairy management	262
33.	Swine	316
	List of Rates	319
	Provincialisms	

THE

THE

RURAL ECONOMY

OF

GLOCESTERSHIRE, &c.

COUNTRIES are characterized by rivers. Mountains are cleft to give vent to their various fources. Or we may fay, and perhaps more philofophically,---rivers receive their general character from countries. In whatever light we view them, it is fufficiently evident that, in moft inftances, they are ftrongly characteriftic of each other. The fiffures uniting form a valley; the united rills the branch of a river. The mountains bow as the fissures widen; and as the hills sink the vallies expand: at length uniting in one open vale; in whose lap the concurring branches form an accompanying river: which as it approaches the sea, widens into an estuary; whose immediate banks are marshes.

But rivers, as all nature's productions, are infinitely various. Each has its differential character.

The HUMBER (the first of British rivers) opens from the sea with an estuary disproportionately small. But its banks spread wide, in due proportion to the vastness of the vale, in which its numerous branches are collected,---and to the magnificence of the mountains and vallies, which give birth to them. The characteristic of the Humber and its accompaniments (its estuary apart) is *greatness*.

The SEVERN is marked by widely differing characters. Its estuary is singularly magnificent; forming a CHANNEL; not unfrequently, nor improperly, styled the SEVERN-SEA; whose banks, on either side, rise from the richest marshes to lofty and most picturesque mountains. Europe, I believe, does not furnish

niſh another River-entrance of equal gran-
deur.

Theſe mountain banks approach; and the
channel contracts with the clifts of Chepſtow
and Auſt; but the *eſtuary* continues; and
the country, above, opens into an extended
vale, which widens as its length increaſes;
until it receive the county of Worceſter, almoſt entirely, within its outline: then contracts, and cloſes with the hills of Shropſhire
and Staffordſhire. A vale, which in *richneſs*
and *beauty*, has no where, perhaps, its equal.

Its banks, to the Weſt, are formed by the
foreſt of Dean, Mayhill, the Malvern hills, and
the hills of Herefordſhire, and Shropſhire: to
the Eaſt, by the Stroudwater and the Cotſwold hills, and by riſing grounds on the border of Warwickſhire; cloſing with the Lickey
and the Clent hills.

By hillocks ſcattered on the area of this ex-
panſe, its entireneſs is not evident: Bredon
hill, with ſome ſmaller hillocks ſtrewed at the
point of the Cleeve hill (a promontory of the
Cotſwolds) croſs the view, and partially di-
vide the vale into three diſtricts: Worceſter-
ſhire; the vales of Gloceſterſhire; and the

 vale

vale of Evefham, which is fhared in a fingular manner between the two counties. But remove thefe hills, and the hillocks near Glocefter,---the whole forms one continued unbroken vale, which accompanies the Severn from the union of its principal branches to its conflux with the Sea.

Probably, however, not having been feen in this light, it has had no general name affigned it. The vale of Evefham lays claim to fome part of it ; but to how much, has not, I believe, ever been fettled. Were it neceffary to affign it a general name,--TEWKSBURY, which is fituated every way in its center, might well claim the honor of giving it.

The upper part of this vale, (its uppermoft extremity excepted) though abundant in *riches* is not *picturefque*. The idea of flatnefs is too predominant: its banks are comparatively tame ; and its furface, though fufficiently broken, for the ufes of RURAL ECONOMY ; is too uniform to give full effect to RURAL ORNAMENT.

Paffing downward, its more finifhed fcenery commences with the Malvern hills: from whence to the rocks of Chepftow, its area and

its

its banks form one continuous scene of pictura-
ble beauty.   A garden forty miles in extent.
A grand suite of ornamental grounds, in nature's best style.   Every part is pleasing. The
banks bold ; and happily varied; and partially
hung with wood.   The area strewed with hillocks, *fertile to the summits*, affording endless
points of view ; while the hillocks themselves
are, in their turns, the cause of infinite beauty.
The soil every where rich ; and mostly in a state
of grass.   The Severn winding with unusual
freedom.   With the Welchmountains rising
in happy distance.   These features well associ-
ated give this passage of country a preference,
in *beauty*, to every other this island is possessed
of ; and, in much probability, to every other
this planet is adorned with. There may be natural situations equal to it : but where shall we
find seasons so favourable to rural ornament
as in this island ; and, in such a climature,
cultivation so highly raised ?

Glocestershire might well be styled the seat
of picturesque beauty.   It is equally a subject
of study for the painter and the rural ornamen-
talist ; not in the outline only, but in the de-
B 3   tail :

tail: the Stroudwater hills, and the banks of the Wye, are full of fecluded beauty.

It is this lower extremity of the Severn-vale which falls within the diftrict I have chofen for my prefent STATION.   Not on account of its *piTurefque beauty*; but by reafon of its *fituation* with refpect to the other ftations I have fixed in; ---its *richnefs*; and the various *productions* it affords.   Had it not been *fingularly* charac-terized by natural ornament, I fhould not have detained the reader a moment on fo *unprofita-ble* a fubject.   But the eye muft be dim, and the heart benumbed, which can be infenfible to the rural beauty of Glocefterfhire.

The popular divifions of the COUNTY are the *Vale*,---the *Cotfwold hills*---the *Stroudwa-ter hills*---the country about Briftol---*Berkley Hundred---Wye-fide*---the *Foreft of Dean*--and *Over-Severn:* the laft a diftrict, which, though it be divided only by the river from what is properly underftood by the *Vale*, differs from it very much in foil and management; both of which partake of thofe of Herefordfhire. The Foreft of Dean a mere wafte, which calls loudly for improvement, and the Wyefide little more than the banks of the river.

Among

Among the eastern divisions we must therefore look for proper subjects of study for RURAL
INFORMATION: and we find three of them entitled to notice.   The vales of GLOCESTER
and EVESHAM, as a rich vale district, equally
abundant in grass and corn.   The COTSWOLD
HILLS, as an upland arable district.   And the
vale of BERKLEY as a grassland dairy country.

The *Stroudwater hills* partake of the Cotswolds and the vale jointly.---A lovely plot of
country: but not a proper subject of rural study ;
as being a seat of manufacture. The Southern
extremity is various in soil and surface.   The
Bristol Quarter is a fine tract of country ; but
lies too near a populous town to be studied for
general information. The *Southwolds*, a ridge
of hill which joins the Stroudwater to the
Lansdown hills,---is in soil, situation, and management, similar to the Cotswolds: the Stroudwater hills lying in a dip between them.

The vales of Glocester and Evesham
The Cotswold hills, and
The vale of Berkley ; as well as
North-Wiltshire, and
Herefordshire ; will be separately described.

B 4   THE

T H E

V A L E S

O F

GLOCESTER and EVESHAM.

THE VALE which accompanies the
Severn, through GLOCESTERSHIRE, has a natural infection, which divides it into two diftricts, very different in produce and rural management.   Thefe diftricts, in diftinction, I
fhall call the *upper* and the *lower* vale ; or the
the VALE OF GLOCESTER, and the VALE OF
BERKLEY.

The upper vale, in whole, or in part, is
fometimes fpoken of as belonging to the VALE
OF EVESHAM ;---at prefent an *imaginary* diftrict, of which no two men have the fame idea.
Some include, not only the vale of Glocefter,
but a principal part of Worcefterfhire within
its limits !   Its *natural* limits, however, are
evident ;

evident; and appear, from old maps, to have
been formerly the received boundaries.

The VALE OF EVESHAM belongs to the
AVON; as the vales of Glocester and Berkley
do to the Severn: being included between the
river and the Cotfwold hills: expanding fouth-
ward to Campden and Morton; and following
the Avon eaftward to Stratford: Evefham
being fituated near the midway between its ex-
tremities: that is, near the center of the VALE
OF AVON; at the fartheft outfkirts of the VALE
OF SEVERN.

The town of Evefham ftands in Worcefterfhire; but much of the vale lies within the
boundaries of Glocefterfhire; and, in point
of fituation, climature, furface, foil, produce,
and management, may be confidered as a continuation of the vale of Glocefter. The fouthern part of Worcefterfhire, likewife enjoys a
fimilar fituation and foil, and is fubjected to a
fimilar management. Therefore, in the rural
Economy of the VALE OF GLOCESTER we fhall
gain a general idea of that of a moft fertile and
extenfive diftrict: one of the richeft rural gardens the ifland has to boaft of.

The

THE VALE OF GLOCESTER

Is, in OUTLINE, somewhat femicircular: the Severn the chord the environing hills the arch: the towns of Glocefter, Tewkfbury, and Cheltenham forming a triangle within its area. Its EXTENT, from the foot of Matfon hill to that of Bredon hill (its *outmoft* limit to the north) is about fifteen miles: from the Severn to the foot of Dowdefwell hill, feven or eight miles. The entire diftrict, therefore, does not contain a hundred fquare miles. It may be eftimated at fifty to fixty thoufand acres.

The CLIMATURE of this diftrict, like that of the vale of Pickering, is *above* its natural latitude, (51.° 55.′) The feafons on this fide of the Severn are a week or ten days later than on the oppofite banks: owing, probably, to the fame caufe, as that which has been affigned for a fimilar effect in the vale abovementioned. The Cotfwold hills rifing high above its level, give a continual fupply of coolnefs and moifture ; while the over-fevern diftrict has no fuch mafs of mountain rifing immediately behind it. The popular idea feems to be that the difference is owing to afpect. The two, jointly,

jointly, may account for it. Diſtricts, every-where, vary as to climature: not altogether through latitude, aſpect, or elevation; but to ſome other cauſe or cauſes;---which are certainly intereſting ſubjects of inveſtigation. Much depends upon climature. A forwardneſs of ſeaſon is always deſirable. The value of land is materially influenced by the climature it lies in.

The SURFACE, an extended plane; ſwelling with gentle protuberances; and ſet with ſome hillocks of remarkable beauty. Church-Down (provincially " Choſen Hill") is, in beauty, next to Matſon's lovely hillock. But Wainlode hill, on the immediate bank of the Severn, commands the broadeſt, beſt view of the vale;---backed by its environing hills.

The common receptacle of the ſurface water of the diſtrict is the Severn: The collecting SHORES*, rivulets which croſs the vale.

The

* SHORE, This word has been cenſured by a critic whoſe remarks are entitled to attention: it is therefore proper to ſay that I do not uſe the word ſhore, as a corruption of iſſue! (Johnſon's idea) but as a word, (probably of ſome centuries ſtanding) analogous with ſewer; which, pronounced as it is written, is become a provincialiſm; while to write ſewer, and pronounce ſhore is an evident impropriety. The eſtabliſhed language has no inſtance analogous with ſuch a uſage.

The Severn being EMBANKED to confine its waters within due limits, during *minor* floods,---the rivulets are let into it by floodgates, which give vent to them at dead water ; and exclude the water of the river in times of floods *.

Near the banks of the Severn, an overflow of thefe rivulets may fometimes be irremediable ; but the area of the diftrict, in general, is placed, by natural fituation, entirely out of the reach of furface water. Neverthelefs, much of it is effentially injured by water lodging upon it, during winter and wet feafons. The rivulets are fhamefully neglected ; and the water ditches choaked for want of timely fcouring. A COMMISSION OF SHORES is evidently wanted in this diftrict, to free it from the evils of fuperfluous water ; one of the moft

ruinous

---

* SEVERN EMBANKMENT. This is not a *publick* work ; nor is it general ; the meadows being in many places ftill left open. The intention of it is merely to fecure the grafs from being filted, and the hay from being fwept away, by fummer floods. The banks being low ; not more perhaps than two to three feet high ; the winter's floods furmount them ; or, if raifed higher, the water at that feafon is, I underftand, fometimes let into the meadows by fluices opened for that purpofe ; fo that the meadows ftill receive a benefit from the floods.

ruinous enemies of hufbandry: yet, by proper management, it is, in general, the moſt eaſy to be overcome.

The SOIL of this diſtrict is moſtly a rich deep loam: fitted, by intrinſic quality, for the production of every vegetable ſuited to its ſpecific nature and the latitude it lies in.   But by a redundancy of moiſture it is chilled, weakened, and rendered much leſs productive than ſoils, which enjoy equal richneſs and equal depth, generally are.   This is in part owing to a want of ſufficient ſhores, and ſurface-drains; and in part to the nature of the---

SUBSOIL, which accords with the theory above offered with reſpect to climature: being in general ſingularly cold and full of water; eſpecially towards the center of the vale; where it appears, in many places, to be compoſed of ſtone and clay, alternately, in thin ſtrata. And here, every ſtone pit is a well of limpid water.   There are parts of the diſtrict, however, which enjoy a more genial foundation; eſpecially round the towns of Gloceſter, Tewkſbury and Eveſham: ſituations admirably well choſen.   But no wonder; they were fixed upon, or raiſed into eminence, by the clergy; who, it

is

is abundantly evident, were judges of foil and climature. The whole diftrict under notice has been ftrewed with monafteries and other religious places.

The ROADS of the vale are fhamefully kept. The Parifh roads moftly lie in their natural flat ftate, with the ditches on either fide of them full of water to the brim. The toll-roads are raifed (generally much too high) but even on the fides of thefe I have feen full ditches. It would, in principle, be equally wife to fet a fugar loaf in water by way of preferving it, as to fuffer water to ftand on the fides of roads whofe foundations are of an earthy nature. For fo long as they remain in immediate contact with water, they never can acquire the requifite degree of firmnefs. The foundation is ever a quagmire; and the fuperftructure, if not made unneceffarily ftrong, is always liable to be preffed into it. Hence the deep, ditch-like ruts which are commonly feen in roads of this defcription. The road between Glocefter, and Cheltenham (now become one of the moft public roads in the ifland) is fcarcely fit for the meaneft of their Majefties' fubjects to travel on,---AND PAY FOR; much lefs fuitable for

their

their Majesties themselves, and their amiable family, to truft their own perfons upon.

Materials are plentiful, and upon the fpot. The ftone of the fubfoil is a blue-and-white limeftone.---Lying, however, in thin ftrata, feparated by thicker feams of clay, the raif- ing of it is fomewhat expenfive, and its du- ration is fhort. But the fhortnefs of the car- riage ftands againft thefe difadvantages. Be- low Glocefter, the roads are made with " flag" copper drofs---and with the ftone of St. Vin- cent's Rock near Briftol. To forty or fifty miles of water-carriage, two or three of land carriage are not unfrequently added!

Townships. The only circumftance no- ticeable, in this place, is the unfrequency of *alehoufes* in the townfhips of the vale: a cir- cumftance which reflects much honour on the magiftracy of this county. Alehoufes are an intolerable nuifance to hufbandry. They are the nurferies of idlenefs, and every other vice. A virtuous nation could not, perhaps, be de- bauched fooner, or with more certainty, than by planting alehoufes in it: yet we fee them every where planted, as if for the purpofe of rendering this nation more vicious than it al- ready

ready is.   If a reform of the lower claſs of
people be really wiſhed for, the firſt ſtep towards it would be, to ſhut up the principal
part of the petty alehouſes which are, at preſent, authoriſed by Government to debauch
them.   Unfortunately, however, for ſo deſireable a reform, alehouſes, like lotteries, are
opened " for the good of the nation"! The
nation muſt be in a tottering ſtate, indeed,
if it require gambling and drunkenneſs, the
two main pillars of vice, to ſupport it *.

INCLOSURES.   Many of the townſhips of
this vale ſtill lie in open common field--" common meadow "---and common paſtures--pro-
vincially " Hams " which are ſtinted for cows
and other cattle.   Perhaps half the vale is un-
divided property.

In the common arable fields, property is
intermixed in a ſingular manner.   Not with a
view

---

* From what will follow it may be ſaid that a want of
alehouſes cannot prevent drunkenneſs. In *this* country it
certainly cannot. Nevertheleſs this diſtrict is a ſtriking evidence that a ſcarcity of alehouſes leſſens the vices which ſeldom fail of aſſociating themſelves with *public* drunkenneſs.
There is a kind of *Peſtrucian* deportment obſervable among
the lower claſs of people, in this diſtrict, which I have not
been able to diſcover, in any other.

view to general conveniency or an equitable diftribution of the lands to the feveral meffuages of the townfhips they lie in, as in other places they appear to have been; but here the property of two men, perhaps neighbours in the fame hamlet, will be mixed land-for-land alternately; though the foil and the diftance from the meffuages be nearly the fame.

A tradition which prevails in the diftrict relates that this intermixture was made intentionally; to prevent the inclofure of the fields; and the crime is laid to the charge of the " Barons ."

The circumftances of intentional intermixture is probable; but the *Barons* were lefs likely to effect fuch an expedient than the *Bifhops*; whofe monafteries were to be fed from the produce of the countries they feverally ftood in. Roads in thofe days were, in all probability, much worfe than they are now; and the bufinefs of diftant carriage much more difficult than it is at prefent. *

C

The

* Every monaftery had its barn. Some of thefe barns, which appear to have been generally of immenfe fize, are ftill remaining. One of them, which I had the opportunity of obferving, is in high prefervation; and ftill in ufe as a barn. Over one of its porches is a room furnifhed with a

fire

The monasteries being thus situated, their existence depended on keeping a due portion of the lands in a state of ARATION. But the lands of this district being better adapted, by the coolness of their situation, to *grafs* than to *corn*, they were no sooner inclosed than converted to grass-lands ; and there appears to have been no other probable means of preventing their inclosure, than by cutting them into shreds too small for that purpose, and intermixing them in the manner in which they too evidently appear.

PRODUCE—principally *corn*. Besides the open fields, a considerable share of the inclosures are arable. However, if we include the common meadows and stinted pastures, nearly half the district may be in *grafs*. The *woodland* is inconfiderable: not a hundred acres in the district. I speak of the area of the vale. The Cotfwold cliffs, which overlook it, are partially hung with wood. Above Witcomb, on the southern limb of the circle, there is a charming tract of woodland. If more of this irregular cliff were planted ; especially the
steeper

fire place and chimney ; and opening into a gallery on the inside of the barn ; probably for the conveniency of the barnyard, in overlooking the workmen.

steeper bolder projections, which are now in a state of waste, the profit eventually might be considerable to the owner ; while beechen mantles thrown over the present baldness of these projections could not fail of being grateful to the observers of rural beauty.

1.

ESTATES.

THIS DISTRICT includes no large estate.—Several Noblemen have off estates within it ; but none of them is extensive. The remainder belongs principally to resident gentlemen ; and to a pretty numerous yeomanry.

The TENURE is mostly *fee-simple* ; with some *copyhold* ; and a considerable proportion of *Church leasehold*. In the VALE OF EVESHAM, one third of the landed property is said to be held by the last mentioned tenure:—mostly by *leases for lives* ;—two in possession, and two in reversion: some by *leases for a term* ; as twenty one years, renewable every seven.

C 2   THE

RENT. The old rent for grafsland 20s. for arable common-field 10s. an acre: landlord paying land tax; which, in moft cafes, runs very high in this diftrict. But eftates in general have been moderately raifed of late years. Grafsland now lets from 20s. to 30s. Common field land 10s. to 15s. Arable inclofures, and " every years' land " 10s. to 20s. an acre.

COVENANTS. Landlord *builds* and *repairs*. Tenant has the care of the *fences*: and is, in the cuftom of the country, allowed to lop and top *bedgerow timber*. *Gateftuff* is, I underftand, pretty generally allowed; and fometimes *plowboot, &c.* In the center of the vale, tenants are reftricted from felling *ftraw*; but, near the towns, they are not under this reftriction.

RECEIVING. The prevailing times of receiving are Michaelmas and Ladyday; landlords allowing their tenants fix months' credit.

C 3

REMOVAL

---

ple, judicious principle of management, which might well be adopted In other arable diftricts, in which a regular courfe of hufbandry is eftablifhed: thus, in Norfolk, fix, twelve, or eighteen years would be a more eligible term of a leafe than feven, fourteen or twenty one;—the prefent term.

REMOVALS. Ladyday is the ufual time of changing tenants. Outgoing tenant fometimes holding part of the grafs grounds to old May-day; and not uncommonly, I underftand, keeping poffeffion of the barns, &c. until the midfummer twelve-month following!:—Har-vefting and thrafhing out all the corn fown upon the farm previous to his leaving it *.

FORMS OF LEASES. The following are the heads of a leafe in ufe on one of the firft off eftates in the diftrict.

LANDLORD AGREES to lett;—certain fpe-cified premifes; from Ladyday;—for a rent, and during a term, previoufly agreed upon.

ALSO to put the buildings into tenantable repair; and to keep them in repair during the term of the demife: (except as hereafter)

LANDLORD RESERVES all mines, quarries, coals, minerals, and metals; all timber, fruit and other trees, ftores, gennins, and faplings; with

* How much preferable, in this refpect, is the *Norfolk* practice; in which the bufinefs of the farm goes on nearly in the fame manner, in the firft and the laft years of the leafe, as in any intermediate year; and in which the in-coming tenant obtains full *poffeffion*, on the day of removal. (fee NORF: ECON:) For the practice of *Cleveland*; a diftrict very fimilar to this; fee YORK: ECON: vol I. P. 37.

with the lops, tops, and shredings thereof; together with all woods and underwoods, coppices, hedges, and hedgerows: (except as hereafter) with full liberty to search for, cut down, &c. &c.

ALSO the right of hunting, fishing, and fowling; " and all other royalties whatsoever."

ALSO free liberty of viewing the premises, and doing repairs.

ALSO a liberty of planting timber or fruit trees, in hedgerows, or on " mounds;" that is, ditch banks.

ALSO to inclose, or to exchange lands, without controul of the tenant; the difference in rental value to be estimated and fixed by arbitration.

TENANT AGREES to take;—and to pay the stipulated rent, half yearly; within fourteen days after it be due;—under forfeiture of the lease.

ALSO to discharge all tithes, dues, levies, duties, rates, assessments, taxes, and payments, (the land tax only excepted) whether parliamentary or parochial, imposed, or to be imposed, on the premises.

C 4

ALSO

Also to do ſuit and ſervice at the Lord's Court, holden for the manor in which the premiſes lie.

Also to do all neceſſary carriage for repairs.

Also to provide wheaten ſtraw, with rods, &c. for thatching.

Also to repair, and keep in good order and repair, and to deliver up in ſuch condition at the end of the term, the pump, and the windows, belonging to the premiſes.

Also the "court yards"—(including the ſtraw and dung yards)—with the cauſeways thereunto belonging.

Also to repair, keep and deliver up in good order and repair, the hedges, gates, pales, rails, ſtiles, mounds and fences; and to find iron work, ſpikes, and nails; (landlord providing and allowing rough timber;) for theſe purpoſes.

Also to ſcour and cleanſe the brook, ditches, watercourſes, drains, and pools; and the ſame to yield up at the end of the term in good and ſufficient order and repair.

Also to occupy, in himſelf or in his heirs, &c. all and every part of the premiſes: and not to aſſign, ſet-over, or lett, the whole, or

any

any parcel of them, (without the licence and consent of the landlord) under forfeiture of the lease.

ALSO not to plow, dig, or break up any of the meadow or pasture ground, belonging to the premises;--under the penalty of ten pounds an acre, yearly, from the time of breaking up to the termination of the demise.

ALSO to grip, trench, hillock, and drain the grass lands.

ALSO to fallow the arable land, every third or fourth year; according to the established course of husbandry of the township it lies in.

ALSO to fold and pen on the premises, and not elsewhere, all such sheep as shall be kept thereon.

ALSO not to sow hemp, flax, or rape seed on any part of the premises. NOR, otherwise, to cross-crop: but to sow the same corn and grain, from year to year, according to the best and most usual course of husbandry used in the respective townships *.

ALSO to rick and house upon the premises, all the corn, grain, and hay grown thereon.

AND

* The arable lands lie chiefly, or wholly in common fields.

AND to spend and employ, on the same, all the straw and sodder arising therefrom, in a husbandlike manner. AND to use on the premises, where most need shall require, and not elsewhere, all the muck, dung, soil, and compost rising thereon. AND not, in these or any other act or acts, negligently, wilsulfully, or willingly, impoverish or make barren, the lands under demise. NOR do or commit, or suffer to be done or committed, any waste, spoil, or destruction whatsoever.

ALSO to plant ———— willows, (six for instance) yearly; on convenient parts of the premises; and to defend, and replace them, if necessary; under the penalty of 20s. a tree, yearly: landlord allowing rough timber for fencing*.

ALSO to preserve and keep all such trees as the landlord shall plant in the HEDGE-ROWS, *from spoil or damage by cattle* (after they have been once well fenced with timber by the landlord)

---

* This is a well conceived clause. In a vale district, destitute, in a manner, of woodlands, the WILLOW becomes a most useful tree: supplying the place of coppice wood, for rails, flakes, handles of tools, edders, withs, and, particularly in this district, for making a species of cattle crib, which will be hereafter described.

lord) AND in case any such trees shall die, *by being hurt or spoiled by cattle*, to plant in their stead the like number, and the same sorts and kinds; and these to preserve and keep; under the penalty of 20s. a tree, yearly *.

ALSO,

* This likewise, *under due limitation*, is an admirable clause. Tempered with the Norfolk regulation in this case, it might be extended, *with propriety*, to PLANTATIONS, and be rendered highly beneficial to an estate, without being *alarming* to the tenants; though, in every case, it must in its nature be *hazardous*.

A clause of this kind,—seeing the difficulty of raising trees on old hedge-banks,— the uncertainty of seasons, and the unskilfulness of planters in general,—ought to be strongly guarded, on the part of the tenant, in the specification of the damage, for which the penalty shall be due; confining it solely to damage by cattle or other stock, or to other neglect, or wilful damage of the tenant.

The penalty, in this instance, appears to me imprudently high. An annual forfeiture of *one* shilling a tree would, during the usual term of a lease, much more than repay the planting, and any increase of value, which could be expected in that time; and would be a sufficient *check*, without being an *obstacle*, to a good tenant.

My remarks on this clause are the fuller, as I have not met with it in the leases of any other district; and I am fully persuaded, that, duly qualified, it would, if generally adopted, be highly advantageous to the landed interest. It avails little to plant; especially in the hedgerows of off estates; unless the occupier be someway interested in the success of the plantation.

ALSO, *in the laſt year of the term*, to ſow ———— acres with clover ſeed (at the rate of 18lb. an acre) AND ſuffer landlord, or incoming tenant, to ſow the remainder of the barley land of that year, with that or other graſs ſeeds. AND not, after the barley crop be cut, to plow in, or break up, or cut, mow, graze, or eat off the young clover, or any part thereof.

ALSO, *in the laſt year*, to weed, hoe, and cleanſe, and to ſuffer landlord, or incoming tenant, to weed, hoe, and cleanſe, the laſt, or " *going-off crop*."

ALSO to rick and houſe, and ſpend on the premiſes, and not elſewhere, all and every part of the " *going-off crop*;" AND to leave in the courts and yards, all the manure made therefrom, for the uſe and benefit of the landlord.

ALSO, *in the laſt year*, to deliver up, on the twenty firſt day of December, to the landlord or incoming tenant,———— acres of the arable land;———as a fallow for the enſuing year.

TENANT TO BE ALLOWED (over and above the rough timber for gates and fences) ſufficient

ficient plow-boot, and fire-boot, neceſſary to be uſed in the management of the premiſes.

ALSO the laſt or " going-off crop" of corn and grain, ſown on the premiſes, in the laſt year of the term;—on ſuch land, and in ſuch kind and ſort, as come, in due courſe of huſbandry, to be ſown in that year*.

ALSO the uſe of the barns, and part of the out buildings and yards, for thraſhing out the grain, and ſpending the fodder of the laſt crop, during twelve months, after the expiration of the term.

FARM

* There is no condition made, in this diſtrict, nor, I believe, in this quarter of the kingdom, for the outgoing tenant to pay the rent and taxes (what in Yorkſhire is termed the onſtand) for his going-off crop: ſo that here (by long cuſtom) the outgoing tenant occupies, and receives the profits of, perhaps, three fourths of the arable land, after the term of general occupation ceaſes; while the incoming tenant is paying rent and taxes for it, without receiving any immediate advantage whatſoever from it. In *this* diſtrict, where wheat is ſown very late, AUTUMN, appears to me, evidently, the moſt eligible time of removal: And I have ſeen the copy of a leaſe, terminating at MICHAELMAS, in which the tenant agrees to plow the fallow field lands twice, and manure them in a huſbandlike manner, in the laſt year of the term; and to give up the reſt of the arable lands, and a part of the buildings, as ſoon as the laſt crops ſhall be off:—a mode of conducting the diſagreeable buſineſs under notice, greatly preferable, in my opinion, to that which is in more general practice.

3.

FARM BUILDINGS.

IMPROVEMENTS in rural architecture are not to be expected in the diſtrict under ſurvey. Nevertheleſs, the leading facts reſpecting its FARM BUILDINGS require to be regiſtered; and ſome peculiarities, as well as ſome few modern improvements, are entitled to notice.

MATERIALS. Timber appears to have been, formerly, the prevailing building-material of the diſtrict. Farm buildings, in general, even to this day, are of frame-work; filled up with ſtrong laths, interwoven in a peculiar manner, and covered with plaſtering; or the ſtudwork is covered with weather-boardery alone; eſpecially outbuildings.

The preſent WALLING material is *brick.* Some few " *clay ſtones,*" dug out of the ſubſoil, are uſed; and, under the hills, "*free-ſtone*"——a ſoft calcarious granate, which is common to the Cotſwold hills, is in uſe.

LIME

Lime is here a heavy article of building.—
From 6d. to 8d. a bushel, of ten gallons level,
at the kiln.

The stones, from which it is burnt, are
brought by water carriage to the towns upon
the Severn; either from Bristol, or from
Westbury &c at the foot of the Forest of
Dean; where the " claystone " of the subsoil
is raised for this purpose. The kilns are built
on the banks of the Severn; so that no land
carriage of the stone is requisite. But the
lime, notwithstanding the exorbitant price at
the kiln is to be conveyed by land into the
area of the district. The margin is supplied
with the calcarious granate (which has been
mentioned), from the Cotswold cliffs; and
from Bredon hill; evidently a fragment of the
Cotswolds.

These stones vary much in general appearance and contexture; and the limes produced
from them are not less various in their qualities.

The " Bristol stone " has a somewhat flint-
like appearance; is of a close, hard, and uniform contexture; and of a dark redish colour;
sparkling with sparry particles; and flying
under the hammer like glass: *no marine shell.*
One

One hundred grains of it afford forty five grains of air, and ninety seven grains of calcarious matter; leaving three grains of residuum;—a dark-coloured impalpable matter.[*] The lime produced from this stone bursts readily in water; and (like that produced from spars) is, when fallen, of a light floury nature: white as snow: covetted by the plaisterer; but is considered by the mason and bricklayer, as being of a *weak* quality.

The Weſtbury-ſtone—which is a ſufficient ſpecimen of the " clayſtones " found in the ſubſoil of moſt parts of the diſtrict—is in colour, contexture, and general appearance, very different from the rock of St. Vincent. It reſembles, in every reſpect, the marble-like limeſtone of the hills of Yorkſhire: generally blue at the core with a grey dirty-white cruſt: the baſe being of a ſmooth, even texture; *interſperſed with marine ſhells.* When it is freſh raiſed out of its watery bed in the area of the vale, it is a ſoft ſubſtance, of a ſomewhat ſoaplike appearance; but hardens (or falls to pieces)

---

[*] In ſolution it riſes to the ſurface as a black ſpume: on the filter it has the appearance of moiſtened ſoot: but adheres to the paper in drying.

pieces) on being expofed to the atmofphere. One hundred grains of this ftone throw off forty grains of air ; and afford ninety one grains of calcarious earth ; leaving a refiduum of nine grains ;—an afh-coloured filt. The lime burnt from it is characterized by *ftrength* ; and is high in efteem for cement ; being found ftrong enough, in itfelf, to be ufed in water-work. It falls flowly ; is of a fomewhat brim-ftone colour ; and is diftinguifhed by the name of " brown lime. " *

The

* Having obferved the reluctance with which the lime of this fpecimen (frefh from the kiln) imbibes water ; while that of the Briftol ftone drinks it with fingular avidity,—I was led to try, by a comparative experiment, whether their powers of imbibing air (that is of regaining their fixed air) were in like proportion. The refult is interefting.

One hundred grains of the firft (in one knob) fufpended in a pair of fcales, got full five grains in twenty four hours. In a drawer (which was fometimes open, fometimes fhut) they got, in twenty four hours more, the fame additional weight. In feven days more (wrapped in paper and lying in a drawer) they got twenty three grains : in all thirty three ; or about three and a half grains a day : moftly air, with, in all probability, fome portion of water.

One hundred grains from the Weftbury ftone, placed in the drawer increafed in twenty four hours not quite one grain ! In twenty four hours more, in the fcale, they barely made up a grain and a half ! In feven days more they gained

The specimen of *calcarious granate* which I have before me was taken from the middle of a " freestone quar ", within the " camp ", on Painswick hill. It is common to the Cotswold and the Lansdown hills; and corresponds exactly with the soft limestone granate of Malton in Yorkshire. It varies in specific quality. The Bathstone is softer and lighter than the specimen under analysis. One hundred grains of which discharge forty four grains of air; yielding ninety eight grains of soluble matter; and two grains of residuum; a snuff coloured impalpable matter. †

The method of *burning lime* in this country has nothing which entitles it to notice; except

the

(in the drawer) exactly nine grains: in all ten and a half grains: not a grain and a quarter a day. Hence we may conceive how widely different may be the qualities of lime. Confequently, how dangerous to draw general conclusions from an experiment, or even experiments, made with one particular species.

† It is proper to say that these experiments were made, and repeated, with great attention, and with exactly the same correspondent results: nevertheless the *proportion of air to diffoluble matter* varies in each specimen. In the Bristol stone the proportion is more than forty six, in the Cotswold less than forty five,—in the Westbury less than forty four, to one hundred.

the practice of riddling and hand-picking the lime as it is drawn, to take out the afhes, cinders, and rubbifh which may have been thrown into the kiln with the ftones or coals. The labour is not great; and the work is valuable. Lime as a building material; efpecially for the plafterer's ufe, cannot be too pure. The refufe pays the labourer, and the quantity of ftone lime lofes nothing by its abfence.*

TIMBER. The old buildings of this diftrict are full of fine oak; in which the lower lands of Glocefterfhire have heretofore, in all probability, been fingularly abundant. But at prefent the vale is entirely ftripped, and even the foreft of Dean (fome few parts of it excepted) is almoft naked of good *oak timber*.

The vale, however, abounds at this time with *elm* of uncommon fize and quality. This and foreign timber are the ordinary materials in

D 2 ufe

---

* The LIMEKILN of this diftrict is noticeable, as being frequently furnifhed with a TOP, fet upon the walls of the kiln, and contracted in a funnel-like form ; the materials being carried in at a door in the fide. In one inftance, the kiln is built within a cone ; in the manner of the brick kilns about London. The principal, if not the fole ufe of thefe tops, is to carry up the fmoke and prevent its becoming a nuifance to the neighbourhood of the kilns.

ufe for farm buildings: oak being ufed only where durability is more particularly requifite.

COVERING MATERIALS. An ordinary kind of *flate*, got out of the fides of the hills, has formerly been the prevailing covering of the diftrict. At prefent *knobbed plain tiles* are principally in ufe. The knob is an obvious improvement of the hole and pin ; which are ftill ufed about the metropolis.

Thatch is ftill in ufe for cottages and farm-buildings. A fpecies of thatch *new* to the reft of the kingdom is here not unfrequently made ufe of; efpecially near the towns, where wheat ftraw is permitted to be fold. In thefe fituations, not only ricks; but *roofs*, are thatched with STUBBLE: a material which is found to laft much longer than ftraw; unlefs this be " helmed " ; that is, have the heads cut off before thrafhing, in the Somerfetfhire manner: a practice which is not common in this country. That ftubble fhould be found to endure is reafonably imagined. It has the advantage of helm (in not being bruifed by the flail) and confifts of the ftouteft part of the ftems. In many diftricts it would be difficult to be ufed on account of its fhortnefs; but in

this

this country, where it is cut eighteen inches or perhaps two feet high, and (in the situations where it is more frequently used) has generally a sufficient quantity of long wirey grass among it to hold it together; there is no great difficulty in thatching with it: except in the raking; which requires a tender hand.   It is first driven up a little with the teeth of the rake; beaten; and then raked gently downward.

FLOORING MATERIALS.   Upper floors have heretofore been laid with *oak*; which is still common in the floors and stair-cases of all old houses.   *Elm* has, perhaps, been more recently used, and is still in use, for the same purposes.   Ground floors are not unfrequently of common *bricks* (a vile material for floors) or of " forest stone "—an excellent freestone grit, raised in the forest of Dean.

FARMERIES.   The farm-buildings and yards, of the district under survey, have not much to recommend them to particular notice. The arrangement has seldom any obvious design. There are however some few exceptions.

The BARNS of the vale are, in size below par: except the monastery barns already mentioned. There are few modern barns; the best, which

                 has

has fallen under my obſervation, meaſures thirty ſix by eighteen feet on the inſide ;—and the plate twelve feet high. The foundation brick. The ſhell elm weather-boarding. The covering knobbed plain-tiles, twelve inches by ſeven ; laid in coarſe mortar ; with four and a half inch gage. The roof, behind, continued down to a plate ſix feet high, ſupported by poſts of elm ſet on ſtone ; forming an open ſhed for cattle to reſt under.

The BARN FLOOR of the diſtrict is moſtly of *plank* ; or of *foreſt-ſtone* ; which makes an admirable floor for beans ; and nor a bad one for barley: even wheat, with due care in keeping the ears bedded among ſtraw, to prevent the flail from breaking the grain, may be thraſhed on a ſtone floor with propriety. Clay floors are here in low eſteem. The price of a ſtone floor, compleat, is about 5d. a foot.

I ſee nothing elſe in the farm-buildings of this vale which is entitled to deſcription ; except BULLOCK STALLS, which are here built in what will no doubt be deemed a ſuperb ſtyle, by thoſe who have been accuſtomed to leſs coſtly buildings for the ſame purpoſe: and CALF STAGES ; an admirable conveniency ;

which

which is peculiar, I believe, to the diftrict; but which ought to be univerfally known; as it may, in any breeding country, be adopted with fingular propriety.

But defcriptions of thefe conveniences will fall better under the articles to which they refpectively belong; namely REARING CATTLE and FATTING CATTLE: fubjects which will be duly noticed in their places.

The CIDERMILL HOUSE, an erection almoft as neceffary as a barn, upon a Glocefterfhire farm, will likewife be defcribed under its proper head.

STACK STAGES are here very common. Moftly upon ftone pillars and caps. The price 18d. to 2s. a pair. A fmall, but fnug frame, is here made with five pillars. Four fet quadrangularly, and one in the center. By making the outfide of the frame fomewhat compaffing, round ftacks are conveniently enough fet on thefe fquare ftages.

YARD FENCES are almoft invariably *broad rails*; the Norfolk battons. Under thefe fences a line of STRAW-MANGERS are ufually formed: and, in the area of the yards, CRIBS of various conftructions are in ufe.

D 4 FIELD-

4.

FIELD-FENCES.

OLD LIVEHEDGES are the ordinary fences of the diftrict. The prefent inclofures, if we may judge from the age of their hedges, are probably fome centuries old.

In the MANAGEMENT of live fences, whether young or old, I have met with nothing, here, that is entitled to particular notice.

It is, however, obfervable, in this place, that one of the fineft hedges I have feen in the diftrict, grows on a cold unproductive fwell: the land not worth, though inclofed, 10s. an an acre: yet, on land worth twice that rent, I have feldom feen a hedge grow fo lux-uriantly. A fufficient evidence, that, *in the valuing of land,* HEDGES cannot be depended upon, as criterions to judge from. The hedge may feed in a fertilizing fubfoil, which corn, or the better graffes, may not be able to reach.

The DITCHES, in every part of the vale, are fhamefully neglected! A vale diftrict, without deep clean ditches, reflects difgrace

on

on the owners, as well as on the occupiers, of its lands. In a diſtrict, that, by natural ſituation, is too cold and moiſt, every poſſible means ought to be uſed to free it from ſurface water: which, if it ſtand only an hour upon the ſoil; or in immediate contact with it; adds, more or leſs, to its natural coldneſs.

The ordinary TEMPORARY FENCE is bar hurdles.

GATES are here made low; with a ſtrong top-bar, in the Kentiſh manner; but want the long upper eye or thimble of the Surrey-Gate*.

STILES are ſingularly abundant. They appear frequently to be placed merely as preſervatives of the hedges; and this may, in many caſes, be good policy. They are frequently made *to open*: the top rail having an iron bolt driven through it, at one end; the other end falling into a notch in the oppoſite poſt, making an opening wide enough to paſs a carriage through occaſionally,

HEDGEROW

---

* HANGING GATES. In this diſtrict, it is the invariable practice to drive the hooks into the *corner* of the poſts, and the thimbles into the *corner* of the hartree; which, in this caſe, ſhuts within the poſt.

5.

HEDGEROW TIMBER.

THE HEDGE TREES of the vale are moſtly ELM and WILLOW. Few of OAK or ASH.

The MAPLE, which grows unuſually large, here, is conſidered as a timber tree, and is put to many uſes for which, in other diſtricts, it is not deemed ſuitable. But the nature of the ſoil, or the variety which is here cultivated, may render its texture leſs brittle than it generally is, in other diſtricts. Hurdles, gates, and even ciderpreſs ſkrews are made of it.

The ELM (chiefly the fine-leaved elm) grows with uncommon luxuriance, and to an unuſual ſize, in the vale ſoil. Its progreſs is quickeſt on the lighter warmer lands; but here the trees ſooneſt decay, and the timber is of the leaſt value. In ſtiffer, more clayey ſituation, its growth is leſs rapid; but its timber is of a much better quality: the colour of iron; and, in ſome inſtances, almoſt as hard.

—The

—The Briſtol ſhip-builders have a ſupply of keel-pieces from this quarter; and I know no country, which is ſo likely to furniſh good ones.

The vales of Gloceſterſhire may boaſt of three of the moſt remarkable trees in the iſland. PIFFE'S ELM, the BODDINOTON OAK, and the TORTWORTH CHESNUT;—but having deſcribed them fully in another work, I forbear to particulaſize them here *.

Hedgerow timber is univerſally *lopped*; few, however, are *beaded* low in the pollard manner; except WILLOWS; which, as has been ſaid, are here, conſidered in a degree neceſſary to every farm.

* See PLANTING and ORNAMENTAL GARDENING; articles FAGUS: QUERCUS: ULMUS,

WOOD.

6.

WOODLANDS.

COPPICES are the only natural wood-lands of the area of the vale. Of thefe there are two or three: one of them, in the center of the vale, is of confiderable extent.

Part of this coppice is a COMMON WOOD ;—*appropriated* to the meffuages of the townfhip it belongs to, but not *divided:* fomewhat analogous with common fields and common meadows. A fpecies of property I have not met with elfewhere.

It is obfervable that, in a part of this coppice, fome ftandard oaks are left as timber trees; which, contrary to common practice, are lopped to the top (as hedgerow trees) every time the coppice wood is cut. This certainly leffens their hurtfulnefs to the underwood; but the timber becomes, no doubt, of a very inferior quality. Their crop of fuel, however, every fifteen or twenty years, muft be confiderable.

confiderable.   The queftion is whether, on
the whole, they are, or are not, more profitable than coppice wood alone: and it appears to me, on reflection, to be a difputable
queftion.   It probably hinges on whether the
trees feed below or among the roots of the
coppice-wood.

This patch of woodland is further entitled
to notice.—The *foil* is an unproductive clay,
mixt with and bottomed by a thin feam of
calcarious gravel; lying on a cold clayey fubfoil; not worth, as arable land, more than
8s. an acre: not eftimated in this country at
more than 5s. an acre.

The *fpecies* of wood is principally *oak*, *afb*,
and *maple*, with fome *fallow*, *white-thorn*, and
bazle.   The *ufes* to which it is applyed are
principally rails, hurdle-ftuff,—hedging materials, and fuel.   The *age of felling* twenty
years.   And its eftimated *value* at that age,
twelve to fifteen pounds an acre! Its growth
is uncommonly luxuriant: the ftools are thick
upon the ground; and, being cut high, afford
numerous fhoots.   In the latter ftages of its
growth, it is the moft impenetrable thicket I
have feen; while the crops of corn and grafs,
which

which border upon it, are remarkably weak and unproductive.

This shows, in a striking manner, the judgment requisite in laying out estates: giving such lands to husbandry, as are adapted to its productions; and converting to woodland, such as are naturally prone to wood.

7.

PLANTING.

THE PLANTATIONS of the vale consist wholly of fruit-trees. Forest-trees may be said to be here in total neglect; excepting some few ashen coppices for cider-cask hoops, a species of plantation common on the Herefordshire side of the county.

If, however, we may judge from the coppice which has been spoken of above; and the hedge noticed aforegoing; it is highly probable,

bable, that many of the cold fwells, which occur in different parts of the vale, might be
planted with great profit.

The timber-oak is, at prefent, almoft entirely banifhed from *this* fide of the Severn;
and although the oppofite banks are, yet,
fufficiently wooded; the prefent woods will, in
all probability, be fallen, long before fuch as
may be now raifed from the acorn, will be
ready for the axe.

F A R M S.

8.

F A R M S.

THE PREVAILING CHARACTERISTIC of farms, in this diftrict, is a mixture of grafs and arable land; in various proportions. Near the towns of Glocefter and Tewkefbury, there are fome few large farms, " all green:"— that is, confifting entirely of grafs-land. But this, alone, makes an inconvenient farm; efpecially in a dairy country, where litter and winter fodder, for dry cows and rearing cattle, are requifite.

The exact proportion of arable to grafs, however, does not feem to be fixed. Too much grafs gives a fcarcity of ftraw: too much arable interferes with the dairy; or, perhaps, more accurately fpeaking, the dairy interferes with much arable land. Even in harveft, let the weather be what it may, the bufinefs of milking and the dairy muft be attended to.

Hence,.

Hence, perhaps, we may conclude, that corn and the dairy ought not to *rival* each other: one of them ought to be *fubordinate*; ought to be rendered fubfervient to the MAIN OBJECT of management. *

In regard to SIZE, the vale farms are of the middle caft. From one to three hundred acres is, I believe, the moft prevalent fize. There are fome made-up farms of much higher magnitude; but no entire farm, in the area of the vale, lets, I underftand, for more than four hundred pounds a year: not many, I believe, higher than two hundred a year. †

PLAN. Some of thefe larger farms; moft of them " manor" or " court" farms; or fimply " the farm" with the name of the townfhip affixed to it; (undoubtedly the ancient

* Neverthelefs, a profeffional man, whofe knowledge of the practice of the diftrict entitles him to be heard with deference, gives the following as the beft proportion of a farm, in the VALE OF EVESHAM: fifty two acres of arable, (fubjected to three crops and a fallow) with fixty acres of pafture ground, and thirty acres of meadow.

† The fame fuperior manager is of opinion, that a double farm of the defcription given in the laft note is the beft fize; and that larger farms are, in the vale, dangerous both to landlord and tenant.

cient demefne lands of the townfhips they refpectively lie in); are very entire; and lie
well round the homefteads. But farm houfes,
in general, ftand in villages; the lands belonging to them being ftill fcattered about in the
extraordinary manner which has been defcribed.
How wrong in their owners *now* to continue
them in that unprofitable ftate. The lofs falls
wholly on themfelves. They let at a rent
proportioned to their prefent difadvantages.

9.

FARMERS.

HUSBANDMEN are much the fame in
all diftricts: plain, frugal, pains-taking, clofe,
and unintelligible. The lower and middle
clafs of farmers, of the diftrict under obfervation, moftly anfwer, in a remarkable manner,
to this defcription:—while fome few of the
fuperior clafs are as ftrongly marked by libe-
rality and communicativenefs:—characters
which begin to adorn fuperior farmers in every
diftrict;

diftrict; and which muft, eventually, do more toward the perfection of the art, than all the applauded fchemes which theory can boaft. Theorifts may draw plans, and fuggeft hints; and in fo doing may do good fervice. But profeffional men, only, can execute, correct, mature, and introduce them into general practice. Should profeffional men become fcientific as well as liberal, what may not be expected? And who, viewing the rifing generation, many of them opulent, well educated, and duly initiated in the profeffion they are defigned for, can apprehend that none of them will become ftudious of the art which alone can render them ,ufeful and refpectable in fociety?

10.

W O R K M E N.

FARM LABOURERS are fufficiently numerous.--they are noticeable as being fimple, inoffenfive, unintelligent, and apparently flow. How different from the farm labourers of Norfolk!

E 2

Their

Their wages are very low, *in money*; being only
1s. a-day. But, *in drink*, shamefully exorbitant. Six quarts a day the common allowance: frequently two gallons: sometimes nine
or ten quarts, or an unlimited quantity.

In a cider year the *extravagance* of this absurd custom (which prevails throughout the
cider country) is not perceived. But now
(1788) after a succession of bad fruit years, it
is no wonder the farmers complain of being
beggared by malt and hops! They are not,
however, entitled to pity. The fault—the
crime—is their own. If a few leading men,
in each township, would agree to reduce the
quantity of labourers' drink within due bounds,
it would at once be effected.

But the origin of the evil, I fear, rests
with themselves. In a fruit year, cider is of
little value. It is no uncommon circumstance
to send out a general invitation, into the high-
ways and hedges; in order to empty the casks,
which were filled last year, that they may be
refilled this. A habit of drinking is not easily
corrected. Nor is an art learnt in youth readily
forgot. Men and masters are equally adepts
in the art of drinking. The tales which are

told

told of them are incredible. Some two or three I recollect. But, although I have no reason to doubt the authorities I had them from, I wish not to believe them: I hope they are not true.

Drinking a gallon-bottle-full at a draught is said to be no uncommon feat. A mere boyish trick, which will .not bear to be bragged of. But to drain a two-gallon bottle without taking it from the lips, as a labourer of the vale is said to have done, by way of being even with master, who had paid him short in *money*—is spoken of as an exploit, which carried the art of draining a wooden bottle to its full pitch.. Two gallons of cider, however, are not a stomach-full. Another man of the vale undertook, for a trifling wager, to drink twenty pints, one immediately after another. He got down nineteen (as the story is gravely told) but these filling the cask to the bung, the twentieth could not of course get admittance: so that a Severn-man's stomach holds exactly two gallons three pints.

But the quantity drank, in this extempore way, by the men, is trifling, compared with that which their masters will swallow at a sitting. Four well feafoned yeomen, (fome of them well known in *ibis* vale) having raifed their courage with the juice of the apple, re-folved to have a frefh hogfhead tapped; and, fetting foot to foot, emptied it at one fitting.

11.

BEASTS OF LABOUR.

HORSES are at prefent, the only beafts of draught, in the vale.

Formerly fome OXEN were worked in it, double, in yoke; but they were found to poach the land, and were on that account, given up. But now, when oxen are worked, on almoft every fide of it, fingle, as horfes, it is fome-what extraordinary they fhould not be admitted into the vale: where their keep would be fo eafy : where grafs and hay may be had at will.

The objection ftill held out againft them is, that, even fingle, they tread the vale lands too much. But in this I fufpect there is a fpice of obftinacy in the old way: a want of a

due

due portion of the spirit of improvement: a kind of indolence: It might not, perhaps, be too severe to say of the vale farmers, that they would rather be eaten up by their horses, than step out of the beaten tract to avoid them.

In harrowing wide ridges, in a wet season, oxen may be less eligible than horses. But shoeing them with whole shoes, as horses, might remedy the comparative evil. If not—let those who are advocates for oxen calculate the comparative difference in *wear* and keep; and those who are their enemies, estimate the comparative mischiefs of treading; and thus decide upon their value as beasts of labour in the vale. *

If after a *fair trial* oxen be ineligible;—let the present *waste of horses* be lessened. Using five horses to a plow, in stirring a loose loamy fallow, not more perhaps than four or five inches deep, is a crime against the community, that ought to be punishable. In the first plowing of a fallow; as well as in plowing for beans or wheat; six, and not unfrequently seven horses, at-length, are used to *one* plow! Yet these five

E 4

six

* I am told, that in the VALE OF EVESHAM, they are gradually coming into use.

fix or feven horfes; with one or two men, and one or two boys; feldom plow three quarters of an acre a day; two thirds of an acre is the day's work of the country! But the plow, in ufe, is a difgrace to prefent hufbandry: thirteen to fourteen feet long, and heavy in proportion.

I am well aware that ftrong land, plowed deep, as it is in this diftrict, requires a ftrong team; and that a long plow is *convenient to the plowman*; efpecially in laying up high fteep ridges. But fimilar ridges are laid up, in the midland counties, with a fhort plow and three horfes. And I know, from experience or adequate obfervation, in various parts of the ifland, that, allowing for the nature of the foil, and the aukwardnefs of the ridges, there is an evident and great wafte of plow horfes in the diftrict under notice: Six horfes, worth perhaps from twenty to thirty pounds each, are not expected to work more than fifty or fixty acres of arable land (with a greater or lefs proportion of grafs land annexed to it.) If thefe fifty or fixty acres be common field land, the intereft of the firft coft, the annual *wear*, and the

the hazard—incident to such six horses, amount nearly to the rental value of the land: and their keep, if they be properly kept up, is worth twice or three times its rental value.

12.

IMPLEMENTS.

THE GLOCESTERSHIRE WAGGON is, beyond all argument, the best farm-waggon I have seen in the kingdom.—I know not a district which might not profit by its introduction. Its most striking peculiarity is that of having a crooked side-rail, bending archwise over the hind wheel. This lowers the general bed of the waggon, without lessening the diameter of the wheels. The body is wide, in proportion to its shallowness; and the wheels run six inches wider than those of the Yorkshire waggon, whose side-rail is six inches higher. Its advantages, therefore, in carrying a top-load are obvious. (see YORKS: ECON: on this subject, vol I. p. 269) And,

for

for a body-load, it is much the ftiffeft beft
waggon I have feen.   The price 20 to 25l.
according to the fize, and the ftrength of the
tire.   The weight, 15 Cwt. to a ton.

This waggon is common to Glocefterfhire
and to North-Wiltfhire.   How much farther
it extends weftward, I know not.   It is a
ftranger in the fouthern, the eaftern, the northern and the midland counties.

Where, and by whom it was firft invented,
I have not learned.   It is fometimes called the
Cotfwold waggon.   It is, by way of preemi-
nence, well entitled to the name of the Farmers'
waggon : for I have not feen another, which,
compared with this, is fit for a farmer's ufe.

S E A S O N S.

13.
SEASONS.

THE PROGRESS OF SPRING, in 1788, in the vale of Glocefter.

> Sallow in full blow—4 April.
> Sloe-thorn in blow—11 April.
> Hawthorn foliated—16 April.
> Cuckoo firft heard—20 April.
> Elm foliated—21 April.
> Pear tree in full blow—27 April.
> Swifts—28 April!*
> Houfe-marten—30 April.
> Swallows—1 May.
> Thermometer—76.° in the fhade—
>   1 May !
> Apple tree in full blow—3 May.
> Oak foliated—4 May.
> Afh foliated—5 May.
> Thunder—6 May.
> Hawthorn began to break 10th; in
>   full blow—17 May.

The

* This is a remarkable circumftance. On the 29th of April SWIFTS were in number, flying high in the atmof-phere, before a fingle SWALLOW had made its appearance.

The

The only circumſtance noticeable, with reſpect to the WEATHER of this year, is that of its *extreme dryneſs*. From the beginning of July to the cloſe of the year, there has been a continuation of dry weather; excepting two or three days' rain in September.

Springs have ſeldom been known ſo low, as they are at preſent (Jan. 1789.) Nature's ſtore rooms appear to be exhauſted. Even in this watery vale, ſurface ſprings, in general, and moſt wells, have been dry ſome months; water having been fetched, and cattle driven, a conſiderable diſtance. The reſervoirs on the ſkirts of Matſon hill, for ſupplying the city of Gloceſter with water, have been empty many weeks: a circumſtance unknown before.

This want of rain, here, is the more remarkable, as throughout a great part of Wales, not fifty miles diſtant, ſummer and autumn were rainy, almoſt without interruption!

In the middle of October, while the lands of this country were ſo dry, that they could

not

The weather unuſually warm. A ſtrong evidence, that the ſwift does *not* migrate. It ſeldom miſtakes the ſeaſon, like the ſwallow. We rarely ſee a ſwift, before the ſpring be confirmed.

not, with any propriety, be worked for wheat; and while, even in Herefordſhire, farmers were breaking the clots with beetles; the farmers in Wales, not twenty miles diſtant, had not been able to put a plow into the ground for near a month, owing to the exceſſive wetneſs of the ſeaſon! While in Yorkſhire, having been miſſed by the rain of September, which gave a looſe to the graſs in this diſtrict, the ſtinted paſtures had been ſo bare, the cattle had been foddered in them!

These circumſtances, ſo remarkable, and ſo nearly connected with our ſubject, I could not paſs over unnoticed. *Showers*, or *a few days' rain*, not unfrequently fall in a partial manner:—but I never before knew a *long-continued rainy ſeaſon*, which was not common to the kingdom.

GENERAL.

14.

GENERAL MANAGEMENT

OF

FARMS.

VIEWING the vale as one farm, its objects of management are the four grand objects of hufbandry:

> Corn;
> Breeding;
> The Dairy;
> Fatting.

There are fome few individual farms, applied, principally, *to grazing:* others chiefly to the *dairy:* and there may be fome few fmall *arable* farms.   But upon the larger farms, in general, the four objects are held in view.

The ARABLE CROPS are principally WHEAT,. BARLEY, BEANS; with fome *peas,* and a *few oats!* Alfo, of late years, fome *clover, vetches,* and fome few *turneps* have been cultivated*.

It

* TURNEPS. In the center of the vale, there are few or none grown. The reafon given is, they cannot be got off the land: and, while the country remains without roads

and

It may, however, be ſaid, with little latitude, that NATURAL HERBAGE is, in this diſtrict, the only SUBORDINATE CROP.

From what has gone before, it may, perhaps, be conceived, that the ARABLE MANAGEMENT of this diſtrict, cannot be entitled to particular notice. This, however, would be deciding too raſhly. The rural management of a country reſembles the moral character. I have not found one that is perfect: nor one which does not comprize ſome portion of good. The arable management, of the country under ſurvey, appears to the obſerver in light and ſhade; and exhibits ſome traits, which the reader, I think, will not be diſpleaſed with. Beſides, in it, we have a ſpecimen of the practice of a claſs of country, which includes a conſiderable ſhare of the beſt lands of this quarter

and ſurface drains, this muſt neceſſarily be the caſe; eſpecially where the ſoil is ſtrong, tenacious, and cold; a ſoil altogether unfit for turneps. There are, however, lands in the vale, well adapted to this crop; and its abſence implies, either a want of the ſpirit of improvement, or no need of *cultivated herbage*. In a vale country, abounding with graſs-lands, turneps are of leſs value, than they are in a hilly country, deſtitute of *natural herbage*. If *arable herbage* were wanted in the vale, CABBAGES would probably be found more eligible than turneps.

ter of the ifland: namely ARABLE VALE. A
fketch of it appears, to me, effentially neceffary, in a REGISTER OF THE PRESENT STATE
OF ENGLISH AGRICULTURE. The reader may
reft affured, that, for my own eafe and gratification, as well as his, I will not dwell longer
on the fubject, than the general defign of the
work I am executing requires.

15.

COURSE OF HUSBANDRY.

THE ANCIENT COURSE of the com-
mon fields was the fame, here, as in moft
other diftricts: namely,

> Fallow,
>
> Wheat, &c.
>
> Beans, &c.—And to this an-

cient courfe, feveral of the townfhips of the
vale ftill adhere.

But fome townfhips in *this* vale, and many,
I believe, in the *vale of Evefham*, have, of
late years, changed the ancient fyftem of management; for one, which, fingular as it may

appear

appear to thofe, who have been accuftomed to fallow for wheat, is founded on good principles; and might well be copied by other ftiffoiled, open-field townfhips: namely,

> Fallow;
> Barley;
> Beans, or clover;
> Wheat.

The reafons given for this change (this ftriking and fingular effort, this promifing dawn of improvement) are,—the bean crop, in the old courfe, came round too quick; the wheat did not do fo well, after fallow, as after beans;—nor the beans fo well, after wheat, as after barley.

Some farmers throw in CLOVER, inftead of beans, between the barley and the wheat crops.

In the neighbourhood of Glocefter, are fome extenfive common fields, under an extraordinary courfe of management. They have been cropped, year after year, during a century, or perhaps centuries; without one intervening whole year's fallow. Hence they are called "EVERY YEAR'S LAND*."

On

---

* Cheltenham, Deerhurft, and fome few other townfhips, have likewife their "EVERY YEAR'S LANDS."

On these lands no REGULAR SUCCESSION of crops is obferved; except that a "brown and a white crop"—pulfe and corn—are cultivated in alternacy.

The inclofed arable lands are under a fimilar COURSE OF MANAGEMENT.

16.

SOILS

AND

TILLAGE.

THE SPECIES OF SOILS have been mentioned as various. Near the towns of Glocefter and Tewkefbury, a DEEP RICH LOAM prevails. Round Cheltenham, a DEEP SAND. The rifing grounds of Deerhurft are covered with a RED LOAM; a remarkable fpecies of foil; common to the hillocks of the over-Severn diftrict, and to the inferior hills of Herefordfhire. It is here called RED LAND;" and refembles much the " RED HILLS" of Nottinghamfhire

The

The area of the vale is a DEEP LOAM; of various degrees of richnefs and contexture. In the center of it, a remarkable fpecimen of vale land appears: a patch of CALCARIOUS GRAVEL: partaking of the nature of the Cotfwold foil!

The particulars noticeable in the SOIL PROCESS of this diftrict, relate folely to TILLAGE: namely,

      1. Breaking up grafs land.

      2. Fallowing.

      3. Laying up ridges.

I. BREAKING UP GRASS LAND. This is not a common operation; yet it fometimes takes place: At prefent, there are many inftances, in which it is much wanted. Old pafture lands, over-run with ant-hills, and the coarfer graffes, are not eafily reclaimed, without the powerful affiftance of the plow.

The method of performing the operation, in this diftrict, is by no means intended to be held out as a pattern. It has, however, fufficient pretenfions to a place in this regifter.

It varies in the firft ftages: fometimes the ant-hills are cut off, carried into heaps, and mixt with ftraw, &c. as manure for corn land. Sometimes they are dried and burnt. But,

in

in the prevailing practice of the country, the ſward and ant-hills are plowed up together, in the ſpring. In ſummer, the land has *one* croſs plowing. In autumn the ſurface is re-duced and levelled; with the harrow; ſown with wheat; and the ſeed buried with the plow, among the graſs-roots and ant-hills.

The enſuing autumn,—the crop being reaped, and the ſtubble mown and raked off,— the ſoil is turned over, and ſown again, (and perhaps a third time), with wheat on one plow-ing! There has, I am told, been inſtances,— there has (I think I am well informed) been at leaſt one inſtance, of wheat being thus re-peatedly ſown (upon a piece of extraordinaryly good land) ſix years, ſucceſſively; the laſt crop being ſaid to be nearly as good as the firſt!!! This, while it diſcovers the indiſcretion of the farmer, evinces the natural ſtrength of the vale lands, and ſhows, in a ſtriking light, the value of old-paſtured turf as a matrice for wheat.

II. Quantity of tillage. In the com-mon fields which are under the improved plan of cultivation,—the number of plowings, in the four years round, is ſix. Three in the fal-

low

low year: one for barley: one for beans: and, generally, one for wheat.

The fallow is broken up after barley feed time; flitting the ridges *down*, by a deep plowing.   In the firft ftirring, they are gathered *up*. On this fecond plowing, the manure is fpread ; and plowed under with a fhallow furrow; which is, likewiife, turned *upward*; to lay the ridges dry during winter.   In the fpring, they are flit *down*, for barley; and, next autumn, gathered *up*, for beans; and the enfuing autumn, again plowed *upward*, for wheat.   Six plowings in four yearts, for three crops and a fallow; four of them being *upward*, two *downward*, of the ridges.   Sometimes the bean ftubble is pared down very thin, previous to the feed-plowing for wheat.   But fometimes the fallow has only two plowings.

With this fmall quantity of tillage, it is no wonder that even the barley ftubbles fhould be foul; or that the bean crop, notwithftanding the extraordinary care which is taken of it, fhould, in fome feafons, be half fmothered in weeds; or that the wheat ftubbles, notwithftanding the fingular attention which is paid to the crop while growing, fhould, not

F 3   unfrequently

unfrequently, be knee-deep in couch and thiſtles.

Two or three plowings of ſuch ſtubbles are not entitled to the name of a *fallow*: they are juſt ſufficient to break the roots of couch graſs and thiſtles into ſets, as it were to propagate and increaſe, rather than to leſſen, their number. While ſeed-weeds, of every genus, are ſuffered to mature, and ſhed their ſeeds, between the plowings. A more ingenious way of propagating weeds would be difficult to conceive.

Fortunately, however, for the character of the vale, as an arable country, this diſgraceful management, though prevalent, is not univerſal. I have ſeen land, in various parts of it, in a high ſtate of tillage, and beautifully clean. But, even for this, I cannot allow an occupier any great ſhare of *merit* ; it is little more than his *duty* as a huſbandman. In keeping land clean and in tilth, and taking a crop every year, ſkill, as well as induſtry, is required, and merit is of courſe due. But to keep it in a huſbandly ſtate, with a whole ſummer's fallow, every third or fourth year, wants common induſtry only: and a man, who with

this

this opportunity, fuffers his crops to be im-
paired, through a want of fufficient tillage,
ought not to be entrufted with the occupation
of arable land.

If, however, we fee caufe of cenfure, in a
redundancy of weeds, and want of tillage, in
the fields, which are fallowed every third or
fourth year,—what fhall we expect to find in
the fields, which are never fallowed? Where
barley is looked up to as the *cleanfing crop*! I
wifh not to exaggerate; and to defcribe their
ftate of foulnefs, with accuracy, would be difficult, or impoffible. I will, therefore, only
fay, that I have found beans hid among muftard feed, growing wild as a weed, but occupying the ground as a crop;—peas, languifh-
ing under a canopy of the cornmarigold and
the poppies;—barley, with fcarcely a ftem
free from the fetters of the convolvulus;—and
wheat, pining away, plant after plant, in
thickets of couch and thiftles.

In the language of cenfure I have no gratification. But, could I pafs over, unnoticed,—
or, having feen, could be filent on—management fo highly blameable,—I fhould be altogether unfit for the tafk I have undertaken,

F 4

It

It is more than probable that one third of the crops, collectively, of some of the best-soiled fields in the district, is every year *lost*, through a WANT OF SUFFICIENT TILLAGE.

These circumstances are mentioned with more readiness, and with greater freedom; as every district of the kingdom lies more or less open, to similar censure; and I make use of this opportuity of mentioning them; because no other district, I have examined, affords evidences so striking, as these which are here produceable.

It might not be far wide of the truth to say, that one fourth of the produce of the arable lands of the kingdom is *lost* through a WANT OF TILLAGE: yet I find men in every country *afraid* to make a whole year's fallow, left they should lessen their produce! But let those who are adverse to fallowing, come here and be convinced of the magnitude of their error.

If land be in a state of foulness, with root-weeds,—as half of the old arable lands of the kingdom may be said to be,—a year's fallow is the *shortest*,—the most effectual,—and the *cheapest* way of cleansing it. Tampering with
fallow

fallow crops, in fuch a cafe, is mere quackery. When land is once thoroughly cleanfed, it may, by fallow crops and due attention, be kept clean for a length of years.

But unfortunately for the occupiers of the fields which are the more immediate fubject of thefe obfervations, they *cannot* be fummer fallowed; *becaufe* every occupier cannot be brought into the fame mind in any one year; confequently, the affiftance of *sheep* cannot be conveniently had.

A Norfolk man, who has always been ufed to make his fallows with horfes only, without having perhaps a fingle fheep upon his farm, might well inquire if the farmers of Gloceftershire ufe fheep in their plow-teams. No. But a Gloceftershire farmer, who has never feen a fallow made, which has not been at the fame time a pafture (and fometimes not a bad one) for fheep, is led to believe, that a fallow cannot be made without them.—I have heard it lamented, by well meaning men, that fuch famous land, as undoubtedly lies in thefe fields, fhould be liable to fuch an inconveniency. But can affure them, from my own practice, that, in

Surrey,

Surrey, where similar fields are not unfrequent, it is common to make pieces of fallow among corn; and without experiencing any material inconveniency from the absence of sheep, during the summer-season.

If land be so foul as to require a whole year's fallow, it ought to have no respite from tillage; no time to form a sheep pasture! Nor if through want of leisure, or through neglect, it should form one,—is it necessary that it should be fed off with sheep. One man we see plowing in a crop of turneps, buck, or vetches, worth perhaps some pounds an acre; while another suffers his land to remain in a state of unproductiveness, lest he should plow in a few farthing's worth of sheep feed!

The *good effect* of fallowing the " every year's land" does not seem to be doubted:—there is, indeed, at this time, evidence, amounting to demonstration, in the center of one of the fields under notice. A plot, which was summer fallowed (by a superior manager) four years ago for wheat, was this year (1788) wheat after beans. In the spring, and during summer, it distinguished itself, evidently by the colour and grossness of the blade; and its superiority

at

at harveſt is not leſs manifeſt. An acre of it is worth four of ſome acres in the ſame field. (Windmill field near Gloceſter.) By obſervation ſufficiently minute, I am of opinion that, taking the reſt of the field on a par, one acre is worth two: and it is highly probable, that, with the unprecedented care, which, in this country, is taken of crops, while growing,—the effects of the fallow will be ſeen for many years henceforward.

I am of opinion that, with the practices of this country, in the ſeed and vegetating proceſſes, which will fall preſently under conſideration, a whole year's fallow *judiciouſly made* every ten, fifteen, or perhaps twenty years, would be found ſufficient to keep the land in a ſtate of cleaneſs and tilth. How extremely abſurd, then, to ſuffer them to remain in their preſent unproductive ſtate!

III. Laying up ridges. The high lands of the vale of Eveſham, have long been proverbial. Thoſe of the vale of Gloceſter are equally entitled to notoriety. It has been ſaid of them, hyperbolically, that men on horſeback, riding in the furrows, could not ſee each other over the ridges. This, we may venture

to

to fay, was never the cafe; though heretofore, perhaps, they have been higher than they are at prefent. Not many years ago, there was an inftance of ridges, toward the center of this vale, which were fo high, that two men above the middle fize, ftanding in the furrows, could not fee each other's heads: I have, myfelf, ftood in the furrow of a wheat ftubble; the tips of which, upon the ridges, rofe to the eye: a man, fomewhat below the middle fize, accidentally croffing them, funk below the fight in every furrow he defcended into. But the ftubble, in this inftance, was not lefs than eighteen inches high. The height of foil from four feet to four feet three inches:—the width of thefe lands about fifteen yards.—I afterwards meafured a furrow near four feet deep.

But an anecdote, relative to the firft-mentioned ridges, will fhew thefe extraordinary moments of human induftry in a more ftriking light, than any dimenfions which can be given. The occupier of them had, at a pinch, occafion to borrow fome plow-teams of his friends; one of whom called upon him, in the courfe of the day, to fee them at work, and was directed to the field, where fix or feven teams were.
plowing.

plowing. He went to the field (a flat inclofure of twelve or fifteen acres) but feeing nothing of the teams, he concluded he had miftaken the direction, and went back for a frefh one. The fact was, the feveral teams were making up their furrows, and were wholly hid, by the ridges, from his fight.

The width of thofe lands was twenty to twenty five yards: but lands in general are narrower, and of courfe lower; the height be-ing, in moft cafes, nearly proportioned to the width. About eight yards wide, and two feet to two feet and a half high, feems to be, at prefent, the favourite ridge. Thefe dimen-fions, though they may appear moderate upon paper, form, in the field, a fteep-fided ridge.

The ORIGIN of high ridges has long been confidered, I believe, as one of thofe fecrets, which antiquity may call its own. They are certainly monuments of human induftry; but are too *lowly* to have engaged the attention of the antiquary; and tradition, at leaft in this diftrict, is filent on the fubject.

They are not peculiar to this, but are com-mon to moft common field-diftricts, in which two crops and a fallow is the eftablifhed courfe

of

of hufbandry. Even upon the wolds of Yorkfhire, I have obferved the thin light chalky
loam, with which they are covered, fcraped
up together into high ridges.

In the vale under confideration, whofe fubfoil is of a nature fo fingularly cold and watery,
there is fome reafon to fuppofe, that the foil
has been thus heaped up, to render it dry
and *warm*. But this could not be the motive
in elevated fituations, where the fubfoil is ab-
forbent. Neverthelefs, we may reft affured,
that they have been raifed on *principle* (true or
falfe) as they muft have been raifed with labour
and expence.

The popular notion, here and in other
places, is, that the foil was thus thrown into
heaps, in order to increafe the quantity of
furface.

I cannot, however, think fo meanly of the
penetration of our anceftors, as to give in to
this improbable notion. For even fuppofing
every part of the fuperficies to be productive,
the advantage accruing to *corn*, through fuch
an expedient, is inconfiderable. It has no
more *room to grow in* than it would have if the
furface lay flat. Its roots, and its ears when
formed,

formed, may gain some addition of freedom, but the stems rise precisely at the same distance from each other, whether the land lie flat, or is raised into the highest ridges.

But in this district, where, in winter and wet seasons, each furrow, in many places, is a canal of stagnant water; and where, even in places in which the furrows lie above the common shore, some yards width of each is a thicket of weeds, without a blade of corn among them; the quantity of *productive surface* is very evidently, and very considerably, *lessened*.

In every district, and in every situation, the skirts of high ridges are weak, and comparatively unproductive. For, in proportion as the ridges are raised, and the depth of soil is there increased, in the same proportion the furrows are sunk, and the depth of soil there diminished; the bottoms of the furrows generally dipping into a dead infertile subsoil.

Besides, the skirts of high lands lie under another heavy disadvantage; especially where the soil is of a retentive nature, and the subsoil cold and watery: in a wet season, after the upper parts of the lands are saturated, the

redundant

redundant water falls down, of courfe, to their bafes, where, meeting with a repellent fubfoil, it is held in fufpence; keeping the fkirts of the lands, fo long as the wet feafon continues, in a ftate much too moift and cold for the pur-pofes of vegetation.

The prefent year (1788) affords numberlefs inftances of this evil effect. Laft autumn was excefflively wet. At wheat feed time, reten-tive foils were in a ftate of mortar; and re-mained in that ftate, until late in the fpring. It is probable that, on the lower parts of the lands, much of the feed never vegetated; and the plants, which reached the furface, dwindled away, as the fpring advanced. In the colder parts of the vale, the fkirts of the lands, in the latter end of May, had the appearance of fal-low-ground: in fome particular fituations, a ftripe upon each ridge, only, was left: not half, perhaps not one third of the furface fully occupied. Whereas, had the fame foil been judicioufly laid up in narrow lands, with crofs furrows to take off the furface water, every foot of furface might have been filled, and every part been rendered equally productive.

But

But extremely difadvantageous as high ridges undoubtedly are, while they remain in a ſtate of aration; they are no longer ſo, when laid down to graſs. In this caſe, the ſurface is indiſputably enlarged. Herbage, eſpecially when it is paſtured, ſpreads every way upon the ground, and does not riſe perpendicularly, as corn. Beſides, in this caſe, there is a variety of herbage, and a variety of ſoil, ſuited to every ſeaſon. If the ſeaſon be moiſt, the ridges afford a plenty of ſweet paſturage, and dry ground for the paſturing ſtock to reſt upon: and I had an opportunity of obſerving, in the year 1783, a dry year, that while the ridges, and flat lands in general, were burnt up with drought, the furrows of high lands continued in full herbage. It is obſervable, however, that in caſes, where the ſubſoil is retentive, every furrow ſhould have its under-drain; otherwiſe the herbage, eſpecially in a wet ſeaſon, will be of a very inferior quality.

The propriety of REDUCING HIGH RIDGES is a matter in diſpute, among men who ſtand high in their profeſſion. To me there appears no room for argument. If they be intended to remain under a ſtate of arable management,

Vol. I.			G			they

they ought to be lowered. On the contrary, if they be intended for a state of herbage, they ought to remain in or near their present form: provided the furrows be sufficiently found, or lie high enough for draining. If not, the ridges ought to be lowered, until the furrows be raised high enough to lie dry, or to admit of underdraining.

In the common fields, no attempts, I believe, have been made to lower them, in any considerable degree. The practice of plowing twice *upward* to once *downward*, as has been explained above, keeps them at, or nearly at, the ancient standard.

There is indeed a disadvantage attending the reduction of high ridges, which those, who have had no experience in them, may not be aware of. The *cores* of the ridges ; though they have been formed out of the original top-foil ; which, in all human probability, was, when buried, of a singularly fertile nature, are now become inactive, unproductive masses of *dead earth*. I have observed, where one of these ridges has been cut across in finking a stone pit, that the present soil forms an arch of dark-coloured rich-looking mould, a foot to eighteen inches deep ;—under which lies a regularly turned cylinder of ill coloured *sub-soil* ; refembling the *natural* fubfoil of the country fo much, that, unlefs we had indifputable evidence of thefe ridges being the work of art, we fhould be led to conclude that nature had moulded them to their prefent form. This appears to me an interefting circumftance, efpecially entitled to the agricultor's attention.

Notwithftanding, however, this difadvantage in reducing high ridges, I have had the opportunity of feeing an inftance of practice, in which fome of the higheft in the diftrict have been brought down to the defired pitch ; and, in the only way perhaps, in which the height of *arable* ridges can be decreafed with propriety: namely that of increafing their number.

The fubjects, in this inftance, were the inclofure particularly noticed in page 76; and a neighbouring inclofure ; which, in 1783, was nearly reduced to the defired ftate. The other had, in 1783, been recently begun upon ; and is now, 1788, in great forwardnefs.

The width of the lands in this cafe as has been faid was twenty to twenty five yards ; the height

                    five

five to fix feet ; the furrows lying much below
the furrounding ditches ; fometimes holding
water enough " to float a barge"!

The method of reducing them was that of
gathering up a new-land in each interfurrow of
the old ones ; which, by this means, were
lowered as the intervening lands were raifed.
To guard againft the difadvantage explained
above, the whole of the manure which would
have been fpread over the entire furface, was
laid upon the crowns of the old or large lands ;
it being found that the new lands, being formed
entirely of made-earth, were fufficiently fertile,
after they got their heads above water, without
the addition of manure ; and the fides of the
large lands were fed from the crowns, by every
plowing, and every fhower. Altogether a
great work, executed in a mafterly manner. *

In the open fields, where the lands lie inter-
mixt, this method of lowering them could not
be practifed. But one equally practicable is
obvious: namely that of forming each large
land into three ; by raifing a fmall one on either
fide of it. Applying the manure as in the
above

* By Mr. George Pitts of Down Hatherly.

above inftance.   If a general inclofure be not
near at hand, fome of the open-field townfhips
might, I fhould imagine, reap great benefit by
fuch a reform.

On the contrary,—where an inclofure is
likely to take place, and the land is naturally
·adapted to a ftate of *grafs,* 'it might be wrong
to leffen the width of the prefent ridges.   All
in that cafe requifite would be to alter their
form ; by reducing them from triangular *roofs*
to *waves,* or fegments of cylinders: a fpecies
of furface, for grafsland whofe fubfoil is any way
inclined to retentivenefs, which has many
ECONOMICAL advantages over a flat bowling-
green furface.

G 3   MANURE.

17.

M A N U R E.

VALE DISTRICTS, whole foils are generally deep and *naturally fertile*, require lefs manure than thin-foiled upland diftricts; which, being *naturally infertile* (if we may be allowed to fpeak of their original nature) require greater exertions of art, to preferve them in a ftate of productivenefs.

Hence, in diftricts of the latter defcription, we fee hufbandmen anxious about manure; making the moft of that which the farm itfelf affords; fetching others from a diftance; and fearching beneath the foil for more;—while in countries covered with more generous foil, manures are in lower eftimation: the degree of eftimation varying, however, in different diftricts of this defcription. *

In

* The PRICE OF TOWN MANURE may be confidered as no mean flandard of the flate of hufbandry, or at leaft the fpirit of hufbandmen, in the neighbourhood of the given town.

A man

In the vale under furvey, there is a confiderable proportion of grafs land. That which is paftured requires little addition of manure. And the grounds which are occafionally mown, have feldom any return made them. While the meadows, being either intrinfically fertile, or liable to be overflowed, pay an annual tribute to the dung yard, without expecting any return. The arable lands, therefore, form the only object of melioration; and DUNG may be faid to be the only manure made ufe of in meliorating them.

MOULD is not in ufe, either in the farm yard, or at the dung heap. I have feen it mixed with litter, or very long dung, layer-for-layer; but this is not the common practice of the diftrict.

MARL

A man whofe intelligence is good, and whofe veracity may be relied on,—has favored me with the prices of manure in the towns of this diftrict. Glocefter 1s. 6d. Tewkefbury 2s. Upton and Worcefter 2s. 6d. to 3s. Evefham 4s. to 5s. a load, of about a ton.

The comparative highnefs of the price at EVESHAM is chiefly owing to the quantity of GARDEN GROUNDS in the neighbourhood of that town; which fupplies Birmingham, and formerly fupplied many other diftant markets, in a great meafure, with garden ftuff. There are now, it is faid, two or three hundred acres under the garden culture.

MARL is not common to the vale. Weakly calcarious clays are frequent. The intervening ſtrata of the ſtone of the ſubſoil are calcarious in a ſlight degree. The only earth I have found, which can with propriety be termed marl, breaks out at the ſkirts, and in the roads of the red hills of Deerhurſt; and is, I believe, common to the red lands weſt of the Severn; where it is ſaid to be uſed as a manure; and it ought to be tried, (if it has not been tried already) in the vale; though its quality appears by analyſis to be of an inferior degree; not more than one fifth of it being a pure calcarious earth.

The ſpecimen I tried was taken near Apperley. Part of it in the hollow way between the common and the village; part from the foot of the hill facing the Severn. The colour a light red, reſembling that of ſalmon-coloured bricks: the contexture inclined to ſhaley; but breaks freely in water. One hundred grains left a reſiduum of eighty grains; a cinnamon-coloured ſilt.

LIME has been tried; and, in one inſtance at leaſt, has been found very beneficial to the vale land. But I do not find that the uſe of it

has

has in any inftance rifen into *practice.*   The argument againft it is, that ftone is expenfive to raife and coals dear.   Stones at 2s. a load are certainly dear; but coals at 10s. to 12s. a ton are very cheap, compared with their price in many diftricts where lime is burnt for manure.

It may be laid upon the land, here, at a much eafier expence than it is in Cleveland (a fimilar diftrict) to which it is fetched, in the ordinary practice of hufbandmen, twenty or thirty miles by land carriage.   But in Cleveland the fpirit of improvement has long been upon the wing: here it might be faid to be ftill a neftling.

In the MANAGEMENT OF DUNG nothing claims particular notice; it is ufually piled in the " courts" in fpring; and, in the common field hufbandry, carried onto the fallows the firft dry feafon of fummer.   One part in the ordering of dung in this diftrict is, however, reprehenfible: if a dung hill be formed in the field, the carriages are drawn upon it; by which means its maturation is very much retarded. See NORF. ECON. vol. I. p. 158.

S E E D

18.

SEED PROCESS.

IN THE SEED PROCESS, the vale farmers are above equality. Beans and peas, are almoſt univerſally SET BY HAND. Barley lands are CLODDED; and wheat "LAND-MENDED:" practices which lower, very conſiderably, the requiſite QUANTITY OF SEED. It appears to me probable, that one fourth of the quantity of ſeed, uſually ſown in moſt other diſtricts, is ſaved in this. The ſeed of barley excepted.

There is a prevailing opinion, backed by common practice, in the more central parts of the vale at leaſt, that it is dangerous *to ſow the freſh furrow of ſtiff land:* which, in this ſtate, is thought to lie "*too hollow!*" A ſtate, which the huſbandmen of the vale ſeem cautiouſly to avoid. Hence the wheat ſtubble is mown off, for beans, and the bean ſtubble drawn, for wheat; and the land ſuffered to lie

ſome

some time between the plowing and the sowing. Yet the lighter soils are sown on the
fresh furrow. In Norfolk, a lightland diftrict, the farmers dread nothing more than
their lands being cold and heavy at the time
of sowing.

Are these practices founded in right reason,
or in custom? If in truth,—how difficult is
the theory of this part of the arable procefs?

19.

CORN WEEDS.

THE SPECIES of cornweeds, pre-
valent in this district, are arranged in the following lift agreeably to their respective degrees of prevalency in the " every years' lands,"
in the neighbourhood of Glocester; or as
nearly fo as the intention of the arrangement
requires.

The first ten are the most destructive.—In
some cases, any one of the species would be
enough to destroy a crop, were they not
checked,

checked, in the manner which will be explained. The laſt nine are naturally the inhabitants of road-ſides and hedges; but, encouraged by the plow's neglect, have ventured abroad into the fields: even the common reed I have ſeen waving its panicles, in number, over wheat, growing ſeveral lands-widths from its native ditch.

LINNEAN NAMES.   ENGLISH NAMES*:

Triticum repens,—couch graſs.
Serratula arvenſis,—common thiſtle.
Sinapis nigra,—common muſtard†.
Convolvulus arvenſis,—corn covolvulus.
Chenopodium viride,—redjointed gooſefoot‡.
Chryſanthemum ſegetum,—corn marigold.

Papaver

* PROVINCIAL NAMES are, in this caſe, neceſſarily omitted. The names of plants; even their provincial names; are known to a few intelligent individuals, only; no one of whom I have been fortunate enough to meet with in this diſtrict.

† COMMON MUSTARD. This is the ſpecies which is cultivated in the north of England for its flour.—It is here the moſt common weed: being, in this diſtrict, what the wild muſtard, or charlock, is in others: a circumſtance, which is leſs extraordinary than that of the diſtrict under notice being free from the latter plant. I have not been able to gather a ſingle ſpecimen in it!

‡ REDJOINTED GOOSEFOOT: This I have heard called, provincially,—" DROUGHT-WEED": an apt name for it.

Papaver Rhæas,——round fmoothheaded
  poppy.
Papaver dubium,——long fmoothheaded
  poppy.
Avena fatua,—wild oat*.

Equifetum

* The WILD OAT, a plant unknown in many parts of the
ifland, is here, as well as in Yorkfhire, a moft troublefome
weed of corn.   In general appearance, this plant refembles
exactly the CULTIVATED OAT: in ftem, blade, panicle,
chaff, and *kernel*, they are the *fame* plant: and, in colour,
their feeds are fubject to the *fame* varieties: namely black,
red, white.   But, examined botanically, the wild oat
differs, in three notable particulars, from *Avena fativa;*
which is defcribed by Linneus, as having " calyxes *two-
feeded;* feeds *polifhed*; one *awned*"; whereas the calices of
the wild oat are *two or three feeded*; the feeds *covered with
long foft hair*; and *all of them* awned.   Neverthelefs,
in one inftance, I found the lower feeds of the panicle
nearly fmooth: this, added to the circumftance of the Poland
oat (a highly cultivated variety) growing in calices *one feeded,*
and *without any awn,* renders it much more than probable, that the various forts of cultivated oats are no more
than CULTIVATED VARIETIES OF THE WILD OAT.

  Be that as it may---the wild oat appears to be as con
firmed a *native* of this ifland, as any other *arable* weed,
which grows in it; and is, perhaps of all, the moft difficult
to be extirpated.   It will lie a century in the foil, without
lofing its vegetative quality.   Ground, which has lain in
a ftate of grafs, time immemorial, both in this county and
in Yorkfhire, has, on being broken up, produced it in
abundance.   It is alfo endowed with the fame inflinctive
                                                        choice

Equisetum arvense,—corn horsetail.
Agrostis alba,—creeping bentgrass.
Alopecurus agrestis,—field foxtailgrass.
Festuca duriuscula,—hard fescue *.
Sonchus oleraceus,—common sowthistle
Artemisia vulgaris,—mugwort.
Sinapis alba,—white mustard †.
Rumex crispus,—curled dock.
Carduus lanceolatus,—spear thistle.
Galium Aparine,—cleavers.

Urtica

choice of seasons, and state of the soil, as other seeds of weeds appear to have. This renders it, what it is considered, a difficult weed to be overcome: for ripening before any crop, it sheds its seed on the soil; where it probably finds safety from the birds in the roughness of its coat. FALLOW-ING; HOING;---and, where it is practicable, giving a final HANDWEEDING, after it shoot its panicle, are the only means of extirpation.

* HARD FESCUE. This plant, which is one of the greatest pests in the arable lands of some districts, (under the name of BLACK COUCH) is seldom met with in the plowed lands of this; notwithstanding their want of tillage: and notwithstanding it is found, (though not abundantly) in the surrounding grass lands.

† WHITE MUSTARD. Its seeds in this district are *red*; some of them inclining to a dark mottle; resembling, in colour, the seeds of the cultivated vetch: none of them lighter than those of the common mustard; *sinapis nigra*; whose seeds, when in perfection, are of a bright sorrel red.

Urtica dioica,—common nettle.

Sinapis orientalis *.

Rumex obtusifolius,—broadleaved dock.

Anthemis Cotula,—maithe-weed.

Matricaria suaveolens,——sweetscented ca-
momile.

Chrysanthemum inodorum,—weakscented ca-
momile.

Mentha arvensis,—corn mint.

Centaurea Cyanus,—bluebonnet.

Polygonum Persicaria,—common mild persicaria.

Sonchus arvensis,—corn sowthistle.

Lapsana communis,—nipplewort.

Atriplex patula,—spreading orach.

Tussilago Farfara,—coltsfoot.

Ranunculus repens,—creeping crowfoot.

Potentilla

---

* SINAPIS ORIENTALIS. A plant which grows here as
a troublesome weed of corn, answering with great exact-
ness, Linneus's description of *Sinapis orientalis,* I have ventured to call it by that name; though I have not been able
to find it, in any list of *English* plants. Its stature is similar
to that of the white mustard; to which its general appearance has some affinity; but, on closer examination, the affinity vanishes. The points, with which its pods and
stem are thickly set, incline *downward*; the body of the
pod is *long*; and the beak *short*; the seeds *numerous, small,*
and of a shining *black.*

Potentilla anserina,—silverweed.
Trifolium Melilotus officinalis,—melilot.
Achillea Millefolium,—milfoil.
Stachys palustris,—clownsallheal.
Veronica hederifolia,—ivyleaved speedwell.
Senecio vulgaris,—groundsel.
Alsine media,—chickweed.
Thlaspi Bursa-pastoris,—shepherdspurse.
Æthusa Cynapium,—foolsparsley †.
Cerastium vulgatum,—common mousear.
Fumaria officinalis,—common fumitory.
Polygonum aviculare,—hogweed.
Plantago major,—broad plantain.
Avena elatior,—tall oatgrass ‡.
Agrostis capillaris,—fine bentgrass.
Heracleum Sphondylium,—cowparsnep.
Centaurea Scabiosa,—upland knobweed.
Scabiosa arvensis,—upland scabious.

Daucus

---

† FOOLSPARSLEY. This is here a very common field weed (a character I have not seen it in before) but coming late, and not rising, in this situation, to a great height, its injury is little perceived.

‡ TALL OATGRASS. This is another fallow-weed which is partial to particular soils or situations. Notwithstanding the want of tillage in this district, I have not once seen its roots turned up by the plow.

Daucus Carota,—wild carrot.

Lychnis dioica,—common campion.

Carduus crispus,—curled thistle.

Lycopsis arvensis,—corn buglos.

Lamium purpureum,—dwarf deadnettle.

Galeopsis Tetrahit,—wild hemp *.

Ranunculus arvensis,—corn crowfoot.

Polygonum pensylvanicum,—pale persicaria.

Polygonum Convolvulus,——climbing buck-weed.

Antirrhinum Linaria,—common Snapdragon.

Hypochæris radicata,——long-rooted hawk-weed.

Euphrasia Odontites,—red eyebright.

Euphorbia Helioscopia,—sun spurge.

Viola

* WILD HEMP. This is another evidence of the same fact. In Yorkshire it ranks with the more prevailing weeds. In the midland counties it is still more prevalent: while here it takes place in the lower part of the catalogue.

These observations will, I am aware, be uninteresting to the reader, who is either unacquainted with the individuals spoken of, or is no way interested in the nature and prevalency of corn weeds. Nevertheless, they will, I am persuaded, be viewed in a different light by the practical farmer, who is, at the same time, a practical botanist; and I believe I may add, that every *good* farmer *is* a botanist, *as far as he is able*; and *ought to be*, as far as botany relates to agriculture.

Viola tricolor,—common pansie.
Prunella vulgaris,—selfheal.
Leont odonTaraxacum,—common dandelion.
Galium verum,—yellow bedstraw.
Malva rotundifolia,—round-leaved mallow.
Vicia Cracca,—bluetufted vetch.
Convolvulus sepium,—hedge convolvulus.
Galium Mollugo,—bastard madder.
Conium maculatum,—hemlock.
Ballota nigra,—stinking horehound.
Erisimum Aliaria,—garlic cress.
Lamium album,—white deadnettle.
Arundo phragmitis,—common reed.

After what has been said, under the head TILLAGE, it will be doing justice, only, to the vale farmers, to apprize the reader, in this place, that, inattentive as they undoubtedly are to the PREVENTION of corn weeds, they must not be considered as the avowed friends and allies of weeds: for, in the DESTRUCTION of them, they indisputably stand preeminent in their profession.

THE HOING OF CROPS IN GENERAL has long been held out as a thing most desirable, in the arable process. Here we find it nearly in full practice. Not only the ligumenous

crops,

crops, which are planted in rows ; but WHEAT, which is fown at random, are hoed: not by a few individuals, only ; but by hufbandmen in general : the wheat crop being hoed, here, as cuftomarily as the the turnep crop is in Norfolk. Barley may be faid to be the only crop, which is not hoed. But this crop is invariably fallowed for ; either by a whole year, or by a winter-and-fpring fallow : fo that EVERY CROP which is taken is, in reallity, a FALLOW CROP.

Hence we fee fields which have borne crops of GRAIN, year after year without remiffion, during time immemorial, ftill affording annually portions of produce, which, in the management of fome individuals, in fome feafons, may be entitled to the name of *crops*. A fact, which nothing lefs than actual obfervation, could have induced me to give full credit to. A fact which proves, in a moft interefting manner, the value of a due ATTENTION TO CROPS WHILE VEGETATING : a fpecies of attention, which, in the management of the kingdom at large, is entirely omitted ; excepting, perhaps, what is beftowed on an imperfect handweeding : In general terms, it may be faid, that, in moft other diftricts, crops re-

H 2

main

main in a ſtate of neglect, from ſeed time to harveſt. While, here, the buſineſs of the arable proceſs does not appear to be ſet about in earneſt, until the crops be above ground !

The origin of this unparalleled attention to crops, WHILE VEGETATING, would now, per-haps, be difficult to trace. In all probability, it originated in a kind of neceſſity, on the every years lands; which, without it, muſt long ago have been wholly poſſeſſed by one continued thicket of weeds. Its good effect being there ſeen, it would be received, by degrees, into the fallow fields: firſt as an ex-pedient to ſave a foul crop; and, at length, as a practice.

The excellency of this cuſtom, and the ex-tent of its utility, are not confined to the field: the HOING OF CORN is done, chiefly, by wo-MEN AND CHILDREN: induſtry is, of courſe, encouraged; and the pariſh levies probably leſſened; or, what is equally beneficial to the farmer, the wages for MEN's labour are low-ered: while, in the ſaving of ſeed, by this practice, the farmer and the community are ſtill more immediately benefited.

HARVESTING.

20.

HARVESTING.

THE WORK OF HARVEST was, formerly, done chiefly by HARVEST MEN; but now, in part, by THE ACRE.

The WAGES of harveſt men are thirty ſhillings for the harveſt; or a ſhilling a-day;—with full board.

The method of VICTUALING harveſtmen, in this diſtrict, is ſingularly judicious. They have *no regular dinner*. Their breakfaſt is cold meat. Their refreſhment in the field bread and cheeſe, with ſix or eight quarts of beverage. At night, when they return home, a *hot ſupper*;—and, after it, each man a quart of ſtrong liquor; in order to alleviate the fatigues of the day which is paſt; and, by ſending him to bed in ſpirits and good humour, to prepare him for the morrow's toil.

There is more than one advantage ariſes from this cuſtom. All work within-doors, in

the

the middle of the day, is got rid of: and the advantage of continuing the work of the field, without a break, through *the prime part of the day*, is obvious; and is highly eſtimated by thoſe who knew the value of it, from experience. Converſing with an active good huſbandman on the ſubject, he exclaimed "Lord, Sir, what ſhould we do now (about noon) if we were to give our men a regular dinner! They muſt either go home to it; or we muſt bring it to them here in the field; and while they were eating, and playing under the hedge, we ſhould loſe the hauling of two or three load of beans."

The hours of work are long;—from dawn to duſk;—eſpecially when diſpatch is more particularly requiſite. The quantity of work done is above par: namely, twenty to thirty loads of corn; with one ſet of men.

FARMYARD

21.

FARMYARD MANAGEMENT.

THE WINTER MANAGEMENT of the vale, as an *arable* diſtrict, affords nothing of excellence; nor includes any noticeable defect; excepting the prevailing one of paying too little regard to the accumulation of manure: nevertheleſs a few peculiarities require to be regiſtered.

Barn management. The *method of thraſhing*, in uſe here, is that of the ſouthern counties: the ears of wheat are occaſionally lifted, and looſe corn from time to time lightened, with the ſwipple; in order to raiſe up the parts unthraſhed, and thereby expoſe them to a more effective ſtroke: a practice which is more eaſy, leſs hurtful to the grain, and perhaps not leſs expeditious, than the north-country method; in which the thraſher keeps on, with one even ſtroke, from the time the corn is ſpread upon the floor, until it be turned, or the ſtraw ſhook off.

H 4

Winnowing

Winnowing is here done with the fail-fan in the fouth-of-England manner.

Chaff is expended on cart horfes. Barley chaff is in good efteem:—fome farmers, at leaft, prefer it to that of the " cone wheat".;—a long-awned grain.

YARD MANAGEMENT. It has been already faid that bottoming farm yards with *mould* is not a practice of this diftrict. They are, how-ever, fometimes littered with *ftubble*.

Straw is given to cattle, loofe, in mangers and cribs of various conftructions. (See FARM-BUILDINGS.)

It is not unufual in the practice of this di-ftrict to let ftraw-yard cattle have a yard, fod-dering ground, or orchard, adjoining to the ftraw yard, to ftray into at pleafure. This in-dulgence may be ferviceable, perhaps, to the health of the cattle ; but is certainly wafteful of manure.

MARKETS.

22.

MARKETS.

THE PRINCIPAL MARKETS of this diſtrict, for CORN, are *Gloceſter* and *Tewkeſbury.* *Cheltenham,* in the ſummer ſeaſon, takes off its proportion of BUTTER and POULTRY. CHEESE is bought up chiefly by *factors* ; and the ſurplus of FAT CATTLE and SHEEP, after the country markets are ſupplied, goes chiefly to *Smithfield.*

MARKET PLACES never ſtruck me as a ſubject entitled to particular attention, until I ſaw the good effect which has taken place, by a reform in the market places of this diſtrict.

In 1783, the markets of Gloceſter, Tewkeſbury and Cheltenham were kept on old-faſhioned *croſſes,* and under open market-houſes, ſtanding in the middles of the main ſtreets ; to the annoyance of travellers; the disfigurement of the towns; and the inconveniency of the market-people, whether ſellers or buyers.

New

Now (1788) thefe nuifances are cleared away, and the markets removed into well fituated receffes, conveniently fitted up for their reception.—A fpecies of reform which moft market towns in the kingdom ftand greatly in need of.

The old croffes and market houfes are generally fmall, inconvenient, and now no longer adequate to the purpofes for which they were originally erected. In winter, they are chilling and dangerous to the health of thofe who have to wait in them; efpecially women; whofe habits of hardinefs may not, now, be equal to what they were in the day in which thefe erections were made. Befides, the corn-market, the fhambles, and the women's market are frequently fcattered in different parts of a town: while, in a fquare inclofed with fhops, fhades, and penthoufes; with fhambles in the center; and a corn market at the entrance;— the whole are brought together; rendering the bufinefs of market commodious and comfortable; epithets which, at prefent, can feldom be well applied to it.

In the inftances under notice, the alterations were made by the refpective towns; at, no doubt,

doubt, a confiderable expence ; the intereft of which is raifed by tolls, payable by the fellers: an inconveniency, which leffens, very confiderably, the magnitude of the improvement.

This is an interefting fubject, and clofely connected with the prefent defign. It would little avail the farmer to raife crops, without a market to vend them at. It is the grand center to which all his labours tend.

We may, I think, venture fafely to ftart as a pofition, that markets are, or ought to be made, the concerns of COUNTIES at large; not of the particular towns they happen to be kept in. They promote, indifputably, the general benefit of towns, and the portions of country which lie immediately round them ; but that of the latter more efpecially: and it would be equally reafonable to expect that a market town fhould build a bridge for the country people to come over to market, as to find them fhops to fell their wares in.

Indeed *weekly markets* are effentially neceffary, in the prefent ftate of things, to the country ; but not fo to towns ; which have markets, *daily*, in the fhops of their own inhabitants: and that they require no weekly markets,

London

London is an inftance.   In wholefale matters, as corn, cheefe &c, towns have no intereft whatever: unlefs the *inns*, as they oftentimes abfurdly are, be confidered as the *town*: the mere *inhabitants* have none.

But although the inhabitants of *towns* have no neceffity for a weekly market; thofe of *villages* would find themfelves aukwardly fituated without one.   They cannot, like the town's-people, go every morning to the fhop. One day in a week is full as much time as they can fpare.

Nor would it be convenient to the *farmer* to depend upon the fhopkeepers' or the huckfters' calling upon him for his produce, and giving him their own price.   It is as convenient,—as neceffary,—for farmers to go to market, as it is for merchants to go to 'change ;—to learn the current price, and take their choice of buyers; as well as to meet each other, and make the requifite bargains between themfelves.

FAIRS are, in this point of view, ftill more convenient to the farmer.   How fhould a grazier or a jobber know that he has ftock to difpofe of, unlefs he had fome means of *publifhing* them ?   At the fame time, how convenient

ent are fairs to the grazier, who can there take his choice of stock; as well as to the breeder, who may there make his election of price.

Towns were no doubt aware of these things when TOLLS were established. But tolls are fetters which all fairs and markets should be freed from. They interrupt the business of the day; are the cause of endless dispute; and may, in these days, well be considered as the impositions of less liberal times, which ought to be cleared away,

Markets, more especially, are a universal good. They bring the producer and the consumer hand to hand. Shopkeepers and hucksters are middle men, who must be paid for their labour; and whatever profit they receive is so much lost, either to the farmer or the consumer.

Tolls have the selfsame tendency. Either the seller or the buyer must pay them; and each has his plea of complaint. The tolls of Glocester market are very high—almost excessive—3d. butter—2d. poultry or eggs.— The market women, of course, complain of the hardship; while the town's people are still louder in their complaints; alleging that the

sellers,

sellers, taking the advantage of the toll, charge them doubly for it. All taxes, eventually, fall on the consumer.

This is a subject which has never, I believe, been agitated; but which is certainly entitled to the *bigbest* attention.

From the observations which are here loosely thrown together, we may venture to draw, as a conclusion, that ALL FAIRS AND MARKETS SHOULD BE FREE:

· And that a REFORM in the MARKET PLACES and FAIR-STEADS* of this kingdom is wanted:

not

---

* FAIR-STEADS in general, are still less commodious than market places. They are mostly confined to the *streets* (barbarous usage) and sometimes every street in the town is a separate fair-stead: so that it is impossible for a buyer to know what stock the fair consists of. When a market is brisk, much of it may be sold before he can possibly have an opportunity of seeing it. While, in other cases, the streets are so narrow, and the fair-stead so confined, that the value of stock cannot be estimated with sufficient accuracy. A square paddock, paled or walled round; with one gate to admit, and another to let out stock; the cattle being placed on the border, properly formed to receive them; and the sheep-pens in the center, (in the manner of Smithfield market) would perhaps be found, in preference to all others, the best form for a fair-stead. How easily might every market town be furnished with such a paddock.

not fo much for the conveniency of towns, as for that of the country.

We have no ground of reafoning, however, to expect that corporations, and lords of manors, will even give up their prefent tolls, much lefs make the requifite reform, without fome adequate recompence.

The COUNTIES, refpectively, have the care of their gaols, and bridges; and it ftrikes me, that the county-rate would be the propereft fund for defraying the expence of a reform in their markets; and for afterward keeping in due order, fair-fteads and market-places.

A reform in WEIGHTS and MEASURES has long been fpoken of as a thing defirable. It would be well if fome GENERAL REFORM, in the fairs and markets of thefe kingdoms, could be brought about. While they remain in their prefent BARBAROUS ftate, we cannot have full claim to the character of a CIVILIZED NATION.

WHEAT.

23.

W H E A T.

THE SPECIES of wheat, in cultivation here, are

1. "CONE WHEAT" or "BLUE CONE":—a variety of TRITICUM *turgidum*. [*] The straw tall and reedy: the ear long, and of a dusky-purple colour: the chaff downy, with a very long awn, which falls off when fully ripe. The grain brown, tolerably well skinned, and of a hard flinty contexture; affording a *thirsty* flour; in good esteem with the miller and baker. This is the prevailing wheat of the district;—whose produce is probably three-fourths of it of this species.

2. "LAMMAS. ·

[*] Not, however, the variety which is entitled to the distinction *cone*; its ears being remarkably *cylindrical*. In Northwiltshire, I met with the TRUE CONE—or *triticum quadratum*—of Miller:—the base of the ear large and square (hence it is there called "square eared wheat") but the upper part is *conical*, tapering to a point. This variety is remarkably *turgid*;—the grains, in the base of the ear, bursting open the chaff, before harvest, showing themselves plainly to the eye.

2. " LAMMAS WHEATS":—varieties of
TRITICUM *bybernum.* Every thing that does
not bear awns is " lammas";—which is divided into " red-ftraw" and " white-ftraw"—
or rather into *red-chaff* and *white-chaff* lammas.
Of the latter there are two entirely diftinct
forts; the chaff of one *fmooth,* the other
villous. They frequently grow together in the
fame piece, and the diftinction probably paffes
unnoticed.

3. TRITICUM *æftivum,*—or SPRING WHEAT:
a fpecies which has been pretty freely tried in
this diftrict; but which is not, at prefent,
likely to gain an eftablifhment.

The CULTIVATION of wheat in this diftrict,
cannot, altogether, be offered as a model:
neverthelefs it muft not be paffed over in fi-
lence. It has one excellency, at leaft, which
entitles it to the higheft attention.

The SUCCESSION has been mentioned. *Beans,*
planted and hoed, may be confidered (except
in the old fallow fields) as its common prede-
ceffor. *Peas* cultivated in the fame manner,
likewife precede it, on light land:—wheat being here grown on every fpecies of SOIL.

The soil process, after pulfe, is fometimes fingular; and is entitled to notice. The *ftub-ble* of beans is pretty generally *drawn* *; and I have feen, in more than one inftance, the fur-face *breaft-plowed*, after peas as well as beans, previous to the feed plowing for wheat.

This is to me a novel practice. I have not, out of this county, feen the breaft plow ufed in any other intention, than that of paring off the furface of grafsland, in whole fods. But the operation, in the practice under notice, is done with a very different defign. The paring is not attempted to be turned in the na-ture of a fod; the intention is merely that of fevering the roots of weeds beneath the fur-face; in order that they may be harrowed out and deftroyed, before the wheat be fown. This, for the clafs of *creeping perennial weeds*, † is a ready and effectual mode of exterpation: alfo

---

* For *fuel*; either by the farmer; or, more generally I believe, by his labourers' wives and children; who have the fuel for their labour; a waggon being generally placed in the field to receive it, as it is drawn. Bean ftubble plowed into the foil is thought to afford refuge for snails; which fometimes do the wheat crop great injury. It is alfo thought *to keep the foil too hollow!*

† See york: econ: vol. 1. p. 375.

alfo the *ftrong-rooted*, and even the *worm-rooted* tribes are, probably, effentially *checked* by this practice ; efpecially as the plow, prefently afterward, makes another feparation at a greater depth ; fo that their feeding fibres, as well as their foliage, are to be produced afrefh.

The only objection to this practice is the expence: namely fix or feven fhillings an acre. In a country, however, where a fingle plowing cofts more money, the expence cannot be deemed exceffive.

But, on a foil free from ftones, as the foils of the vale almoft invariably are, the fame or a fimilar effect may be produced, in a much eafier way. For although I had not feen a breaft plow ufed in the operation ; the utility and effects of the operation itfelf are familiar to me. In my own practice, in Surrey, I purfued the operation of SUB-PLOWING to, perhaps, its fartheft limits: gaining a full view of its merits and defects. The greateft difficulty lies in getting an implement to work, in all foils, and in all feafons. A light wheel-plow,— with a broad fharp fhare, and without a mould board,—drawn by one or two horfes, is, I believe, the beft implement which can be ufed in this operation: which, in some cafes, is very valuable.————See MIN. OF AGRI. dates 16 Auguft, 10 and 20 October 1775, and 16 Auguft 1776.

The TIME OF SOWING, November and December! If a farmer get his feed wheat into the ground before Chriftmas, he is thought to finifh in due feafon. How widely different are the cuftoms of countries, with refpect to this important operation. Cuftoms which are, no doubt, founded, in fome degree at leaft, on the experience of ages. This country is nearly a month behind the reft of the kingdom. It is argued, by men of experience, in fupport of this extraordinary practice, that, " late-fown wheats are apt to be better headed"—are more productive of *grain*—than crops which are fown more early: and the argument, duly limited, may have fome foundation. But it is very probable, that the *peculiar* latenefs of wheat feed time, in this diftrict, is not effentially neceffary to the natural fituation of the vale, or to the nature of its foil, but arifes, in fome degree, out of its prefent peculiarity of management. The unproductivenefs of the early fown crops may be, in part, owing to the

the hoſt of weeds with which they have to en-
counter; while thoſe which are ſown late, eſ-
caping the autumnal vegetation, have fewer
enemies to contend with, the enſuing ſummer.

There are two diſadvantages evidently at-
tend late ſowing. The ſeaſon is uncertain, and
the requiſite quantity of ſeed is increaſed.
Much of it never vegetates, and much of that,
which, if ſown in due ſeaſon, might have vegetated, falls unavoidably a prey to vermin of
different kinds.

Nevertheleſs, ſuch is the ſtrength of the
vale lands, and ſuch the advantages of hoing,
that the QUANTITY OF SEED ſown in this diſtrict is *conſiderably leſs*, than that ſown, I believe, *in any other part of the kingdom*. Even at
Chriſtmas, the quantity ſeldom exceeds *two
buſhels* an. acre! *Six pecks*, in September--
October, would afford as full a ſufficiency of
plants; and, in the more early part of the
ſeaſon, *ſeven pecks, ſown broadcaſt*, is the uſual
quantity of ſeed! *

I 3

The

* SETTING WHEAT. This practice is not here in uſe;
except on a ſmall ſcale. In the little encroachments round
Corſe Lawn (a well ſoiled and very extenſive common-
ſheep-walk weſtward of the Severn) I have obſerved ſeveral
patches of wheat, planted in rows, with " ſetting pins", in
the manner beans and peas are planted in this diſtrict.

The meafure, it is true, is large: full nine gallons and a half: fo that the feven pecks contain near feventeen gallons. But, in Norfolk, three bufhels containing near twenty five gallons, is ufually fown, fome weeks, perhaps, before the feed time commences in this country: two bufhels and a half; about twenty two gallons, may be taken as the middle quantity of feed wheat, throughout the kingdom.

But, in the vale of Glocefter,—WHEAT IS UNIVERSALLY HOED: a fact which does honor to ENGLISH AGRICULTURE; and which I enter in this regifter with more than ordinary fatisfaction.

The hoing of wheat is one of thofe valuable operations in hufbandry, which are lefs difficult, and more effectual, in practice than in theory. I have examined it with extraordinary attention; and fhall beftow upon it a minute analytical defcription.

     1. The number of hoings.
     2. The times of hoing.
     3. The width of the hoe.
     4. The method of hoing.
     5. The price.
     6. The advantages.

1. THE

1. THE NUMBER OF HOINGS. Two ho-
ings are generally fpoken of; but are executed
only in the practice of fuperior hufbandmen.
One hoing and a handweeding, however, are
effential to good management. Two hoings,
the laft likewife a handweeding, might be
deemed perfection. The firft hoing, if given
in due time, will unavoidably mifs many weeds,
which will afterwards run up to feed, and foul
fucceeding crops.

Sometimes the crop is HARROWED early
(about the time of the firft hoing) and ho'ed
fome time afterward. It is likewife not unfrequently HARROWED prefenting after the firft
hoing: a good finifh, which not only loofens
the foil, and lets down a fupply of air to the
roots of the corn; but effectually difengages
the weeds from the foil; in which they are
liable to be refixed by the feet of the hoers.

2. THE TIMES OF HOING. The firft hoing
is begun in April, or as foon as the feafon will
permit. It ought to be finifhed before the
plants begin to " branch" ftock—tiller—or
make their vernal ramifications. The fooner
the fecond hoing fucceeds the firft, the lefs
difficulty there is in doing it; but the later

it is given, the more ferviceable it proves ;
provided the crop be not immediately injured
in the operation.

3. THE WIDTH OF THE HOE. It is generally underftood, that the fize of the hoe
ought to be proportioned to the fullnefs of the
crop: a thin crop requiring a wide hoe—one
which is thick upon the ground, a narrow
one. The narroweft I have meafured has
been three inches; the wideft five inches.
The form is that of the turnep-hoe: except
that the corners are, or ought to be, rounded
off.

4. THE METHOD OF HOING. If the plants
ftand fufficiently wide to admit the hoe between them, the entire furface is ftirred.
Where they ftand clofely, and weeds do not
appear, they are paffed over. Thus, the tops
of high ridges are frequently too rank to admit
the hoe, while the fides of the lands are entirely
worked over with it.

The *art* of hoing wheat is much lefs difficult
than that of hoing turneps; which require a
quick eye and a fteady hand, to fingle them
out at proper diftances: whereas, in hoing
wheat, the plants, and of courfe the fpaces
between

between them, are *given*; all the hoer has to do, is to cut over the vacant patches, and draw the hoe between the plants;—length-way, if the plants will admit of it; if not, and weeds intervene, to force through the end, or the corner: in doing which the plants are not much endangered; unlefs the hoe be very fharp: for the fame hoe, which will ftir the ground, and cut up feedling weeds, will flip over wheat without injuring it. Wheat, rooting deep, is not eafily eradicated; and fhould part, or even the whole of the blades be cut off, they will, provided the crown be left, re-fpring.

Hence women and children may, with fufficient fafety, be trufted with hoes among wheat; and, where the foil is tolerably free from root-weeds, foon become fufficiently expert.

But if couch grafs abound among wheat, which it too frequently does, not only more labour, but greater fkill is requifite. Couch grafs bears the fame affinity to wheat, as the wild muftard does to turneps; an adept will generally diftinguifh the plants with fufficient readinefs; but in fome cafes, they refemble

each

each other so nearly, as to be easily mistaken for one another, by the inexperienced. Besides, in this case the hoe is obliged to be kept with a sharp edge; otherwise it will not take the couch: this, of course, renders it a more dangerous implement in the hands of the inadept. Therefore, under these disgraceful circumstances, men ought to be, and frequently are, on the every years lands, employed in the hoing of wheat.

This, however, does not operate against the general principle of HOING WHEAT BY WOMEN AND CHILDREN. No man, who has any regard for his interest, or to his character as a husbandman, *attempts* to cultivate wheat in a bed of couchgrafs.

The requisite *distance* between the plants, depends on the species of wheat, and the state of the soil. Cone wheat is found to branch more than lammas.; and either of them will spread wider on a rich, than on an impoverished soil. If the plants be strong, ten or twelve inches is not deemed too great a distance.

It might, however, be wrong to set-out close-growing plants at that distance: plants
may

may acquire, during the autumn and winter, habits agreeable to their refpective fituations: the fingle plants to fpread,—thofe in groups to run upward; and it might be injurious, in the fpring, to place them in new fituations. Neverthelefs, it is probable that, in many cafes, the crop would be improved, if the underling plants, which rank wheat generally abounds with, were in due time removed. Crouded plants produce feeble ftraw, and puny imperfect grain: and, from the attention I have paid this fubject, I am of opinion, that a five-inch hoe might be ufed, freely, in the fulleft crop. I do not mean in fetting the plants out, fingly, like thofe of turneps; but merely in leffening their number; thereby giving thofe which were left a fufficiency of air and headroom. A turnep requires room at the root; wheat at the ear: and it is a thing of no great confequence, perhaps, whether a given fquare foot of atmofphere be filled with ears from one, two, or a greater number of roots.

5. PRICE. The ordinary price is half a crown an acre, for the firft hoing. But the
requifite

requisite labour varies with the state of the crop, and the nature of the soil. A full clean crop, on a free soil, wants little labour. Nor on such a soil, though foul with seed-weeds, is the labour difficult; provided the crop has not been suffered to run up and hide the surface. On the contrary, a thin tall crop, foul with couchgrass, on a stubborn soil, in a dry season, requires more labour than is ever paid for. I have seen a man hoing wheat under the last mentioned circumstances, at 3s. an acre. But he barely earned day-wages; yet did not half do his work. If the soil be tolerably free, the season kind, and the crop taken in a proper state as to growth, notwithstanding it may be foul with seed weeds, there are women who will hoe half an acre a day. Such a crop is not unfrequently done at 2s. an acre.

The second hoing is frequently more tedious than the first; by reason of the crops, hiding the ground, and being in the way of the hoe.

6. The ADVANTAGES of hoing are many. The seed weeds are cut off; the root weeds checked; and the crust of the soil broken.

By

By thus giving the roots a full fupply of air,
and the plants themfelves the full poffeffion of
the furface,—they acquire a vigorous habit,
and are induced to branch out, fpread over
the furface, and fill up every vacancy; by that
means increafing their own ftrength, and
keeping their enemies under. If a fimile
might be ufed on this occafion, we might fay,
that the foil is a country contended for; the
corn and the weeds contending armies:—By
deftroying, or checking the advancement of
one, we give the other an opportunity of gaining full poffeffion.

Befides the advantages to the growing crop,
thofe of future crops ought to be confidered.
The hoe deftroys, in the firft hoing, a clafs
of weeds, which handweeding feldom, if ever
ftoops to. Indeed, before that operation ufually takes place, they are fhrunk beneath notice: they flourifh, however, at a critical
time;—the time of branching;—and are probably the caufe of greater mifchief, than rifes
to common obfervation. The fpecies which
come moft particularly within this clafs are the
ivyleaved fpeedwell or *winterweed*,—*chickweed*,
and *groundfil*: while *hairough*, one of the worft

weed

weed of wheat, falls an eafy victim to the hoe.
The *fhepherdspurfe,—common* and *fcorpion moufe-
aars, fumitory, bogweed,* and other low-grow-
ing weeds, are cut off imperceptibly in HOING;
but are feldom the objects of HANDWEEDING:
confequently, fhed their feeds upon the foil,
and remain, from year to year, a nuifance to
the growing crop.

In the HARVESTING of wheat, we find nothing particularly noticeable; except the
practices of letting it ftand until it be unrea-
fonably ripe,—of cutting. it very high,—and
of binding it in remarkably fmall fheaves.
The laft requires fome attention.

The fize of the fheaf is here proportioned,
in a great meafure, to the height of the crop.
The fheaves being invariably bound with one
length of ftraw. The practice of making
double bands—a practice common to the fouthern, eaftern, northern, and midland counties, appears to be unknown in this diftrict.
This year, the ftraw being fomewhat fhort,
the fheaves (if fuch they may be deemed) are
mere handfuls—many of them may be grafped
with the fingers.—Few of them are equal to
half a common fheaf; three or four of fome

of

of them (efpecially in the every years fields, where, perhaps, there are more weeds than corn to bind up) would not make a fheaf of fome diftricts.

The advantages and inconveniences of this extraordinary practice require examination.

The inconveniences arife chiefly from the number of fheaves.   The crop takes more binding.—The trouble of band-making, however is evaded.   But it is certainly more tedious to ftook, pitch, load, unload, ftack &c. &c. than it would be if bound in larger fheaves; and, in thefe operations, without any obvious counter advantage.

The practice, neverthelefs, has its advantages.   Small fheaves require lefs field room, as it is termed; that is lefs time between the cutting and the carrying; than large fheaves do.   And, what is equally valuable, if they be caught in wet weather, they are much fooner dried again: confequently, the danger of growing is not fo great as when the crop is bound in large fheaves; which frequently require opening, when a fmall one may be got dry without that tedious and dangerous expedient.

The

The practices of cutting high and binding
with single bands, have probably arisen, like
that of hoing wheat, out of a kind of necessity
on the every year's lands; on which if the
weeds as well as the wheat were to be reaped,
by cutting the latter low; and the whole bound
up together in large sheaves;—scarcely any
length of time would cure them to the center.
The great length of cone wheat may have af-
sisted in establishing the practice.

The size of sheaves, uninteresting as it may
appear to those who are unpracticed in the minutiæ of husbandry, is a subject of some importance.—That the sheaves of wheat are made
much too large in many districts, and perhaps
in general, is as evident as that, in this district,
many of them are made smaller than any good
purpose can require.   The difficulty lies in as-
certaining the happy medium.   We may venture to say, without risque, that the size ought
to bear some proportion to the state of the crop.
At present, it may be said to vary from a handful to an armful.   How far it ought to vary,
and what the proper sizes of the two extremes
are, I dare not, here, take upon me to deter-
mine.

The

The STUBBLE and weeds are generally mown off in ſwaths, ſoon after harveſt, for litter. It is not unuſual to ſell the ſtubble on the ground. The price ſometimes ſo high as 5s. an acre ; off which perhaps the buyer will carry a full waggon load ! A quantity, perhaps, equal to that carried off in ſheaves at harveſt.

The PRODUCE of wheat, in this diſtrict, is below par : notwithſtanding the ſuperior quality of the ſoil. The par produce of the diſtrict is laid at *eighteen* buſhels an acre (the meaſure large). I have heard men talk gravely of *twelve* buſhels ; even in the ſallow fields. I have myſelf ſeen, in one of the every year's fields, not leſs perhaps than twenty, perhaps not leſs than forty acres, which could not be laid at more than *eight* buſhels an acre !

I do not mention theſe things to expoſe the huſbandmen of the vale of Gloceſter—I have no motive whatever to lead me to ſuch a conduct—nor do I, on any occaſion, I truſt, ſuffer any motive whatever to lead me to cenſure, other than the facts which appear before me, I have no partiality to this or that diſtrict. To enable me to proſecute with greater diligence the deſign I have entered upon, I en

Vol. I.   K   deavour

deavour to view *each* diſtrict *as my own*: and wiſh to ſee the ſeveral parcels of my wide domain; or,—in language more ſuitable to the ſubject,—the ſeveral cultivated diſtricts of this iſland, on a par as to cultivation; and as near perfection as the preſent ſtate of the art is capable of raiſing them. On the preſent occaſion, I wiſh to prove, by the moſt ſubſtantial evidence, the neceſſity of a CHANGE OF MANAGEMENT.

The diſtrict contains, without diſpute, ſome plots of cold unproductive ſoil. Every acre of it, which lies out of the water's way, may neverthcleſs be ſaid to be WHEAT LAND. Three fourths of it is land of ſuch a quality that it ought never to be ſown with wheat, without a fair probability of THREE TO FOUR QUARTERS AN ACRE. The preſent unproductiveneſs is a loſs to the community; and reflects equal diſgrace on its owner and its occupiers.

There muſt be ſome cauſe or cauſes of this ſtriking deficiency of produce; and it behoves the landowners to aſcertain and remove them: their intereſt is the moſt materially concerned.

If the deficiency be owing to the open fields being worn down by arable crops, (which I believe is one very great caufe of it)—why let them remain in their prefent unprofitable ftate? Why not inclofe them, and let the lands be laid to grafs?

If the deficiency be caufed by the land's being chilled with furface water (as much of the central parts of the vale undoubtedly is) why not obtain an act of fhores: and under it keep them, as they may undoubtedly be kept, fufficiently free from it.

If the coldnefs of the fubfoil be the caufe, (as it may be in fome places) encourage underdraining.

If, on examination, the caufe of a deficiency of produce fhould appear to be principally owing to a deficiency of tillage (as in the every year's lands it affuredly is)—give due encouragement to fallowing; and check, by every other poffible means, the prefent difgraceful practice of growing eight bufhels of wheat an acre, on land which is by nature enabled to bear four times that quantity.

The reform which is here offered is wanted in various other diflricts of the kingdom; in

which

which the wheat crop, by injudicious management, is too frequently difgraceful to Englifh
hufbandry.   The wheat crop, above all others,
fhould not be *rifqued*.   No man ought to fow
wheat where he has not, with a common feafon, a moral certainty of a crop.

24.

BARLEY.

THE QUANTITY of barley grown in
this vale is very confiderable.   For, notwithftanding the uncommon *coldnefs* of much of the
vale lands, this is the only fpring *corn* which is
cultivated on them.

The only SPECIES that I have feen cultivated
in the diftrict is the common LONG-EARED
BARLEY: HORDEUM *zeocriton*.

In the CULTIVATION of barley, one circumftance, only, is noticeable: namely that of its
being made ufe of, on the every year's lands,
as the *cleanfing crop*.

It

It appears to be a leading article of faith, among the occupiers of thefe lands, that if a week or ten days fine weather, in the fpring, can be had for the operation of harrowing out couch; and if, after this, a full crop of barley fucceed; efpecially if it fhould be fortunate enough to take a reclining pofture; the bufinefs of *fallowing* is effectually done:—the foil being thus raifed to a degree of cleannefs and tilth fufficient to laft it through a feries of fucceeding crops.

Hence, to catch a few fine days to fallow in, barley is fown, on thefe lands, very late:—the middle of May—fometimes the latter end of May—fometimes the beginning of June—this year (an aukward feafon) barley was fown towards the middle of June.—And, to obtain a full crop, three to four bufhels an acre is invariably fown; under the idea that a full crop of barley, efpecially if it lodge, fmoothers all forts of weeds; even couch grafs itfelf. And true it is, that under lodged barley the foil grows mellow, and weeds get *weak*.

Neverthelefs, I mean not to recommend a practice which is already too prevalent; not in

 this

this diftrict, only, but in others: where we fee men catching at a barley fallow, as a twig which will keep their corn above the weeds a few crops longer. The confequence is, the barley crop, by being fown out of feafon, is of an inferior value, and fucceeding crops, by having a hoft of weeds to ftruggle with, are rendered equally unproductive.

If the land be tolerably clean, and the feafon favourable, a barley fallow may no doubt be of effential fervice. But there is not one year in five, in which, even land which is tolerably clean, can be fown in feafon and at the fame time be much benefitted by it for future crops.

I am well aware that even land which is foul with couchgrafs, may, by harrowing, raking and handpicking, at an unlimited expence, and fowing the barley fome weeks behind its time, be made to appear, to the eye, perfectly clean at barley feed time; but whoever will examine it after harveft, or the enfuing fpring, and compare its ftate then, with that of land which has had a turnep or a whole year's fallow, will fcarcely beftow the labour of harrowing, and raking,

'and

and picking; and rifque the lofs of his barley crop, a fecond time. *

I have faid the more on this fubject, becaufe
it is an important one. I know no practice fo
popular, and at the fame time fo deftructive
of good hufbandry, as that of tantalizing foul
land with a barley fallow. And I offer my
fentiments upon it, in this place, becaufe I
hope I fhall never have a more fuitable opportunity.

Barley is HARVESTED loofe: mown with
the naked fithe; lies in fwath till the day of
carrying; and is cocked with common hay
forks.

The MARKETS for barley are Glocefter and
Tewkefbury. The buyers, malfters of the diftrict, and factors who buy for the Briftol brew-
ers.

The PRODUCE, on a par, three quarters an
acre: the meafure very large.

K 4   The

* I fpeak, here, of land which is kept under a courfe of
arable crops; rather than of that which is occafionally broken up from grafs, and laid down again, when two or three
crops of corn have been taken: a practice which I may
have occafion to fpeak of fully, in another place.

The QUALITY of the vale barley is such as recommends it to the malster, in preference to hill barley that affords a more sightly sample. But there seems to be a quality in the soils of these vales which gives strength and richness to every article of their produce.

25.

O A T S.

OATS, it has been said, are not a produce of this district; at least none of the CULTIVATED varieties are: the WILD OAT grows every where with unusual strength and productiveness.— Many lasts of it are, every year, no doubt produced.

I have never however yet seen a low-situated, strong-soiled, cold-bottomed country, which has not been found, on experience, to be better adapted to oats than to barley. And I have not, in this district, met with any experience, or indeed with any reasoning, which attempts

tempts to prove the contrary.   Cuſtom alone is pleaded. *

This excluſion of the oat crop from the lands of the vale,—extraordinary as it appears at firſt ſight,—may perhaps be accounted for in this way.   The monks preferred ale to oaten cake: barley of courſe became the favorite crop: the monaſteries were numerous: the lighter lands were not adequate to the demand:—the barley crop, therefore, was neceſſarily extended to the ſtrong lands. The monaſteries, it is true, have long been diſſolved ; but the ſpirit of improvement

---

* Since writing this article, I have received, (from very reſpeĉtable authority) in anſwer to a query on this ſubjeĉt, that " the vale land is natural to oats ; which, if once ſown and ſhed their ſeed, will remain in the land for ever ;" that is, will become a weed to future crops: and further, that under this idea, " few oats are given, in the vale of Eveſham to farm horſes (uſing beans in their ſtead) as they are ſuppoſed to paſs through them in a vegetative ſtate." Theſe fears, however, appear, to me, to be groundleſs. I have not, in any diſtriĉt, found the *cultivated oat* lie lpnger than one winter in the land : nor have I, in this diſtriĉt, found a *cultivated oat* in the charaĉter of a weed: for although I have diſcovered ſome few individuals with the grains of the lower part of the panicle, nearly ſmooth ; yet the upper parts of the panicle have always evinced them, plainly enough, to be the *genuine wild oat* : the NATURAL SPECIES.

provement (excepting a partial reform which has lately taken place in fome of the fallow fields) has flept ever fince. The prefent fyftem of management (of the arable land at leaft) was probably formed under the influence of the monafteries; and has fallen thro' fucceeding generations, without receiving any material change.

This, however, by the way. I do not mean to cenfure the vale hufbandmen for not fowing oats, in preference to barley. I have had no opportunity of comparing their produce. Neverthelefs, I would wifh to recommend a trial of oats, on the ftronger colder lands, in the area of the vale. Thefe lands can feldom be got fufficiently fine for barley. Much feed muft every year be buried in them. I have feen barley fown over a furface on which fome men would have been afraid to truft oats. The clotting beetle, it is true, fines the immediate furface, and gives relief to many grains which lie near it: neverthelefs thofe which fall down the deeper fiffures muft, in the tender nature of feedling barley, be irretrievably loft.

On

On the contrary, oats might, almoſt in any year, be ſown without hazard or difficulty; and, in the fallow fields, might be got in ſoon enough to break up the fallows, without ſix or ſeven horſes to one plow. Beſides, in a dairy country, the ſodder from oats, if the ſort were well choſen, would be found of much more value—more of it—and of a better quality—than that of barley. While the produce of grain,—if theory and compariſon may in any caſe be truſted,—would more than over-ballance, in quantity, the comparative difference, in price: more eſpecially as oats would be a crop new to the vale land. See YORK: ECON: vol: II. p. 21.

PULSE.

26.

P U L S E.

A T length we have paſſed the ground
of cenſure ; and are now entering on a ſubjeꝗ
of praiſe, to which it will be difficult to do
juſtice: ſo *mixed* is the management of this intereſting diſtriꝗ.   Its cultivators might be
called, without incurring a paradox, THE BEST
AND THE WORST FARMERS IN THE KINGDOM.
Were they as attentive to the SOIL, in freeing
it from *ſuperfluous water*, and from the *roots*
and *ſeeds* of weeds, as they are in freeing the
CROPS from the *herbage* of weeds—they might
well be ſtyled the firſt huſbandmen in Europe.

PULSE, whether BEANS or PEAS, ſeparate or
mixed, are, in the ordinary praꝗice of the diſtriꝗ, PLANTED BY WOMEN, and HOED BY WO-
MEN AND CHILDREN, once, twice, and ſometimes thrice ; giving the crop, when the ſoil
is ſufficiently free from root weeds, a gardenly
appearance, which is beautiful to look on, in
the

the former part of the summer; and which, at harvest, if the season prove favorable, seldom fails of affording the cultivator more substantial gratification: while the soil, under this practice duly performed, is left in a state extremely well adapted to future crops; particularly the wheat crop.

The SPECIES of pulse in cultivation, here, are

1. BEANS—the large hog-bean: a variety of VICIA *faba*.

2. GREY PEAS; and

3. WHITE PEAS: varieties of VICIA *pisa*.

4. PEABEANS; namely a mixture of beans and grey peas; in various proportions. Generally, a few peas among a large proportion of beans: I have however seen, on the lighter lands, a few beans among peas; by way, I suppose, of natural rods to the crop.

The CULTIVATION of pulse in this district requires to be registered in detail.

I. SUCCESSION. Pulse succeeds invariably a corn crop: namely, wheat in the old fallow field course; barley in the new;—either wheat or barley on the every year's lands.

SOIL.

II. Soil. Every species. The ſtronger ſoils beans, or beans and peas mixed;—the middle ſoils generally the ſame; the lighter ſoils in the neighbourhoods of Gloceſter and Cheltenham, peas, of various ſorts. But, in the area of the vale, few peas are grown; except among BEANS; which are, throughout, the prevailing crop; and which, alone, are entitled to particular attention.

III. TILLAGE. Begin plowing as ſoon after Chriſtmas as the ſeaſon will permit; fetching up the ſoil as deep as the plow will turn it:—nine, ten or more inches deep; and let it lie in whole furrow " to take the froſt."

IV. MANURE. The bean crop, in the common practice of the diſtrict, is ſeldom manured for.

V. SEED PROCESS. This will require to be particularized.

1. THE TIME OF SETTING. Begin about Candlemas; or as ſoon after that time as the land can be got upon with the harrows, to break the plits and level the ſurface for the ſetters. The ſoils of this vale are moſtly of ſuch a nature that, after being frozen, they fall like lime; once going over with the harrows being

being on the colder foils fufficient to reduce the furface to powder as fine as afhes ; leaving not the trace of a whole furrow.

2. The METHOD OF SETTING varies in different parts of the diftrict. In the central and fouthern quarters, the prevailing practice is to fet *acrofs* the ridges, *by the eye*, without a line ! About Cheltenham and along the northern border, it is a practice, equally prevalent, to fet *lengthway* of the ridges, *by a line*. While about Tewkefbury, and towards Deerhurft, it is common to fet *by a line, acrofs* the ridges.

In theory, a *line* appears to be neceffary. In practice, however, it is otherwife. Women, who have been long in the habit of fetting without one, are able to go on, pretty regularly, by the eye alone; and the young ones are trained up, by putting one of them between two who are experienced. Upon the whole, however, a line appears to have its ufes. The foil becomes, in all probability, more evenly occupied by the roots ; and the plants are fomewhat more conveniently hoed ;—when the feed is planted in ftraight lines, with equidiftant intervals.

Each

Each fetter is furnifhed with a " fetting pin," and a " tuckin;" namely, a fatchel (hung before, by a ftring round the waift) to carry the beans in. The *fetting pin* refembles the gardener's dibble: with, in general, however, a valuable improvement: a crofs pin, or half crutch, near the top, to reft the palm upon; with a groove on each fide of the main pin to receive the forefinger and the thumb. The length of the dibble (which is about two inches fquare in the middle tapering conically, to a fharp point) is about eight inches; of the handle, about four.

In *fetting*, the women walk fideway, to the right; with their faces toward the ground which is fet: the laft row, therefore, is immediately under the eye, and the difficulty of fetting another row, nearly parallel with it, is readily overcome by practice. An expert hand will fet with almoft inconceivable rapidity.

The *diftance* between the rows varies from ten to fourteen inches. Twelve inches may be confidered as the prevailing width throughout the diftrict. The diftance, in the rows, about two inches; making the holes as clofe

as

as can well be done, without their interfering with each other;—and about two inches deep; dropping one bean in each hole *.

3. The QUANTITY OF SEED—from two and a half to three bushels an acre.

4. The PRICE OF SETTING—sixteen to eighteen pence a bushel: costing from 3s. 6d. to 4s. 6d. an acre.

The practice of setting *by the bushel,* appears to be, in one particular at least, very injudicious. Instead of a single bean being assigned to each hole, two and sometimes more, are put in;—that the bushel may be sooner emptied: for the same purpose, and with the same dishonest intention, a handful will not unfrequently be thrust into a hole, and covered up with mould. The only danger, in setting *by the acre,* would be that of the seed's being put

in

* In the Cheltenham quarter of the district, I have observed a singular method of setting *peas*;—not in continued lines; but in clumps; making the holes eight or ten inches from each other; putting a number of peas in each hole. This is called " bunshing" them. The hoe has, undoubtedly, in this case, greater freedom: all the danger arising from the practice is, that the soil is not so evenly and fully occupied by the roots in this case, as they are when the plants are distributed in continued lines.

in too thin. But it being a notorious fact, that beans, which stand thin, are (under the same circumstances) invariably better podded, than those, which stand in a close crouded state;— it is highly probable that, of the two evils, setting by the acre would be found the least.

5. The COVERING is generally done with tined harrows, drawn once in a place. If, however, the soil be in so light, so floury a state, that the tines pull up the beans, a thorn harrow is generally made use of for the purpose of covering the seed.

VI. VEGETATING PROCESS. Presently after the beans are above ground, the surface is sometimes loosened with the HARROW; previous to the HOING.

TIME OF HOING. The first hoing is given as soon as the plants are free from the danger of being buried by the hoe. They ought, if the weather permit, to be begun upon, before they be a hand high.

The METHOD OF HOING is the common one, which is practised by gardeners, in hoing drilled crops. The intervals are cut-over, as close to the plants as can be done with safety: and, if a gap or vacancy occur in the row, the

the hoe is drawn through it: the hoer taking two, and fometimes three intervals at once.

The WIDTH OF THE HOE for beans, I believe, is invariably five inches. In this cafe, the corners may be kept on, and the edge kept fharp, with little fear of injury.

The SECOND HOING is, or ought to be, deferred as long as it can be with fafety. It is, however, or ought to be, always finifhed before the beans begin to blow: it being·confidered very injurious to the crop, to hoe it when the " blows are on."

The fecond hoing is ftill *flat*,—as the firft. I have not feen an inftance in this diftrict, of beans being earthed up.

In the fecond hoing, the rows are, or ought to be, carefully HAND-WEEDED. Not a weed fhould be left ftanding. Beans cannot blow among weeds: and every one now left, furnifhes the foil with a frefh fupply of feeds for the annoyance of future crops.

GENERAL OBSERVATIONS ON HOING. The fecond hoing is effentially neceffary to common good management. Without it, the firft is of little avail: it may loofen the foil, and give a temporary relief to the young plants; but the number of weeds, *at harvest*, will be nearly the fame, as if it were not to take place; for though, no doubt, it deftroys numbers, it unlocks the feeds of others, which rife up in their ftead,—high enough to injure the growing crop; and to give a fupply of feeds to the foil.

Weeds injure beans, and all pulfe, in a way, in which they have it not in their power to hurt corn. Corn bears its feed on the fummit of its ftem. The weeds muft be afpiring, indeed, if it cannot blow in defiance of them. Nor, during the maturation, is the grain (in ordinary cafes) liable to be over-fhaddowed and crouded by weeds. On the contrary, beans throw out their feed from the fides of the ftems; down to within a few inches of the ground; provided they have room, air, and fun enough to encourage them to throw out bloffoms, and to enable them to bring the pods to due perfection. And it is obfervable, that a crop of beans feldom turns out productive, unlefs the pods farm low on the ftems.

Hence the utility of the firft hoing;—to prevent the weeds from crouding the beans; and thereby give them a tendency to run upward;

as well as prevent them effectually from forming the neceſſary rudiments below: and of the ſecond;—to give the beans an opportunity of blowing; as well as of maturing their pods without the interference of weeds.

Hence, likewiſe, the unproductiveneſs of a thick-ſtanding rank crop; which, by drawing up the individuals, tall and ſlender, forms a ſhade below, and prevents a due circulation of air; the plants, in this caſe, operating as weeds to each other. And hence the uſe of THINNING a rank crop of beans, whenever they ſhow a tendency to draw each other up tall and "rammelly;"—a ſpecies of crop, which, it is well underſtood in this diſtrict, fills the rick-yard, but not the granary*.

The PRICE OF HOING, is generally ſix ſhillings an acre, for the two hoings and the "handpulling;"—more or leſs, according to the nature of the ſoil, the height of the crop, and its degree of foulneſs †.

L 3 6. HAR-

---

* TOPPING, if done in due ſeaſon, aſſiſts in the ſame intention.

† The HORSE HOING of beans is not in any degree of practice; the only inſtance of deviation from the common practice of handhoing, was one, in which an ASS was made

uſe

VII. Harvesting.   The method of harvesting varies with the length of the crop.

A ſhort low-podded crop is neceſſarily
mown;—uſually with a naked ſithe;—letting
the plants drop upon their roots.   Having
lain ſome time to wither, in this ſcattered
ſtate, they are gathered, with common forks,
into ſwath-like rows, on the ſides of the lands:
where, having lain a further time, proportioned to their ripeneſs, their weedineſs, and
the ſtate of the weather, they are made up
into wads or bundles, with the ſame implement, and ſet upon the ridges of the lands;
and there remain, in that ſtate, until they be
fit for hauling.   If the crop be ſtouter, it is
ſometimes bound after the ſithe, and dried in
ſhuck.

But tall beans are uſually cut with a reaping hook, and a hooked ſtick; with which,
inſtead of the hand, they are gathered.

Reaping beans.   The larger end, or handle, of the *gathering hook* is eighteen inches
long

----

uſe of in this operation?   Seeing the ſmallneſs of the feet,
and the narrowneſs of the tread of this animal, it appears
to be ſingularly adapted, on free light ſoils, to the operation.

long, the fhorter end, or hook, twelve inches;
its point ftanding out about twelve inches
from the handle. The *reaping book* in this
operation, is ufed in a fingular way; *ftriking*
with it beneath the gathering hook; making
a fweep as with a fithe; driving the cut beans
forward, until about half a moderate fheaf be
collected.

In this cafe, they are left awhile to wither
in open reaps, and are afterward either bound
in fheaves and fet up in ftooks; or, much
more ufually, are fet up in what are termed
" HACKLES :"—finglets of unufual fize; and of
a conftruction fufficiently fingular to merit
defcription.

The reaps are generally gathered up by
two boys; who, taking them in their arms,
fingly, adjuft their butts; by letting them
fall upon them; thereby giving a level even
bafe. Three or four of thefe reaps (about
half a fheaf each) are fet up in a hollow cone-
like form; as flax is fometimes fet up after
being rated; or as hop poles are fometimes
piled. A man follows, and ties a band, made
of three or four bean ftems—a length of peaf-
halm, or a twifted rope of long grafs,—near

L 4

the

the top of the hackle, as it stands: and, to secure it still more from the wind, as well as to prevent its yet leafy broom-like top from catching driving showers, and conveying the rain water down into the body of the hackle, —he draws a single stem from the middle of it, until only a few inches of its butt remain; or enters one which he finds loose, a similar depth: then, taking the whole top in his hand, with the long stem in the center of it, twists it round in a spiral manner; thus making the hackle a perfect cone; its apex resembling the point of a snail-shell; and fixes it in this form, by winding the single stem round the top; burying its end within the hackle.

The crop remains in this state, until it be taken up by the carriages;—the *Glocestershire hackle* not being rebound, like the *Yorkshire gait*, previous to the carrying; the band and the twist at the top hold them together, until they be got onto the waggon, at least.

In " *hauling*," it is customary for boys or others (employed by the farmer) to pick up the scattered beans, by hand, after the waggon.

7. In

VIII. In the center of the vale, BEAN HALM is thrown into the horſe rack, and the offal ſtrewed about the yard as litter.   About Gloceſter, great quantities of it (as well as ſome ſtraw) are bought up at a potaſh manufactory, and burnt for the aſhes!

IX. The MARKETS for beans are the market towns of the diſtrict; at which they are bought for horſes and for hogs, (of which they are here a principal article of fatting:) and Briſtol; whoſe factors buy up great quantities for the inns; (beans being throughout this diviſion of the kingdom ſtill uſed as a provender of horſes) and for the Guinea ſhips; as food for the negroes, in their paſſage from Africa to the Weſt Indies.

X. The PRODUCE of beans, on a par of years and crops, is about three quarters an acre.   Four quarters—that is, about thirty eight Wincheſter buſhels, are not a very extraordinary crop: though much of the land which produces them has borne beans every 3d year, and ſome of it, perhaps, every ſecond year, during a ſucceſſion of ages.   Something may be due to management, and much to the nature of this plant; which appears to
flouriſh,

flourish, unabatingly, on strong, deep land.
The rest may be owing to the natural richnefs and peculiar depth of the vale foils.—
Beans strike deep, and probably feed, in some
meafure at leaft, beneath the ordinary pafture of plants.

27.

CULTIVATED GRASSES.

IN A COUNTRY, whofe lands lie chiefly
in common arable field, or in old grafs inclofures,—the CULTIVATION OF GRASSES, either
as *temporary* or as *perennial* ley, is, of courfe,
confined within narrow limits: neverthelefs,
the two fpecies of cultivation require to be
noticed in this place.

I. TEMPORARY LEY. Pafture lands are
too abundant, and hay too cheap, to require
much temporary ley to be made. In the
improved courfe of the fallow-field land, fmall
pieces are, however, not unfrequently fown
with CLOVER (common red clover) inftead of
beans;

beans; by way of *green herbage* for farm-horses; and sometimes larger pieces; for *feed clover*.

The quantity of CLOVER HERBAGE, which some of the vale lands throw out, is extraordinary. The lighter lands are thought to be " too free for clover!" Running it too much to *balm*; which trails upon the ground like that of peas! It will not, it is said, answer on this soil, either for soiling or for feed; for if mown, even twice, the third crop will be rotten before the feed be ripe!

But the stronger lands produce a more upright clover-like crop;—generally, however, of uncommon luxuriance. It is usually mown, as green herbage, three times in the course of the summer. If made into hay, the quality is found to be extremely good. If cut in due season, and properly made, it is thought to be equal to meadow hay, as an article of fatting for oxen.

• Such is the value of the CLOVER CROP on *fresh lands*,—on lands which are new to it: and such, we may fairly add, is the *natural strength* of the lands of this district. How truly absurd, then, to suffer the common

fields

fields to remain in their prefent unproductive ftate. Not clover, only, but every other fpecies of CULTIVATED HERBAGE, adapted to the feveral foils, would, no doubt, be productive.

In the fame unprofitable ftate lay the lands of the vale of Pickering*. They had borne *grain* until they would barely pay for the labour of cultivation. The yeomanry ftarved on their own lands. They were not worth, as arable lands, 10s. an acre. But, having been inclofed and kept in a ftate of *herbage*, they now, many of them let from 30 to 40s. an acre.

It muft be allowed, that fome confiderable expence attends the inclofure of open lands; and that it is fome years before the herbage arrives at its moft profitable ftate. In the cafe here inftanced, the land lay feveral years nearly in a ftate of wafte †. But it does not follow, that, in thefe more enlightened days, the fame method of leying fhould be practiced. They might, now, on a certainty, be
rendered

---

* See YORK. ECON. I. 291.
† See YORK. ECON. II. 84.

rendered productive from the day of inclosure. But of this in the next section.

In the management of SEED CLOVER, I have met with nothing worthy of notice; except the practice of thrashing it in frosty weather: or rather the idea of giving the preference to such weather for thrashing it in. The advantage is evident, when the idea is known; but it does not seem to have struck universally: I therefore give it a place in this register.

II. PERENNIAL LEYS. The recent attempts at laying down arable land to grass, in this district, have been made principally on the lands mentioned aforegoing, as being broken up from a state of rough pasture, and sown repeatedly with wheat (see page 67.)— But these attempts, I believe, have generally been unsuccessful. The soil reduced to a state of foulness, by repeatedly cropping it on single plowings, had no other cleansing, perhaps, than a barley fallow; and, in this foul state, was probably rendered still fouler, by sowing over it the seeds of weeds, under the name of " hay seeds."—No wonder that land laid down to grass, in this manner, should,

in

in a few years, require to be given up again
to corn.

Hay seeds, however, is an indefinite
term. Seeds collected from known hay, of a
well herbaged ground, cut young, shook or
thrashed upon a floor, and sifted through fine
sieves, to take out the large seeds of weeds,
with which all old grafslands abound, might
be eligible enough; provided still purer feeds
could not be had.   But what is generally
thrown upon land, under the denomination of
" hay feeds," is a collection of the feeds of
the ranker weeds, with few or none of those of
the finer graffes.

One of the fineft grafs grounds, I have feen
in the vale, was laid down with hay feeds,
about five and twenty years ago; but it was
with feeds of the former defcription; and the
management in every other refpect equally
judicious. The land had been in bad hands,
and was become extremely foul with couch;
it was, therefore, fummer fallowed. But the
feafon proving unfavourable, it was deemed,
the enfuing fpring, not yet fufficiently clean.
It had, therefore, a fecond year's fallow!—
By repeated plowings and harrowings, acrofs
the

the ridges, they were pulled down from from roofs to waves. The next enfuing fpring, it was fown with barley and hay feeds: the moft *fpirited* inftance of practice, I have met with in this moft important branch of rural economics. And the event proves its eligibility in a ftriking manner. Before this two year's fallow, the land let for 10s. an acre: foul as it was, at the time it was broken up, no crop could grow in it; it was worth nothing to the occupier for one year. It is now worth from 25 to 30s. an acre.

On the other hand, I have had opportunities of obferving feveral inftances of lands, which have been laid down with "hay feeds," and which, at prefent, lie a difgrace to Englifh agriculture. This fpring I lifted the plants of a piece laid down in this difgraceful manner.

In *May*, the only *grafs* was the brome-grafs—(oat grafs—loggerheads—lob.) and of this but a very fmall quantity. The *weeds* were as follow: *corn horfetail,—broad plantain,— common thiftle,— groundfel,—crowfoots, —convolvulus,— docks,* &c. &c. Half the furface was actually bare: no appearance of a

quarter

quarter of a crop; even of weeds. In *September*,—I found it over-run with the *ox-tongue* *(picris ecbioides)* whose feeds were blowing about, to the annoyance of the neighbourhood. And this, I am afraid, may be taken as a specimen of the present method of laying land down to *grafs*, in the vale of Glocefter.

The only reafon given for perfevering in this unpardonable practice is, that no better feeds are to be had; RAYGRASS being " ruinous to the vale lands"!—" Smothering every thing: and impoverifhing the foil, until it will grow nothing"!

In the next article, it will appear, by the catalogues there given, that the predominant herbage of the old grafs lands of the vale is RAYGRASS. But left the general account which will there be given of the grafTes fhould not be thought fufficiently conclufive, I will here copy a feries of memoranda, made on the fubject, in the autumn of 1783: before I became acquainted with the rooted antipathy, which I have fince found to be formed, againft raygrafs.

" *Hatberley*, 10 *Sept*: 1783. Obferving in a fmall inclofure, which has been lately laid
down

down (or more accurately fpeaking is laying itfelf down) to grafs, fome green fwardy patches beginning to make their appearance through a carpet of couch and other foulnefs, I examined the fpecies which were thus employed in rendering the land, in defpite of bad management, ufeful to the occupier; and found them to confift wholly of raygrafs and white clover. This led me to a more minute examination of the adjoining ground, efteemed the beft piece of grafsland in the neighbourhood, and, from the feed ftems which are now remaining in the ftale patches, I find the bladegrafs to be chiefly raygrafs, with fome dogstail, and a little foftgrafs."

"*Sept:* 11. In my ftroll this morning, in the center of the vale, I met with an extenfive fuite of cow-grounds (by the fide of the Chelt in Boddington) the foil five or fix feet deep. The herbage white clover and raygrafs: the young fhoots of the raygrafs as fweet as fugar! Much fweeter than any I have before examined. Thefe grounds (late Long's) are, it feems, very good ones for grazing; but are difficult to make cheefe from."

" I have no longer a doubt about the herbage of church ground confifting *at prefent* (the middle of Sept.) in a manner wholly of ray grafs and white clover; for in my walk this evening, I carefully examined feveral plants of raygrafs, which had both feedftems and blades belonging to them; and, on examining the blades with a glafs, and comparing them with the turf of this field, I find they are identically the fame. In *tafte*, however, the different fpecimens vary confiderably; and *perbaps* the tafte of raygrafs might be taken as a criterion of foils; and *perbaps*, with the affiftance of a glafs, not only this but any other grafs may be known, with certainty, by the blade alone."

" *Sept:* 15. Tewkefbury lodge, a charming grafsland farm: a bold fwell covered with a rich warm foil, occupied by a luxuriant herbage; chiefly raygrafs! Some white clover; and fome other of the finer bladegraffes. " All green": not a foot of plowed land!"

" Below Apperley,—an extenfive whole year's common, ftocked with horfes, young cattle, fheep and geefe: the fite a dead level, fubject to be overflowed; the foil a redifh loam; the herbage raygrafs—(faccharine in a fuperior degree—literally as fweet as fugar!)—
with

with fome white clover, and from what I can judge by its growth, fome marfh bent. It is eaten down fo level and fo bare, that the geefe, one would fuppofe, could fcarcely get a mouth-full; yet the young cattle are as fleek as moles: it is efteemed, I underftand, without exception, the beft piece of land in the country."

In proof, however, of raygrafs being wholly unfit for the vale lands, I have been fhown a piece which was laid down with " ryegrafs:" and, certainly, a more fhameful piece of ley was never fhown. Perceiving, however, from the rubbifh upon it, that the feeds of rubbifh, not thofe of raygrafs, muft have been fown, I made enquiry into the complection of the feed, and found that it was brome-grafs--lob--loggerheads--fetched from the hills, where that grafs abounds, which had " fmo-thered every thing" (even the ray grafs which might have been fown among it) except a few of the ranker weeds. And fimilar evidences of the ruinous nature of " rye grafs" I have met with in other diftricts.

The bromegrafs and other weeds, which have been fown hitherto under the name of rye grafs, are certainly improper for the vale foils ; and it is poſſible that even the *variety* of *real* raygraſs which is cultivated may not be eligible.   In Yorkſhire, I found a variety (in a garden) which had evidently a *couchy* habit.

But how eaſy to collect the NATIVE SPECIES, which abounds on the old graſslands ; and thus raiſe a new variety, adapted, on a certainty, to the vale land.   The difficulty of doing it would vaniſh the moment it were ſet about: it only wants a little exertion: a ſmall ſhare of indolence to be ſhook off.

If *real* raygraſs has ever been tried alone and without ſucceſs, it has probably ariſen from too great a quantity having been ſown. Be it raygraſs or rubbiſh, I underſtand, ſeldom leſs than a ſackfull an acre is thrown on: whereas ONE GALLON an acre, of CLEAN-WINNOWED REAL RAYGRASS-SEED, is abundantly ſufficient, on ſuch ſoil as the vale in general is covered with.

Or perhaps the miſcarriages have ariſen in the ſtrength of the vale lands ; in their being naturally affected by raygraſs, and in the want of theſe valuable qualities being duly tempered by proper management.   (See YORK: ECON: vol. ii. p. 89.)

The

The *forcing* quality of the firſt ſpring of graſs ſeems to be, here, well underſtood. "No matter how ſhort the graſs at this time of the year, ſo the cattle can get hold of it;—they are ſure to thrive amain."

The reaſon is obvious: there is not, at that ſeaſon, a blade of any other graſs than ray graſs: no alloy to lower its value: it has then full ſcope; and, in this caſe, the Gloceſter-vale graziers experience its uſe, as ſenſibly as the Norfolk farmers: theſe, however, are grateful; becauſe they know the effect proceeds from raygraſs: but thoſe, unaware of the gratitude they owe, ſtand foremoſt to revile its character.

In Norfolk, and on the Cotſwold hills, the lands are comparatively weak, and have perhaps long been uſed to ray graſs: the graziers, there, find no difficulty in keeping it down in the ſpring. Here, on the contrary, the land is rich, is peculiarly affected by raygraſs, has much of it lain, for ages, in a ſtate of aration, and is of courſe peculiarly prone to the graſſes. The graziers, it is highly probable, are not aware of the ſtock it will carry, for a few weeks

M 3

in

in the fpring ; twice, perhaps three times, as much as their old grafs grounds.

Some men fenfible of the mifchievoufnefs of foul " hayfeeds",—and believing in the diabolical influence of *raygrafs*, have laid down lands with WHITE CLOVER alone ; or with a mixture of white clover and TREFOIL ; without any bladegrafs whatever.

This is certainly preferable to fouling the turf with weeds ; but it is returning one ftep back to the obfolete cuftom of letting land lay down in its own way. There is a certain lofs of nutritious herbage in the outfet ;—and the weeds, already in the foil, will of courfe occupy, in fome degree, the vacancies which would be better filled by blade graffes.

That land may be leyed without blade graffes is certainly true: I have long ago practifed this method of leying. (See MINUTES OF AGRICULTURE, date 20. May 1775.) But it was before I had feen the extraordinary effects of raygrafs, when properly managed, in the eftablifhed practice of Norfolk, See NORF: ECON. vol. i. p. 303.)

It is equally true, that moft excellent grafs land may be obtained, without fowing any

feed

feed whatever.   (See YORK: ECON: vol. ii.
p. 84.)   The impropriety of the practice is,
however, evident.   And fowing one clafs only
appears to be, no more than a middle way
between that and good management.

Who would not wifh to fee the herbage of
his leys, the firft year, refemble the better
herbage of his old grafslands, without their
weeds?

It is evident, that the prevailing herbage of
the beft grafs grounds of this diftrict is com-
pofed of raygrafs and white clover. In Spring
and Autumn, the furface is in a manner wholly
occupied by them.   All that the art of leying
wants, to make it perfect, is a SUMMER BLADE
GRASS, to fupply the place of the natural fummer grafTes of the old fward.

But if we are unable to reach perfection,
there is no reafon why we fhould not approach
it as nearly as we can.   A nutritious bite, in
fpring and autumn, is certainly better than a
want of it at thefe times.   By fowing a *fmall
quantity* of raygrafs, and keeping this *clofely
paftured in the fpring,*—the fummer grafTes,
natural to the given foil, have little more impe-

M 4   pediment

diment to their rifing, than they would have, if no raygrafs were fown.

If, inftead of a *gallon* of *clean raygrafs*, a *fackful of rubbifh* be fown, or if even a gallon of clean raygrafs be fown and the herbage be fuffered to run away wild in the fpring, and get poffeffion of the furface, its evil effects cannot be faid to be owing to the nature of the plant, but to a want of judgment in the growers of it. Under proper management, it can do no harm: it can *fmother* nothing but the bones of the cattle that eat it;—nor *exhauft* any thing, but the pockets of their purchafers.

I have been induced to fay more on this fubject, and to exprefs my ideas in ftronger language, as fome of the leading men of this diftrict are *afraid* to cultivate raygrafs ; and one, more particularly, whofe management is defervedly looked up to, is an open enemy to it. All I have to fay farther on the fubject is, that, *I verily believe*, I have no undue affection for any particular fpecies of grafs. My leading principle of conduct, throughout the irkfome undertaking I have engaged in, is to ftand with all my ftrength againft FALSE-GROUNDED PARTIALITIES;

PARTIALITIES: whether I perceive them in myself, or obferve them in others.

The fubject before us is of the firft importance, in rural economics: converting worn-out arable lands to a ftate of profitable fward is one of the moft important operations in hufbandry; and is, perhaps, of all the other operations in it, the leaft underftood. The diftrict under furvey contains twenty thoufand acres of land, which ought to undergo this change, with all convenient fpeed. And, whenever it take place, ten to fifteen thoufand pounds a year, for fome years afterward, will depend on whether it be judicioufly, or injudicioufly conducted.

NATURAL

28.

NATURAL GRASSES.

THE OLD GRASSLANDS of this diſtrict fall moſtly within the ſpecies LOWLAND GRASS and MIDDLELAND GRASS. The UPLAND it contains is too inconſiderable to claim particular notice; conſiſting merely of the marginal ſlopes; and the ſides and contracted ſummits of the hillocks which are ſcattered on its area.

I. LOWLAND GRASS. This conſiſts moſtly of COMMON MOWING GROUNDS,—provincially "meadows" *: in part, of COMMON PASTURE GROUNDS,—provincially "hams" †. Some incloſed

* It is obſervable that the GLOCESTERSHIRE MEADOWS do not lie in long *ſwaths*, as thoſe of the YORKSHIRE INGS, but in ſquare *plots*, marked by boundary ſtones. The HAY is private property, but the AFTERGRASS is generally common to the townſhip; either without ſtint; or is ſtinted by the " yard lands" of the common fields.

† HAMS are moſtly ſtinted paſtures: one, near Gloceſter, is however an exception.

inclofed property likewife comes within this divifion of grafslands: which, it is obfervable, are uniformly found and fully fwarded; their levelled furface rifing in fome places twelve or fifteen feet above the level of dead water. No *fens*, or *watery marfhes*, mix in the lowlands of the vale of Glocefter.

By NATURAL SITUATION, however, thefe lands are fubject to be overflowed; either by the Severn, or by the rivulets which crofs the vale; and owe no doubt the prefent elevation and levelnefs of furface to the fediment of floods.

In the immediate neighbourhood of Glocefter, there are not lefs than a thoufand acres of this defcription of grafsland; moftly of a rich productive quality. The ISLE OF ALNEY (a holm, or river-ifland, formed by a divarication of the Severn) confifts wholly of it. It is not, however, peculiar to the Severn; but accompanies, on a more contracted fcale, the Chelt and other brooks and rivulets, into the area of the vale.

The soil of thefe lowlands is invariably deep: and of the fame quality and contexture at different depths. That of the ifle of Alney,

and

and the other meadows near Glocefter, is about
fix feet deep; an uniform mafs of fomewhat
redifh loam.

It is obfervable, however, that the quality
of this loam varies in different fituations, At
the upper point of the ifland it inclines to a
coarfe fand; while toward the lower extremity,
it is fine almoft as filt. It is alfo obfervable
that the furface lies higher in that than in this
fituation. But thefe circumftances are ftri&ly
agreeable to the general effe&s of floods: that
is, of foul water in a current ftate.

Another obfervable circumftance relative to
the foil of thefe meadows is, that it is uniformly
CALCARIOUS, in the degree of about five grains
to a hundred; except near the furface; *in the
immediate fphere of vegetation*; in which it dif-
covers no figns of calcariofity! A circumftance that appears to me extremely interefting.

Near Glocefter, this bed of loam is ufed as
BRICKEARTH: and, without any admixture,
affords bricks of an excellent quality. A new
county jail, on the Howardian principle of feparate cells, and on a very extenfive fcale, is
now building with bricks made from this
earth; one hundred grains of which, in the fituation,

tuation, from which the earth of thefe bricks is taken, affords, by analyfis, five grains of calcarious earth, twelve grains of fand, and eighty three grains of filt.

Another obfervable circumftance relative to this foil is, that it refembles, in COLOUR, the waters of the Severn in the time of floods. The waters of rivers, in general, are, in the time of flood (during frefhes or land-floods as they are ufually called) of a light brown, or ftone colour. But thofe of the Severn, in their paffage through this part of Glocefter-fhire, are moftly a light red, or what is ge-nerally underftood by a cinnamon colour; owing, moft probably, to particles of the red foils, weft of the Severn, being fufpended among thofe wafhed from the vales of Glo-cefter and Evefham: the colour varying as the rain, which caufed the fwell, fell more or lefs, on the redland country.

The banks of the Avon and the Chelt are free from this rednefs; as are the rifing grounds on either fide of the Severn meadows in this neighbourhood: facts which, to my mind, demonftrate, that thefe meadows are a crea-tion of the floods of the Severn, fince the

rifing

rifing grounds received their prefent form: confequently, that the extenfive flat, which they
now occupy, was heretofore (and, perhaps,
not many centuries ago) a WASH; over which
the tide flowed; in the manner in which it
ftill flows, over a yet more extenfive tract of
furface in the neighbourhood, of Newnham.
A tract of furface, which ftill remains in an
unprofitable ftate; but which, may we not
venture to fuggeft, might poffibly be reclaimed.

The nature of the SUBSOIL, likewife favors
the above pofition. Beneath the mafs of loam,
which I have termed the foil, lies a ftratum of
earth, of a fomewhat lighter colour, but evidently partaking of the nature of the foil,
which refts upon it; beneath this, a yet lighter
coloured filt, exactly refembling the mud,
which is ftill brought up from the fea, or from
banks formed in the lower parts of the Severn,
and left in quantity by every tide, wherever
it can find a lodgement: and beneath this bed
of mud (mixed in fome places with a coarfer
fandy earth) lies, in red and white ftrata, the
natural fubfoil of the country,—the ORIGINAL
SURFACE;—as left by nature, or the convul-
fions

fions of nature, which appear evidently to have thrown the earth's furface into its prefent form.

This original furface would be covered by the tides with filt from the fea, long before the lands, lying above it, were brought into an ARABLE STATE; to furnifh the river-floods with materials to give much addition to the covering; and yet a longer time before ART affifted (as in all human probability it has) in raifing the furface to its prefent height *.

The

---

* By obfervations during a flood, while the general le-vel was covered, a part near its center (the town ham, &c.) appeared fome two feet above the water. This part, in much probability, was the original ISLE OF ALNEY: an ancient name, which the prefent holm bearing that appel-lation, was the lefs likely to obtain, as tradition relates that the minor divifion of the Severn, which now winds by the kays of Glocefter, was originally a cut, made for the con-veniency of navigation: a circumftance that is corroborated by the plan of an ancient fortification, which appears to have extended confiderably beyond the prefent river; and whofe foundation, probably, is now buried, among the accumulation of foil, fome feet below the prefent furface.

Thefe obfervations, I acknowledge, are not effential to a regifter of the prefent ftate of rural affairs: neverthelefs it is interefting to obferve the changes which the face of na-ture, and with it rural affairs, have undergone: not in this inftance only; but in various others of a fimilar nature, in every quarter of the ifland.

The HERBAGE, with which the floods, time, and other circumſtances have furniſhed theſe lowlands, varies with the manner in which they have been occupied.

The herbage of the " hams"—or commons is, (as has already been intimated) in the ſpring, and in autumn more particularly, one continuous mat of RAYGRASS and WHITE CLO-VER, with a portion of the CRESTED DOGS-TAIL: the bladegraſſes being of a ſuperior quality; ſaccharine in the firſt degree: particularly thoſe of the commons that are fed with ſheep; which keeping down the weeds, the finer graſſes are in full poſſeſſion. But the ſuperior quality and productiveneſs of theſe paſture grounds are not matters of ſurprize:— for, beſides the annual tribute of the floods, they have had the whole of their own produce regularly returned to them: while the mowing grounds have been annually robbed of a principal part of their produce; without having, perhaps, in general, had any return whatever made.

The herbage of the " MEADOWS" appears in the following liſt; the individuals of which were collected in the Iſle of Alney, and other
diviſions

divisions of the extensive flat, which has been more particularly noticed. They are arranged agreeably to their degrees of frequency in those meadows; or as nearly so as the intention of the arrangement requires:

LINNEAN.   ENGLISH.

Lolium perenne,—raygrass.
Trifolium repens,—creeping trefoil *(a)*.
Trifolium procumbens,——procumbent tre-
. foil *(b)*.
Hordeum murinum,—common barleygrass.
Phleum nodosum,—bulbous catstailgrass.
Cynosurus cristatus,—crested dogstailgrass.
Carices,—sedges.
Anthoxanthum odoratum,—vernal.
Alopecurus pratensis,—meadow foxtailgrass.
Festuca fluitans,—floating fescue.
Festuca elatior,—tall fescue.
Agrostis alba,—creeping bentgrass.
Agrostis capillaris,—fine bentgrass.
Alopecurus geniculatus,—marsh foxtailgrass.
Holcus lanatus,—meadow softgrass.

Bromus

(a) CREEPING TREFOIL; or *white clover.*
(b) PROCUMBENT TREFOIL; or *trefoil.*

Bromus mollis,—foft bromegrafs.

Bromus   .—fmooth bromegrafs

Avena flavefcens,—yellow oatgrafs.

Poa trivialis,—common poe.

Poa pratenfis,—meadow poe.

Poa annua,—dwarf poe.

Sanguiforba officinalis,—meadow burnet.

Lathyrus pratenfis,—meadow vetchling.

Trifolium pratenfe,—meadow trefoil *(c)*

Lotus corniculatus,—birdsfoot trefoil.

Ranunculus repens,—creeping crowfoot *.

Chryfanthemum Leucanthemum,—— ox-eye daifey.

Centaurea nigra,—common knobweed.

Achillea Millefolium,—common milfoil.

Rumex Acetofa,—forrel.

Rumex crifpus,—curled dock.

Rumex

(c) MEADOW TREFOIL, - or *red clover.*

* CREEPING CROWFOOT;---- provincially " creeping crazey"——is here efteemed as a valuable fpecies of herbage, while the common and the bulbous fpecies, of this genus of plants, are confidered as extremely pernicious; efpecially among hay. This is a diftinction, which does the attention of the vale farmers great credit. The fact appears to be, on examination, that the two latter are extremely acrid, and probably have a cauftic effect on the mouths of the cattle, which eat it; while the firft is perfectly mild and agreeable to the palate. A circumftance, that is not generally underftood.

Rumex obtusifolius,—broadleaved dock.
Leontodon Taraxacum,--common dandelion†
Hypochæris radicata,—— longrooted hawk-
  weed
Galium verum,—yellow bedstraw.
Ranunculus Ficaria,—pilewort.
Bellis perennis,—common daisey.
Dactylis glomerata,—orchardgrass.
Briza media,—tremblinggrass.
Aira cæspitofa,—haffock airgrass.
Avena elatior,—tall oatgrass.
Festuca duriufcula,—hard fefcue.
Juncus articulatus,—jointed rufh.
Scirpus cæfpitofus ?—fluted clubrufh ?
Peucedanum Silaus,—meadow faxifrage.
Oenanthe pimpinelloides ?—meadow drop-
  wort ?
Heracleum Sphondylium,—cowparfnep.
Carduus paluftris,—marfh thiftle.
Serratula arvenfis,—common thiftle.
Urtica dioica,—common nettle.
Vicia cracca,—bluetufted vetch.
Phalaris arundinacea,—reed canarygrass.

N 2   Cardamine

† The Gloceftershire dairymen have alfo obferved, that cows have an averfion to the " bitter graffes"—(the DAN-DELION and HAWKWEED tribes) but that fheep are particularly partial to them ; eating even their " blows."

Cardamine patensis,—common ladysmock.
Senecio aquaticus,—marsh ragwort.
Spiræa Ulmaria,—meadowsweet.
Lychnis Flos-cuculi,—meadow campion. .
Ranunculus acris,—common crowfoot.
Ranunculus bulbosus,—bulbous crowfoot.
Pastinaca sativa,—wild parsnep.
Achillea Ptarmica,—goosetongue.
Potentilla Anserina,—silverweed,
Potentilla reptans,—creeping cinquefoil.
Cerastium vulgatum,—common mousear.
Galium palustre,—marsh bedstraw.
Prunella vulgaris,—selfheal.
Ajuga reptans,—meadow bugle.
Myosotis scorpioides,—scorpion mousear.
Plantago media,—middle plantain.
Plantago lanceolata,—narrow plantain.
Rhinanthus Crista-galli,—yellow rattle.
Colchicum autumnale,—autumnal crocus.
Allium vineale,—crow garlic.
Tragopogon pratense,—goatsbeard.
Thalictrum flavum,—meadow rue.
Tanacetum vulgare,—common tansey *.

Cerastium

---

* TANSEY. A very common plant, in this district; particularly on the banks of the Severn.

Ceraſtium aquaticum,—marſh mouſear.
Galium Mollugo,—baſtard madder.
Antirrhinum Linaria,--common ſnapdragon.
Geranium pratenſe,—crowfoot craneſbill.
Valeriana dioica,—marſh velerian.
Orchis maculata,—ſpotted orchis.
Polygonum Perſicaria,—common perſicaria.
Lythrum Salicaria,—ſpiked willowherb.
Symphytum officinale,—common comfrey.
Ranunculus Flammula,—common ſpearwort.
Caltha paluſtris,—marſh marigold.
Mentha hirſuta,—velvet mint.
Siſymbrium ſylveſtre,—water rocket.
Siſymbrium amphibium,—water radiſh.
Sparganium erectum,—common burflag.
Poa aquatica,—water poe.

The PRODUCE of theſe meadows varies: near Glocefter they are occaſionally manured, with aſhes and ſweepings of different kinds. The par produce, in a midling year, is, I underſtand, about a ton and a half an acre; not unfrequently two tons. The hay of a fine quality.

II.   MIDDLELAND GRASS. The principal part of the grafslands of the diſtrict belongs to this clafs. The MEADOWS and HAMS, tho'

extenfive, are not equal, in quantity of furface, to the " grounds:" of which fome of
the inclofed townfhips principally confift; and
which ought, indifputably, to form the principal part of every townfhip within the diftrict: the area of the lower vale is in a manner wholly occupied by this fpecies of grafsland.

The soil is the fame as that of the arable
lands. Almoft every acre of it having, heretofore, been under the plow: lying in ridge
and furrow, like the lands of the common
fields. In the parifh of Churchdown, there
are grafslands which lie in high fharp ridges,
with fides nearly as fteep as thofe of a modern
pitch-roof. In general, however, they appear to have been fomewhat lowered, previous to their being laid down, or fuffered to
lie down, to grafs. Toward Glocefter the
lands in general are narrower, and fome of
them nearly flat.

On examining the foil of a ground, which
is defervedly efteemed the beft piece of land
in the neighbourhood it lies in (Down Ha-
therley); and which, though a rifing ground,
bears no veftige of the plow;—I found it as
follows :

follows :—The firſt ſix inches, a ſtrong loam (a mixture of clay and ſand) free from calcarious matter:—from ſix to nine inches, a dark brown clay, very weakly calcarious:—at twelve inches, a ſimilar ſoil, but ſomewhat more ſtrongly calcarious:—from fifteen to eighteen, a ſtronger bluiſh clay ſtill more ſtrongly calcarious: a ſoil, or rather a ſubſoil, which probably runs a conſiderable d epth

The firſt ſix inches I found thickly interwoven with fibres ; which leſſened in number as the depth increaſed ; but, even at eighteen inches, the ſubſoil appeared to be full of them. Hence appears the value of a rich ſubſoil to grafsland. This piece has never been plowed ; becauſe, perhaps, it never required plowing ; its ſward never failed it ; continuing in full vigour through ſucceſſive generations. It is obſervable, however, that the ground under notice does not ſhoot early in the ſpring ; but its ſap once in motion its growth is uncommonly rapid.

The Herbage of the grounds varies much with the nature of the ſoil ; or, perhaps, more accurately ſpeaking, with the quality of the subsoil. The colder clayey ſwells (ſome of which are shamefully neglected) naturally run to an almost worthless herbage: the *wood fescue,* the *coltsfoot,* the *silverweed,* the *fleabane,* the *common scabious,* and the *sedges,* are too frequently suffered to occupy their surfaces: while the boggy tumours,. which rise at the feet of the hills, and bulge out by the sides of rivulets; and the swampy bottoms which the rivulets too frequently are obliged to ooze through;—are nurseries of the whole palustrean tribe.

The herbage of the grounds, in general, is however, of a superior quality. The PASTURES, in spring and autumn, are (as has been mentioned) covered with carpets thickly woven with a few of the finest grasses. In summer, however, the MOWING GROUNDS display a most ample variety. The individuals, which form it, are arranged in the following list, agreeably to their degrees of prevalency; or as nearly so as the intention of the arrangement requires.

LINNÆAN.	ENGLISH.
Lolium perenne,—raygrass.	
Trifolium repens,—creeping trefoil.	
Cynosurus cristatus,—crested dogstailgrass.	

Trifolium

Trifolium pratense,—meadow trefoil.
Poa trivialis,—common poe.
Trifolium procumbens,—procumbent trefoil.
Lathyrus pratensis,—meadow vetchling.
Lotus corniculatus,—birdsfoot trefoil.
Bromus mollis,—soft bromegrass.
Bromus   ,—smooth bromegrass.
Hordeum murinum,—common barleygrass.
Phleum nodosum,—bulbous catstailgrass.
Avena elatior,—tall oatgrass.
Anthoxanthum odoratum,—vernal.
Agrostis alba,—creeping bentgrass.
Agrostis capillaris,—fine bentgrass.
Poa annua,—dwarf poe.
Festuca sylvatica,—wood fescue *.
Ranunculus repens,—creeping crowfoot.
Ranunculus bulbosus,—bulbous crowfoot †
Ranunculus acris,—common crowfoot.
Achillea Millefolium,—common milfoil.

Centaurea

---

* WOOD FESCUE. Very common on the *cold swells*; and every where on *ant-hills*: an interesting circumstance.

† The BULBOUS CROWFOOT is singularly prevalent in this district. In the middle of May, some of the grounds near Glocester, were hid under its flowers. The *leaves* of this species are more acrid even than those of the common sort.

Centaurea nigra,—common knobweed.
Heracleum Sphodylium,—cowparſnep.
Paſtinaca ſativa,—wild parſnep.
Serratula arvenſis,—common thiſtle.
Rhinanthus Criſta-galli,—yellow rattle ‡.
Euphraſia Odontites,—red eyebright.
Leontodon hiſpidum,—rough dandelion.
Leontodon Taraxacum,—common dandelion.
Hypochæris radicata,—longrooted hawk-
weed.
Galium verum,—yellow bedſtraw.
Potentilla reptans,—creeping cinquefoil.
Plantago media,—middle plantain.
Plantago lanceolata,—narrow plantain.
Ranunculus Ficaria,—pilewort.
Bellis perennis,—common daiſey.
Dactylis glomerata,—orchardgraſs.
Holcus lanatus,—meadow ſoftgraſs.
Briza media,—common tremblinggraſs.
Alopecurus pratenſis,—meadow foxtailgraſs.
Avena flavescens,—yellow oatgraſs.
Poa pratenſis,—meadow poe.
Feſtuca elatior,—tall feſcue.
Aira cæſpetoſa,—haſſock airgraſs.

Alopecurus

‡ YELLOW RATTLE. For obſervations on this plant
ſee forward.

Alopecurus geniculatus,—marſh foxtailgraſs.
Juncus articulatus,—jointed ruſh.
Chryſanthemum Leucanth:—oxeye daiſey.
Peucedanum Silaus,—meadow ſaxifrage.
Rumex criſpus,—curled dock.
Rumex Acetoſa,—ſorrel.
Rumex obtuſifolius,—broadleaved dock.
Carduus lanceolatus,—ſpear thiſtle.
Urtica dioica,—common nettle.
Ceraſtium vulgatum,—common mouſear.
Stellaria graminea,—meadow ſtarflower
Plantago major,—broad plantain.
Prunella vulgaris,—ſelf heal.
Primula veris,—cowſlip.
Viola hirta,—hairy violet.
Convolvulus arvenſis,—corn convolvulus.
Veronica Chamædrys,—germander ſpeed-
    wel.
Veronica ſerpyllifolia,—thymeleaved ſpeed-
    wel.
Juncus campeſtris,—graſs ruſh.
Feſtuca duriuſcula,—hard feſcue.
Avena pubeſcens,—rough oatgraſs.
Trifolium fragiferum,—ſtrawberry treſoil.
Vicia Cracca,—bluetuſted vetch.
Orchis Morio,—fool's orchis.

Tragopogon

Tragopogon pratense.—goatsbeard.
Daucus Carota,—wild carrot.
Agrimonia Eupatoria,—agrimony.
Artemisia vulgaris,—mugwort.
Chærophyllum sylvestre,—orchardweed.
Galium Mollugo,—bastard madder.
Geranium pratense,—crowfoot cranesbill.
Geranium dissectum,—jagged cranesbill.
Vicia sativa,—meadow vetch.
Vicia sepium,—bush vetch.
Lathyrus Nissolia,—grasleaved vetchling.
Primula vulgaris,—primrose.

The above constitute the herbage of the sounder, better soils: the following are suffered to inhabit ; and, in some instances, to occupy exclusively ; the colder less fertile swells ; or the bogs and swamps that are suffered to remain in more genial situations.

Festuca sylvatica,—wood fescue.
Ononis arvensis spinosa,—restharrow.
Tussilago Farfara,—coltsfoot.
Potentilla Anserina,—silverweed.
Hieracium Pilosella,—mousear hawkweed.
Carices,—sedges.
Melica cærulea,—purple melic grass.
Cineraria palustris,—marsh fleabane.

Scabiosa

Scabiosa Succisa,—meadow scabious.
Carduus palustris,—marsh thistle.
Spiræa Ulmaria,—meadowsweet.
Stachys palustris,—clownsallheal.
Juncus inflexus,—wire rush.
Juncus effusus,—common rush.
Achillea Ptarmica,—goosetongue
Ajuga reptans,—meadow bugle.
Orchis maculata,—spotted orchis.
Orchis latifolia,—marsh orchis.
Myosotis scorpioides,—scorpion mousear.
Mentha hirsuta,—velvet mint.
Polygonum Persicaria,—common persicaria.
Polygonum ampbibium,—amphibious persi-
  caria.
Caltha palustris,—marsh marigold.
Veronica Beccabunga,—brooklime.
Sisymbrium Nasturtium,—water cress.

The PRODUCE of these up grounds varies
with the quality of their respective soils. An
acre and a half to two acres, of the better
grounds, are allowed as *pasturage* for a cow:
there are grounds which will nearly carry a
cow an acre. The produce of *hay* from one
to two tons an acre.

The

The MANAGEMENT OF GRASSLAND, as practifed in this diftrict, requires an outline of defcription, fimilar to that which was found requifite, in defcribing the fame important branch
of hufbandry, as practifed in the vale of Pickering.   See YORK: ECON: ii. 123.

The GENERAL MANAGEMENT comprizes
  1. Draining   3. Dreffing   5. Manuring
  2. Clearing   4. Weeding   6. Watering
  1.   DRAINING.   Many of the grounds are
fhamefully liable to furface-water.   The fubject of fhores, ditches, and furface-drains, has
been repeatedly touched on, in the courfe of
this volume: it might here be reiterated.   A
vale without fhores, ditches,   and SURFACE-
DRAINS, is a difgrace to its owners and occupiers.

  Befides a deficiency of furface drains much
UNDERDRAINING is wanted: efpecially in the
boggy tumours which have been noticed.
The *flats* of cold blue clay, fome few of which
there are, would be found more difficult to be
improved by underdraining: the caufe of their
infertility is probably owing more to the retentive nature of the foil and immediate fubfoil, themfelves, than to internal waters rifing
                                              toward

toward the furface. *That* gives a general coldnefs, which is difficult to remove: but the effect of *thefe* is partial; being caufed by collected or communicating waters, too fmall in quantity, or lying too low, to force themfelves out at the furface, as *natural fprings*; but are ready to efcape from their confinement as foon as an *artificial vent* is made for them. *

The colder *fwells* might probably be aſſiſted very much by throwing the lands acrofs the flopes. See YORK: ECON: vol. i. p. 324.

2. CLEARING. The grafslands of this diftrict, confidering their age, may in general be faid to be well kept: owing perhaps to their having, in general, been occafionally mown for hay, or fwept in a ftate of pafturage. Bufhes and anthills are lefs common here than in many other grafsland diftricts. Some grounds are in high prefervation: not a bufh or an ant hill left to disfigure their polifhed furfaces. There are others, however, in the oppofite extreme of neglect. Their furfaces hid, and in a manner occupied, by reftharrow and the
ant

* In the VALE OF EVESHAM, I am informed, much underdraining has been done, and with good fuccefs.

anthill fefcue: a ftage of diftemper which nothing but the plow can cure.

Some of thefe lands, it has been faid, have
been given up to tillage. The reft have a
right to undergo the fame falutary operation.
It is voluntary wafte, in their owners,—to let
them lie in their prefent ftate; and that, too,
without being repaid in any counter gratification. An oak-wood may be an object of *pride*
to its owner; and grows venerable as it grows
old: but a rough grafs-ground is an eye-fore;
a fcab which disfigures the face of a country;
and grows offenfive with age.

Their motive, however, for fuffering thefe
grounds to remain under circumftances fo difgraceful, may be more pardonable than may
appear at firft fight. It may proceed from the
evident ill ufage of thofe which have been permitted to be broken up. But this only leffens,
and does not wholly wipe away the *crime* of
keeping them in an unproductive ftate. If they
have not been properly laid down again to
grafs, the *neglect* is their own. See YORK:
ECON: vol. ii. p. 94.

3. DRESSING. Molehills and dung are
here fpread with common hay-forks; ufed with
.the

the back downward; fwinging them right and left: tolerable implements for the purpofe. Sometimes a bufh-harrow is drawn over the furface of the mowing grounds; which are fometimes rolled; efpecially thofe which have been foddered on, and trodden up by the cattle. No moulding hedge, nor any thing adequate to it, is here in ufe; though it would be obvioufly ufeful. The fledge which is now in common ufe for carrying hedging thorns &c. might, with a little alteration, be made to anfwer both purpofes. (See YORK: ECON: vol. i. p. 279.)

One particular in the practice of dreffing meadows, here, is noticeable. If a mowing ground be fed late in the fpring, fo as to render it doubtful whether, if the dungbe fpread, it would be wafhed down below the cut of the fithe before mowing time, it is picked off the ground and carried to the dunghill.

4. WEEDING GRASSLANDS. With refpect to the *eradication* of weeds, I have met with nothing praife-worthy in this diftrict. Some of the meadows are fhamefully overrun with *docks*; while the hams, being unappropriated, are too frequently occupied by *thiftles*

VOL. I.   O   which

which I have feen growing in beds of an acre each.

But with refpect to the *topping* of weeds, in the inclofed pafture-grounds, the vale merits fingular praife. It is the only diftrict, in which I have obferved this piece of good hufbandry, in any thing like common practice. Here, not only weeds of pafture-grounds are topped, generally once (about midfummer) and fometimes twice; but the grafs of the furrows is mown, and the broken grafs of the ridges fwept off for hay. Several loads of good fodder will fometimes be got from a ground by this practice. A practice which ought to be adopted in every diftrict. Befides the loads of fodder which are obtained,—feveral acres of autumnal pafturage are probably gained:—or in other words a frefh ground is added to the farm—by the operation. See NORF: ECON: min. 7. and YORK: ECON: vol. ii. p. 150.

5. MANURING. The manuring of grafslands will, I believe, fcarcely admit of being called a practice of *this* vale. The lowlands in general are configned to the benevolence of the floods: cowgrounds, which are every year paftured, require no manure; and mowing
grounds

grounds are feldom, I believe, afforded any. The arable lands, alone, require more than the diftrict produces. However, by bottoming the courts with mould, to abforb and retain that which now runs wafte out of them, a confiderable quantity of grafsland manure might annually be obtained, without robbing the arable lands of a fingle load of their prefent quantity of dung. See YORK: ECON: i. 405.

This deprivation of manure may account in fome meafure for the unproductivenefs, compared with the intrinfic quality, of fome of the vale lands; which may not, perhaps, have received any other melioration than the *teathe* of pafturing cattle, and perhaps fome good effect from being foddered on in the winter, fince the time they were converted into grafslands.

6. WATERING. The watering of grafslands, on the modern principle of float-and-drain, is not the practice of either of the vales of Glocefterfhire. I have not feen even a fingle inftance in either of them; though there are many fituations which would admit of its introduction. This circumftance is the more remarkable, as in Northwiltfhire, a neighbouring diftrict, it is in common practice. In

                    the

the more weftern counties it is, I underftand,
ftill more prevalent.

This is another inftance of the ftagnant ftate
of the hufbandry of thefe vales.   It is highly
probable, that, at the time of the diffolution of
the monafteries, they ftood pre-eminent in
Englifh Hufbandry.   But, through an evident neglect of MODERN IMPROVEMENTS,
they are now left, in many refpects, beneath
the reft of the kingdom.   This appears to
.me a circumftance well entitled to the attention of the landed intereft of thefe vales.

The OBJECTS of the grafsland management
are *hay* and *pafturage.*

It feems to be well underftood here, that
grounds ought to be mown and paftured alternately ; and in fome inftances the principle
may be attended to in practice.   But it is
generally convenient to have the " cow-
grounds" near the milking yard.   The diftant
grounds are of courfe more convenient as
" mowing grounds :" they are, however,
" grazed" occafionally by fatting cattle.

It is obferved here, and is obfervable almoft
every where, that if grafs land be mown every
year it is liable to be overrun with the YEL-
LOW

LOW RATTLE (Rhinanthus) which, being a biennial plant that sheds its seed early in the spring, is increased by mowing. But pasturing the ground, even one year, is found to check it. The reason is obvious: the major part of the plants, being eaten off with the other herbage, are prevented from feeding. Pasturing two years, succeflively, and carefully sweeping off the stale herbage, when this plant appears in full blow, would go near to extirpation.

The MANAGEMENT of
   1. Mowing grounds,
   2. Pasture grounds.

I. MOWING GROUNDS.
   1. Spring management
   2. Hay.
   3. Aftergrass.

1. SPRING MANAGEMENT of MOWING GROUNDS. In this diftrict, where grafslands vary much as to their times of vegetating in the spring, the time of shutting up the *inclosed grounds* for hay, provincially " hain-" ing" them, is regulated by the nature of the land. Cold backward lands are seldom eaten in the spring: while the free-growing

more early grounds are paftured till the beginning of May.   This diftinction is a maf-
terftroke of management, which I have not
obferved in the ordinary practice of any other
diftrict.

The time of fhutting up *meadows* is guided
by cuftom.   Some Candlemas, others Ladyday, others May-day.   A very extenfive meadow, immediately below the town of Glocefter, is, by ANCIENT PRIVILEGE, paftured,
even with fheep, until the middle of May.
The confequence of this cuftom is, that in
cafe the fpring fet in droughty, the crop of
hay is in a manner loft.   This year (1788)
the worm-cafts were not hid, until the latter
end of June !

But injudicious as that RELICK OF ANCIENT
LORDLINESS may now be, viewed in a general light, another, in its tendency abundantly more mifchevous, is preferved in a meadow
of fome hundred acres, in the fame neighbourhood.   Over this valuable tract of mowing ground, two horfes range at large, *while
the crop is growing!!!* with, of courfe, the
privilege of doing all the mifchief to which
the wantonnefs of horfes turned loofe in fo

large

large a pasture can stimulate. The reader,
I am afraid, will scarcely give me credit for
what I am relating. No other authority than
my own sight could, I confess, have induced
me to believe, that an evil so great—an ab-
surdity so glaring—could, in these enlightened
and liberalized times, have existed in the rural
economy of this country. Tradition says,
that stallions, alone, were formerly entitled to
this diabolical priviledge; but, at present,
any two horses are admitted to it. Whatever may have been its origin, it would be
doing injustice to the present laws of England
to suppose them capable of giving countenance to any act whose main tendency is the
wanton destruction of the produce of the
soil. No man has now a privilege of doing
the community wanton mischief. The full
value of the pasturage is, no doubt, the right-
ful property of the *claimant*.

2. HAY. The state of ripeness—*the age*—
at which a crop of grass ought to be cut—is a
subject of no small importance. In the ordinary practice of this district, as in that of every
other district I have observed in, grass is suf-.
fered to stand much too long, before it be

O 4

mown

mown for hay. This evil practice may have
originated in common meadows, whose aftergrass is unstinted, (or frequently belongs to a
separate owner): a species of mowing ground,
which, formerly, was common to this and
most other countries.

There are, however, in this district, men
who are well aware of the advantages of early
cutting ;—who know, from experience in
grazing, the value of the aftergrass of early
mown grounds ; as well as the fatting quality
of hay, which has been mown in the fullness of
sap. Hence we find in this country, more advocates for early cutting, than in most others,
where the fatting of cattle on hay is not a practice. There is, in an ordinary season, much
grass cut, in different parts of the district, *at
six or seven weeks old.*

In *mowing,* it is observable, the Glocestershire labourers cut remarkably level. In some
cases not a stroke, or scarcely a swath-balk, is
discoverable. This is chiefly owing to the
narrowness of the swath-width, and the short-
ness of the sithe, in use in this country. The
mowers of Glocestershire and those of Yorkshire work in opposite extremes of the art.
The

The Yorkshireman drives a width of nine or ten feet before him, the Glocestershireman of six or seven feet only. I have measured across a series of swaths which, one with another, have not measured six feet wide. The one makes . the operation unnecessarily laborious, and causes, almost unavoidably, a waste of herbage,—the other renders it unnecessarily tedious. A good workman may take *half a rod* (eight feet and a quarter) with sufficient ease to himself, and at the same time leave his work sufficiently level. It is prudent, however, on the part of his employer to see that he keeps within due bounds ; and, generally, that he does not exceed the *medium width*.

The *making* of hay is an inexhaustible subject. Every district, if we descend to minutiæ, has its shades of difference. The practice of this district resembles very much the practices of Yorkshire ; not only in the first stages, but . in the remarkable expedient of forming the hay into stacklets (here called " windcocks") previous to its being put into stack. But the practice is here carried a stage farther ; the hay being sometimes made into small stacks, of several loads each, in the stack yard ;

yard; and, while yet perhaps in a degree of heat almoſt ſuffocating to work among, is made over again into one large ſtack.

The ſame reaſons are given for this practice, here, as in Yorkſhire: namely that of being able to make it fuller of ſap in this way than it can be by the ordinary method. There ſeems, however, to be an additional motive to it in this country: namely that of being enabled, by this means, to make it into *very large ſtacks*—of fifty or perhaps a hundred loads each. Such ſtacks are faſhionable. They are ſpoken of with pride: and it ſeems probable that the *pride of great ricks* has ſome ſhare, at leaſt, in the practice of giving hay a double heat.

Be this as it may, however, it is a fact, well aſcertained, that the hay of theſe vales is of a ſuperior quality. It is found to bring on *fatting cattle* nearly as faſt as the green herbage from which it is made, paſſing thro' them with the ſame appearances. And the produce of *butter* from hay in this diſtrict, is extraordinary. But whether this ſuperior quality be owing, in part, to the method of making it, or wholly to the.ſoil and the herbage

bage from which it is made, is by no means well afcertained. That there is a *fomething* in the foils of thefe vales, which gives a peculiar richnefs to whatever they produce, is to me evident; and to endeavour to preferve in hay, as much as poffible of this richnefs, is indif-putably, good management.

The *degree of heat*, which hay ought to be fubjected to, is an interefting fubject, which is feldom agitated, and little underftood; even in this country, where fome little attention is paid to it. Something may depend on the fpecies of ftock it is intended for. The pre-vailing opinion, here, feems to be that, for fatting cattle, it ought to be moderately or fomewhat confiderably heated. For cows, however, there are dairymen, who fay it fhould have little, or no heat; giving for a reafon,— that " heated hay dries up their milk."—Thefe, however, I mention merely as opinions. They may be well grounded. If not, they may excite a fpirit of enquiry into a fubject of fome importance in a grafsland country.

The *expenditure of hay* in this diftrict is chiefly on cows and fatting cattle; to which

it

it is given either in sheds—yards—foddering grounds—or the ground it grew on;—in the manner, which will be mentioned in the articles cows, and FATTING CATTLE.

3. AFTERGRASS. I find no regular management of it here. The unstinted meadows are frequently turned into, the instant the hay is off the ground; and sometimes while no inconsiderable share of it remains in the meadow! Horses, cows, sheep, fatting-cattle, and haycocks being mixed in a manner sufficiently *grotesque* for the purpose of the painter; but in a way rather disgusting to those, who are aware of the waste they are committing: not of the hay, but of the after-grass. In eight and forty hours after the whole of the hay is out, the meadow, thus misused, has the appearance of a sheep common in winter: not a bite of green herbage to be seen; the whole being nibbled out by the sheep and horses, or trodden into the ground by cattle: nothing but the stubble, or dead stumps of seed stems, being left to cover the soil. These meadows, however, being free of growth, sheep, and even horses, may continue to get a living on them; and cattle may

be

be kept from ftarving;— but cannot bring home any advantage to their owners*.

Nor is this illjudged practice confined within the unftinted meadows; but is frequently extended to inclofed grounds. A full bite of aftergrafs is (this year at leaft) a rare fight in the country: I have feen very little fit for the reception either of cows or fatting cattle.

The line of right management is frequently difficult to draw. Different directions have their advantages and their inconveniences. By turning into mowing grounds as foon as the hay is out of them, the Glocefterfhire farmer gives a loofe to his pafture grounds: it is a *move* for his cattle: and if he would forbear a few weeks, to let his aftergrafs rife to a fufficient bite, his management would, in my judgment, be much preferable to the Yorkfhire practice; in which the cattle are kept in the pafture grounds, without moving, until the aftergrafs be overgrown. See YORK: ECON. article AFTERGRASS.

II. PASTURE

---

* This, however, is not general. Some of them, by ancient cuftom, are kept till the middle of September, before they be broken.

II. PASTURE GROUNDS.

    1. Spring management.

    2. Stocking.

    3. Summer management.

1. SPRING MANAGEMENT. The hams and inclofed pafture grounds are fhut up at different times, and opened about Old Mayday. Some of the hams much too late: thereby encumbering the furface, unnecef-farily, with weeds and ftale grafs; and leffen-ing, of courfe, the quantity of pafturable land*.

2. STOCKING. It feems to be a prevailing cuftom to mix a few *fheep*, in the pafture grounds,——whether with *cows*, or *fatting cattle*.

3. SUMMER MANAGEMENT. This appears in what has gone before. They are fwept, and fometimes mown; and have a refpite from ftock, while the *ftubbles* of the mowing grounds are picked over.

* See YORK: ECON: ii. 149.

HORSES.

29.

HORSES.

THE BREEDING OF HORSES for ſale is not, here, a practice. Moſt farmers rear their own plow-horſes ; and a few ſaddle horſes are alſo bred: but I have met with nothing in the practice of breeding horſes, in this diſtrict, which requires to be regiſtered.

The farm horſes are of the fen breed :— but very uſeful ones of that ſort: ſhort and thick in the barrel ; and low on their legs. —Colour moſtly black, inclinable to a tan-colour.

The price of a ſix-year old cart horſe, of this breed, is twenty five to thirty five pounds !

SHEEP.

30.

S H E E P.

THE SHEEP is a MOUNTAIN animal. Even in its prefent cultivated ftate, HILLS are its NATURAL ELEMENT. Uplands (or very found dry middlelands) are the loweft ftage on which fheep can be *kept*, with any degree of fafety to them; or with any degree of certainty to their owner. Vale lands, in general, are, without great caution, certain ruin to both.

Formerly, fome confiderable flocks were kept, or attempted to be kept, in this vale: even breeding flocks were not uncommon in it. But the wet fummer of 1782, fwept the country of them. One farmer, who had, for three or four years back, been recruiting his flock, and got it up to eight or nine fcore, had not, I was informed, in the autumn of 1783, more than three individuals left!

The low fituation of this vale,—the fingular retentivenefs of its fubftrata,—and the wa-

terinefs

terinefs of its foils, through a want of fur-
face-draining,—confpire to render it,—what,
from experience, it is too well known to be,—
fingularly fatal to fheep.

How unaccountable, then, is the conduct
of thofe, who attempt to keep ftore flocks in
it ? Nothing but the common error, which
pervades almoft every diftrict,— that fheep
are effential to farming,—can account for it.

At prefent, however, the vale, fully convinced of the folly of attempting to keep ftore
flocks, changes its ftock of fheep every year.

This fpecies of ftock, now, confifts chiefly
of ewes, bought in autumn, and, having fatted
their lambs in the fpring, are themfelves finifhed in the courfe of the enfuing fummer.

I. The SPECIES of fheep ufed in this practice are moftly the *Ryland*, and the *Cotfwold*,
both of which will be defcribed in the courfe
of thefe volumes.

II. Some little FOLDING was formerly
done in the fallow fields: " but all the folding
flocks are dead of the rot".! What folly!
What *cruelty*—to drive this animal from its
native heights ; and force it into a fituation,
where it muft inevitably become a prey to dif-

eafe; and at length, (if not releafed by the humanity of a butcher), fall a victim to folly, by a loathfome, tedious, lingering death.

III.   In a diftrict fo notorious as this for the ROTTING OF SHEEP, fome accurate ideas of this fatal diforder were of courfe enquired after.   An experienced hufbandman, on opening a fheep which he had killed for his own family, and finding a collection of water within it, pronounced the reft of his flock to be tainted.   Water he has always found to be the firft ftage of the diforder: a " white fcum" upon the liver the next: the laft flukes. From thefe circumftances, and from all the obfervations I have myfelf been hitherto able to make on this fubject, it appears to me *probable,*—that *an unnatural redundancy of water* —unavoidably taken in with the food—is the caufe of the diforder.

CATTLE.

31.

CATTLE.

CATTLE are the natural inhabitants of a vale country; and in this vale we find every description of them abound:—cows ;—REARING STOCK ;—FATTING CATTLE ;—and each of these of various species, or breeds.

Formerly, and perhaps not long ago, *one* breed of cattle might be said to possess the vale; a breed which still predominates in some parts of it. It is known by the name of the GLOCESTERSHIRE BREED ; and has, I understand, been common to the district time immemorial. WELCH CATTLE, no doubt, may have long been brought into the district, as *fatting cattle* ; and of late years some considerable number of HEREFORDSHIRE OXEN have been fatted in it. But still the *cows* and *rearing cattle* were of the Glocestershire breed.

Of still later date, however, an alien breed of *cows* has been introduced: the long-horned

P 2   breed

breed of Staffordshire and the other midland counties;--by the name of the " NORTH-COUNTRY SORT."   A breed, that, in a few years, has made rapid advances; and is likely to dispossess, in no great length of time, the naturalized species.   In 1783, dairies were mostly of the Glocestershire breed: in some, a mixture of the longhorned sort was observable;—and, in the lower vale, a few dairies were mostly of that breed.   Now (1788) few dairies are left without admixture; and, even in the upper vale, are some entire dairies of the longhorned breed.   In general, however, they are an unsightly mixture of the two species; with, not unfrequently, a third sort, a mongrel kind, reared from an aukward cross between them.   In the fairs and markets of the vale, scarcely any other than the north-country sort and this mule breed are to be seen.

Of the LONGHORNED CATTLE of the midland counties I mean to speak fully at a future time.   WELCH CATTLE are extremely various: every province of the principality seems to send out a separate breed.   They are invariably of the middlehorned species; but in regard

gard

gard to fize they vary, in regular gradation, from the largeft ox to the loweft Welch runt. The Herefordshire breed will be fpoken of under the head FATTING CATTLE ; and in the article HEREFORDSHIRE, toward the clofe of thefe volumes. The Glocefterfhire, therefore, is the only breed which requires to be defcribed in this place.

The GLOCESTERSHIRE BREED OF CATTLE is a variety of the MIDDLE HORNED SPECIES. (See YORK: ECON: article CATTLE.) In fize, it forms a mean between the *Norfolk* and the *Herefordfhire* breeds. (See NORF: ECON: art: CATTLE.) The head moftly fmall; neck long; fhoulder fine; and all of them generally clean. The carcafe moftly long, with the ribs full and the barrel large in proportion to the cheft and hind-quarters. The huckle of due width; but the nache frequently narrow. The bone, in general fine; the hide thin and the hair fhort. The charadteriftic colour, dark red,—provincially " brown";—with the face and neck inclining to black; and with an irregular line of white along the back. The horns fine and rather long; but, in fome individuals, placed aukwardly high on the fore-

P 3   head,

head, and near at the roots: in others, however, they ſtand low and wide ; winding with
a double bend, in the middle-horn manner.

The principal objections to the Gloceſterſhire breed of cattle are, a deficiency in the
chine, and too great length of leg; giving
the individuals of this deſcription, an aukward, uncouth appearance.

But no wonder.   The breed has not had a
fair chance of excelling.   I have heard of only
one man, within memory, who ever paid any
eſpecial attention to it ; and this one man, * by
ſome election ſtrife (a curſe in every county)
was driven out of the vale about ſeven
years ago: ſo that, at preſent, it may be ſaid
to lie in a ſtate of neglect.   Nevertheleſs, it
ſtill contains individuals which are unobjection-
able ;—particularly the remains of the Boddington dreed ; and, with a little attention,
might, in my opinion, be rendered a very
valuable breed of cattle.

For *dairy* cows, I have not, in my own
judgement, ſeen a better form.   It is argued,
however,

---

* Mr. ―― Long of Boddington.

however, that the northcountry cows, being *hardier*, ſtand the winter better in the ſtraw-yard; and *fat* more kindly when they are dried off. It ſhould be recollected, however, that Gloceſterſhire is a *dairy* country: and remembered that it was the Gloceſterſhire breed which raiſed the Gloceſterſhire dairy to its greateſt height. Beſide, the breed has long been naturalized to the ſoil and ſituation;—and certainly ought not to be ſupplanted, without ſome evident advantage; ſome clear gain, in the outſet; nor even then, without mature deliberation; leaſt ſome unſeen diſadvantage ſhould bring cauſe of repentance in future.

The three claſſes, enumerated at the head of this article, now require to be ſeparately conſidered.

I. Cows. This being a dairy country, the *procuring* of cows, and the *ſize of dairies*; as well as the *treatment*, the *application*, and the *diſpoſal* of cows, will require to be ſhewn ſeparately.

1. Procuring. Dairymen in general *rear* their own cows: ſome, however, *purchaſe* the whole, and others part, of their dairies.

                    The

The *point* of a milch cow which is here
principally attended to,—and which, no doubt,
is the main object of attention,— is a LARGE
THIN-SKINNED BAG: I have, however, heard
a large tail spoken of, in the true tone of su-
perstition.

The following are the dimensions of a cow
of the Boddington breed. A genuine, and a
fair specimen, as to form; but not as to size:
the cows of that celebrated breed were, in general, considerably larger. As a *milker* she
has had few equals; and, in my eyes, she is,
or rather was, one of the handsomest and most
desireable *dairy* cows I have yet seen. These
dimensions were taken when she was five
years old, off; she being then several months
gone with her fourth calf.

Height at the withers four feet three inches,
————of the fore dug twenty one inches.
Smallest girt six feet and half an inch.
Greatest girt seven feet eleven inches.
Length from shoulder-knob to huckle four
    feet one inch.
————from the huckle to the out of the
    nache twenty inches.
Width at the huckle twenty two inches.

Width

Width at the nache fourteen inches.

Length of the horn twelve inches.

The eye full and bright.

The ears remarkably large.

The head fine and chap clean.

The bosom deep; and the brisket broad, and projecting forward.

The shoulders thin with the points snug.

The thigh likewise thin, notwithstanding the great width at the nache.

The bag large and hanging backward; being leathery and loose to the bearing.

The teats of the middle size; gives much milk, *and holds it long.*

The tail large, the hide thin, and the bone remarkably fine.

The colour a " dark brown"; marked with white along the back and about the udder; with the legs, chap, and head, of a full, glossy, dark, chocolate colour.

The horns a polished white; tipped with black.

The reasons given, by the dairymen of this district, for *rearing* their own cows are, " that they should soon be beggared if they had their cows to buy"; and " that they know what they breed,

breed, but do not know what they buy." The latter has much the moſt reaſon in it; for, as they obſerve, if a heifer is not likely to turn out well, they ſell her: on the contrary, if they went to market for their cows they muſt buy the outcaſts of other breeders. Beſides, they endeavour to breed from known good milkers; ſuch as milk well, not only preſently after calving; but will *hold their milk*, through the ſummer, and the lattermath months: whereas in the market they are ſubject to chance, and the deceptions of drovers: the moſt they have to judge from is the *ſize* of the bag at the time of the purchace. In ſuitable ſituations, there can be little doubt of the propriety of every dairyman's rearing his own cows.

The *place of purchaſe*, in this diſtrict, is chiefly the market of Gloceſter, held every Saturday; to which, in the ſpring, from fifty to a hundred cows, of different breeds, *with calves by their ſides*, are brought; by dairymen and drovers; but principally longhorned cows, brought from a diſtance by the latter.. In the Ladyday fair at Gloceſter, there were not leſs than four hundred cows.

Some

Some of the larger dairymen go themſelves into the midland counties, to purchaſe cows. But ſeldom, perhaps, with much advantage; the expence of the journey; the time loſt; and the danger of a long drift, by unſkilful hands, probably, more than over-balance the dealer's profit. In caſes, in which ſtock is required to be transferred from one diſtrict to another, dealers become a uſeful claſs of men.

The *price* of a cow and calf of the Gloceſterſhire breed, has been for the laſt ten years eight to ten or eleven pounds; of the north country ſort ten to twelve or thirteen pounds.

2. THE SIZE OF DAIRIES. In *this* vale dairies are not very large: twenty or thirty cows are a full ſized dairy. Forty, I believe, the higheſt*. But farms are ſmall, and of courſe numerous; and the number of cows kept are collectively very conſiderable.

3. TREATMENT OF COWS. Notwithſtanding, however, the number of cows which are kept in this diſtrict, and the length of time which it has been celebrated as a dairy country,

* In the VALE OF EVFSHAM dairies are larger; fifty, ſixty, ſeventy, and one or two of eighty cows each.

try, I have met with few particulars in its management of cows, that are entitled to a place in this regifter.

The *fummer* management confifts chiefly in turning them out, in the beginning of May, fooner or later, according to the feafon and the nature of the foil,—into a ground, or fuite of grounds lying open to each other,—and there letting them remain until fome after-grafs be ready to receive them. The *fhifting* of cows, from pafture to pafture, is fpoken of, and may be fometimes practifed by a few individuals; but it is not the general practice of the country.

The *winter* management varies with the characteriftic of the farm, as to grafs and arable. On farms which have much plowland belonging to them, the dry cows are kept in the ftraw yard, until near calving; when they are put to hay in a feparate yard, or a foddering ground. On farms which are principally " green," they are kept all winter at hay; in the open air, or under loofe fheds; the practice of houfing cattle in winter, in the north-of-England manner, being, it may be faid, unknown, in this quarter of the kingdom.

4. The

4. The APPLICATION of milk in this diftrict, is to *calves, butter, cheefe*; principally to the latter; which forms no inconfiderable part of the produce of a vale farm; and the DAIRY MANAGEMENT becomes, in this cafe, too important a fubject to be confined, as heretofore, within a fubdivifion of the article CATTLE; requiring, in the prefent volumes, a feparate fection. (fee the next general head).

5. DISPOSAL OF COWS. *Dairy cows* are fold, *with calves at their fides*, in the manner which has been mentioned. *Heifers* which mifs the bull, or do not anfwer for the pail; alfo *young cows* that pafs their bulling; and *aged cows*, which are ufually thrown up at eight or nine years old, are, in the ordinary practice of the country, *fatted on the farm*, (in the way which will prefently be defcribed) and fold to the country butchers.

Thus, we find the dairymen of the vale of Glocefter, not only rearing their cows from their own ftock, but continuing them in their own grounds, after they have done their work as dairy cows, until they be fit for the flaughter:——a fyftem of management, which is

pleafing

pleafing to the obfervation; and which, by reafon of its fimplicity and perfection as a whole, affords the reflection equal pleafure and fatisfaction. There may be fituations, which will not admit of this practice, in its full extent; but, in moft cafes, there can be no doubt of its eligibility.

II. Rearing cattle. Breeding is here confined, in a manner wholly, to heifers for the dairy.

The number reared from a certain number of cows varies with circumftances; fometimes it may depend on the number of cow calves dropped within the feafon of rearing; the demand for young cattle; the circumftances of the farm; and the individual opinion of the dairyman,—likewife influence the proportional number. The firft breeder in the vale, feldom reared more than ten or twelve calves from forty cows;— while another judicious dairyman reared nine or ten from twenty cows.

In giving a fketch of the management of young cattle, in this diftrict, it will be proper to feparate the three diftinctions: namely,

Calves.

Yearlings.

Two-year-olds.

1. The

1. CALVES. The *season of weaning* lasts from Chriftmas to Ladyday: feldom longer: late-weaned calves interfere with the dairy.

The *method of rearing* is pretty uniform: at leaft in the outline. The calf is ufually taken from the cow at two or three days old, and put to *heated milk*. The degree of heat, how-ever, varies. In the practice of the firft breeder in the vale, the milk was given to the calves *fcalding hot !* as hot as the dairy-girl could bear her hand in it. The lips of the calves were not unfrequently injured by it. His reafons for this practice were, that the heat of the milk prevented the calves from fcouring; made them thrive; and enabled him to put his rearing calves to fkim milk, immediately from their being taken from the cow, at two or three days old. They never tafted " beft milk" after they were taken from the teat at that age !

This is an interefting inftance of practice; and merits a few moments' reflection. Na-ture has evidently prepared milk of a pecu-liar quality for the infant calf; and this milk is ufelefs in the dairy: it is therefore doubly good management to fuffer the calf to remain at the teat, until the milk becomes ufeful in the dairy; which it ufually does in two or three days. But although it becomes, to general appearance, fimilar to that of a cow which has been longer in milk, it is highly probable, that it is *ftill* fingularly adapted to the yet infant ftate of the calf. In the *fuckling* houfes, round the metropolis, it is well underftood, that putting a young calf to a cow, which is old in milk, will throw it into a fcouring. It, no doubt, requires a degree of correction to render it fully acceptable to the ftomach of the calf, at fo early an age : and, if we may venture to judge from this inftance of practice, *fufficiently authenticated*, fcalding the milk, very highly, gives it the due correction.

Befides the fcalded milk, this judicious manager allowed his calves fplit beans, oats, and cut hay. When they took to eat thefe freely, water was, by degrees, added to the milk.

In the fpring they were turned into a large well herbaged ground; allowing them fo good a pafture, that it was generally mown after them : and, during the whole of the firft

fummer

ſummer, they had the firſt bite wherever they went.

"CALF-STAGES." The calf-pen of this diſtrict is of an admirable conſtruction: extremely ſimple; yet ſingularly well adapted to its intention.   Young calves,—fatting calves more eſpecially—require to be kept narrowly confined: quietneſs is, in a degree, eſſential to their thriving. A looſe pen, or a long halter, gives freedom to their natural fears, and a looſe to their playfulneſs. Cleanlineſs, and a due degree of warmth, are likewiſe requiſite in the right management of calves.

A ſtage which holds ſeven, or occaſionally eight calves, is of the following deſcription.— The houſe or room-ſtead, in which it is placed, meaſures twelve feet by eight. Four feet of its width are occupied by the ſtage;— and one foot by a trough placed on its front; leaving three feet as a gangway; into the middle of which the door opens. The floor of the ſtage is formed of laths, about two inches ſquare, lying lengthway of the ſtage, and one inch aſunder. The front fence is of ſtaves, an inch and a half diameter, nine inches from middle to middle, and three feet

VOL. I.   Q   high:

high: entered at the bottom into the front bearer of the floor; (from which cross joists pass into the back wall) and steadied at the top by a rail; which, as well as the bottom piece, is entered at each end into the end wall. The holes in the upper rail are wide enough to permit the staves to be lifted up and taken out; to give admission to the calves: one of which is fastened to every second stave; by means of two rings of iron joined by a swivel; one ring playing upon the stave, the other receiving a broad leathern collar, buckled round the neck of the calf. The trough is for barley-meal, chalk, &c. and to rest the pails on. Two calves drink out of one-pail; putting their heads through between the staves. The height of the floor of the stage from the floor of the room is about one foot. It is thought to be wrong to hang it higher, lest, by the wind drawing under it, the calves should be too cold in severe weather: this, however, might be easily prevented by litter, or long strawy dung thrust beneath it.

It is observable, that these stages are fit only for calves, which are fed with the pail; not for calves which suck the cow.

Fatting

Fatting calves are here kept on the ſtages, until they be ſold : rearing calves until they be three weeks or a month old ; or until they begin to pick a little hay; when they are re-moved to a rack, and allowed greater freedom.

2. YEARLINGS. The firſt winter they are uſually allowed the beſt hay on the farm : and the enſuing ſummer, ſuch a paſture as con-veniency aſſigns them.———A diſtant rough ground, if ſuch a one belong to the farm, is generally their ſummer paſture.

3. TWO-YEAR-OLDS. The ſecond winter, heifers are generally kept at ſtraw; except they have had the bull the preceding ſummer; in which caſe they are wintered on hay. But the moſt prevalent practice is to keep them from the bull until the enſuing ſummer; *bring-ing them into milk, at three years old.*

III. FATTING CATTLE. The diſtrict un-der ſurvey, does not anſwer fully the deſcrip-tion of a GRAZING COUNTRY: the DAIRY forms its grand characteriſtic. Nevertheleſs, there are numbers of cattle annually fatted within it.

There are two diſtinct ſpecies of grazing carried on in this vale. The one natural to

Q 2

a dairy

a dairy country : namely that of fatting barren and aged cows : a species of grazing, which is purfued by *dairymen* and *farmers* in general : the other is that which more particularly characterizes a grazing country : namely, the practice of purchafing cattle for the immediate purpofe of fatting : a species of grazing, which is here carried on by a few opulent individuals only. Some of them, however, purfue it on an extenfive fcale ; and in a manner, which entitles it to particular attention.

Thefe two species of grazing require to be examined feparately. They are not only profecuted by two diftinct orders of men ; but the food—the cattle—the method of fatting—and the market of each is different. In one, the cattle are generally finifhed in *yards* or foddering grounds, abroad, in the open air, on hay alone. In the other they are moftly finifhed in *ftalls*, on hay and oil cake.

1. FATTING IN THE YARD. The *foods*, or fatting materials, in this cafe, are folely GRASS and HAY. Sometimes the cattle, in this mode of fatting, are frefhened with fummer grafs, and finifhed with lattermath ; but, more

frequently,

frequently, they are brought forward with grafs, and finifhed with hay; which, of this country, if well got, is found to force them on nearly as faft as grafs.

Befides the CULLINGS of the DAIRY, a confiderable number of WELCH CATTLE, of the fmaller kinds, and generally cows or hei-fers; and fome few HEREFORDSHIRE OXEN; are fatted in this way.

The principal *place of purchafe* of the Welch cattle is Glocefter market; to which, every Saturday, in the fummer, the autumn, and the winter months, confiderable numbers are brought.

The *fummer management* of this clafs of fat-ting ftock is no way extraordinary, nor par-ticularly inftructive. A diftant ground is generally affigned them, for the double pur-pofe of keeping them from the bull, and of giving the dairy cows the grounds which lie more conveniently to the yard.

The *winter management* is entitled to more attention. It commences in the field, while the cattle are yet at grafs; they being fod-dered, there, with hay, as foon as the grafs begins to fhrink; or fharp weather fets in.

The

The graſs done, or the weather becoming ſevere,—they are either brought into a *ſmall dry graſs incloſure*, (near the homeſtall)—provincially a " ſoddering ground"—where they have their fill of hay, given them three times a day, in round rodden cribs*, which are

rolled

---

* RODDEN CRIBS. Theſe are a kind of large baſket; made of the topwood of willow pollards. A utenſil common to this country and to Lincolnſhire; though ſituated on oppoſite ſides of the iſland: but they are alike graſsland countries, wherein 'cattle are fatted on hay. They are about ſix feet diameter. The height of the baſket-work is two feet and a half; of the ſtakes three feet and a half; their heads riſing about a foot above the rim of the baſket. The width between the ſtakes twelve to fourteen inches. The ſize, that of large hedge ſtakes. The ſize of the rods vary from that of a hedge ſtake, down to a well-ſized edder.

In making theſo hay baſkets,—the ſtakes are firſt driven, in a ring of the required ſize, firmly into the ground.—— Some of the larger rods are then wound in at the bottom, in the baſket work manner. Upon theſe the ſmaller rods are wound; the middle part of the work requiring the leaſt ſtrength; reſerving the largeſt for the top. In the winding and due binding of thoſe, the principal part of the art of " withy cub making" reſts. Some makers warm theſe thick rods in burning ſtraw: others wind them cold; one man drawing them in with a rope; while another beats them at the ſtake with a wooden beetle, until they acquire a degree of ſuppleneſs. They are moſtly made by men, who go about the country; and who, by practice, make

them

rolled upon the ridges of the lands, as the ground gets foul or poachy;—or in *yards*—provincially " courts"—in which the hay is given to them in mangers, formed by a rodded hedge, running parallel with the outfide fence; or in cribs—provincially " cubs"—of different forts and defcriptions, placed in the area of the yard.

Out of thefe cribs and mangers the cattle not unfrequently feed to their knees in dirt; having perhaps an open fhed to reft under; or perhaps only a fmall portion of the yard littered for that purpofe: yet fuch is the fagacity and cleanlinefs of this fpecies of animal, that when they are at liberty to make choice of their bed, they will, if poffible, choofe it warm and clean.　I have feen half

Q 4

a dozen

them very completely; winding in the top-rods fo firmly and fo regularly, that it is difficult to know, which has been the laft put in.

In ufe, the cattle lay their necks between the tops of the flakes.　Each being thus kept in its place, the mafter cattle are, in a degree, prevented from running round, and driving away the underlings.　The clofenefs of thefe cribs prevents a wafte of hay, either by the wind, or by the cattle.

On the whole, they are ufeful, fimple, cheap; and, if well made, will laft feveral years.

a dozen fine oxen, worth, at the time I repeatedly obferved them, twenty to thirty pounds a piece, fatting on hay, actually to their knees in dung; with only a corner of the fmall yard they were penned in, littered with ftubble; and this corner fo fmall there appeared to be fcarcely room for the fix to lie down together: neverthelefs, their coats were always clean; and, if one might judge from the condition they were in, and the appearance of health and good habit they wore, they were perfectly fatisfied with their fituation. A fact which appears to me extremely interefting. The yard in this cafe was entirely open, (excepting fome trees which overhung it) but was well fheltered from the north and eaft.

The *progrefs* of this clafs of fatting cattle depends much on the given fize. The Welch fort, if purchafed early in fummer, will generally get fufficiently fat, with grafs alone; and fome cows the fame: but in general thefe are finifhed with hay. If cows, which are put to lattermath, do not get fat on hay, by Mayday, they are fometimes fold, as forward ftock, to *graziers* of this or other diftricts.

tricts. The oxen are not expected to be finished completely in less than ten or twelve months.

The *purchasers* of this class (the oxen generally excepted) are the butchers of the district.

In estimating the value of fat cattle, here, the *butcher's allowance* of profit, on a cow of ten or twelve pounds price, is from one to two guineas.

The *proof* expected from this class of cattle, at head keep, is—Welch cows 1s. 6d. to 2s. dairy cows 2s. to 3s. oxen 3s. to 3s. 6d. a week, at grass ; and somewhat considerably more at hay.

2. STALL FATTING. This may be considered as a modern practice, in the RURAL ECONOMY OF ENGLAND.

GRASS is the NATURAL food of fatting cattle. HAY was probably first in use for WINTER fatting. CORN has probably been used, on a small scale, time immemorial, for the same purpose. TURNEPS may have been applied to this purpose, in Norfolk, about a century. But OILCAKES, the residuum or bran of linseed from which oil has been expressed,

(the

(the grand material made ufe of in the practice
under notice) has not perhaps been uſed, in
this intention, more than half that period.
They have not in this diſtrict been uſed, in
quantity, more than 20 to 30 years.

At prefent, they are become a ſtaple article
of food, for winter fatting, in various parts of
the iſland; but in no one of the five widely
diſtant ſtations, I have obſerved in, are they
uſed on ſo ample a ſcale as in the diſtrict now
under ſurvey.   There are two individuals fi-
niſh, annually, from one hundred to one hundred and fifty head of large bullocks each.
And a third, who fats a ſtill greater number:
not however on oilcakes, alone; but on the
foods, and in the manner, which will be mentioned.

In giving a detail of this practice, it will be
proper to take a feparate view of

1.   The fituation and foil of the diſtrict.
2.   The foods or materials of fatting.
3.   The breed, ſex, and age, of the cattle
      fatted.
4.   The places of purchafe and the obſer-
      vable points.
5.   The ſummer management.

6. The

6.   The winter management.

7.   The market.

8.   The produce.

1.   *Situation.*   This ſpecies of "grazing" is confined chiefly to the vicinities of Glocefter, Tewkeſbury, and Upton.   The *ſoil*, whether of upland or meadow, is moſtly rich, ſound, and early.   The upgrounds affording paſturage, and the meadows hay, of the firſt quality.   If we except the margins of ſalt marſhes, few ſituations are better adapted to ſummer grazing ; and the navigation of the Severn is favourable to winter fatting.—We may add to theſe advantages, the circumſtances of one of the fineſt breeds of cattle, the iſland affords, being reared on one hand ; while the market of the metropolis is within a moderate diſtance on the other.

2.   The *foods* in uſe for ſtall fatting are HAY, CORN, " CAKES", LINSEED.

Hay is a ſtanding article of food in the ſtalls ; being uſed jointly with one or more of the other articles ; moſtly, I believe, in its natural ſtate ; ſeldom, I underſtand, cut with ſtraw into what is termed chaff ; a practice in ſome other diſtricts.

The

The species of *corn* in use are barley and beans, ground, and given dry, alone. But this is not a common material of fatting in the diftrict under notice, where

Oilcake, as has been faid, is, next to hay, the main article of ftall fatting. But the price of this article is at leng thbecome fo exorbitant, that it no longer, I am afraid, leaves an adequate profit to the confumer. Some years back, I recollect, it was the idea of men of experience, that it could not be ufed profitably as an article of fatting for cattle, at a higher price than three pounds a ton. Now (1788) it is, in fome places, more than twice that price. The loweft price, at the more diftant mills, is, I am well informed, five pounds ; at Berkeley mills, fix pounds ; at Evefham, fix guineas ; at Stratford, fix pounds ten fhillings a ton. †

This extravagant price of the cakes has induced fome fpirited individuals to try the *linfeed*, itfelf, boiled to a jelly, and mixed with

flour,

---

† Thefe prices fluctuating, from time to time, fo much as 20s. a ton. Some few years ago the price was higher than it is at prefent.

flour, bran or chaff; and, from the information I have had, with favorable fuccefs. *

This novel practice requires a few minutes reflection. From the prefent fcarcity and dearnefs of cakes, it may be inferred that the demand is greater than the quantity in the markets. If, therefore, the feed can be profitably ufed; though with only a fmall increafe of profit, and with this even on a contracted fcale; the ufe of it may operate very beneficially; by leffening the demand, and thereby lowering the prefent exorbitant price, of the cakes.

It is highly probable, however, that it may be ufed with much greater advantage than cakes at their prefent price. I have by me a fample of American feed, (nearly equal to the beft Dutch feed I have feen), which may now be imported for 38 to 40s. a quarter, of eight winchefter bufhels. Suppofing the bufhel to weigh 50lb, the price of this prime feed is not twelve pounds a ton. Ordinary feed might be had cheaper.

It is farther *probable* that the fuperior kind of nutriment, which the cakes afford, proceeds

from

---

* In Herefordfhire, *linfeed oil*, I am told, is ufed in a fimilar manner.

from the unexpreſſed oil they contain, rather
than from the huſks of the ſeed of which they
appear to conſiſt.   This being admitted, and
ſeeing the exceſſive power which is uſed in ex-
tracting the oil, we may without riſque conclude that a ton of ſeed contains more than
twice (*perhaps* five times) the nouriſhment
which remains in a ton of cakes. *

Viewing the preſent ſubject in a partial light,
it might be ſaid, that an unlimited and exceſſive

* LINSEED-JELLY. The principal objection to this material is the trouble of preparing it. In an inſtance in which
it was uſed with ſucceſs, the method of preparing was this.
The proportion of water to ſeed was about ſeven to one.
Having been ſteeped, in part of the water, eight and forty
hours, previous to the boiling, the remainder was added,
cold ;—and the whole boiled, gently, about two hours ;
keeping it in motion during the operation, to prevent its
burning to the boiler ; thus reducing the whole to a jelly-
like, or rather a gluey or ropy conſiſtence. Cooled in tubs :
given, in this inſtance, with a mixture of barley meal, bran,
and cut chaff ; each bullock being allowed about two quarts
of the jelly a day ; or ſomewhat more than one quart of
ſeed in four days : that is, in this caſe, about one ſixteenth
of the medium allowance of cake.

This however is thrown out as a general idea ; not drawn
as an inference: the comparative effect of theſe two materials of fatting forms an important ſubject for the deciſion
of experiment.

five ufe of a foreign article of farting for cattle, might leffen the demand, and thereby
lower the value of our own productions, applicable to the fame purpofe ; to the injury of
the landed intereft.   If, however, we confider
that, by the ufe of foreign linfeed, an influx of
the firft vegetable manure we are acquainted
with would be diffufed over the foils of this
country ; and that wheat may be exported at
a price more than equivalent to the prefent
price of linfeed; the landed intereft would feem
to have no caufe of alarm ;—while in a more
general point of view, the importation of linfeed from AMERICA might be a national good.
I underftand from intelligence of the firft authority, that fome of the fineft provinces of that dif-
ftrefsful country, are in a manner deftitute of
marketable returns, for the produce and ma-
nufactures of this kingdom ; and further, that
linfeed, which can there be grown in unlimited
quantities, is at prefent a drug in the American markets.

But this by the way, FLAX SEED cannot yet
be confidered as an eftablifhed article of food
for cattle, in this diftrict ; in which GRASS,
HAY, and OILCAKE are the prevailing foods
of

of the species of fatting cattle now under confideration ; and to thofe, only, I fhall confine.
myfelf in the following remarks.

3. *The cattle* which are fubjected to this
mode of fatting are chiefly HEREFORDSHIRE
OXEN, which have been worked in the breeding country, and thrown up after barley feed-
time, in working condition ; or have been kept
over the fummer, and fold " frefh"—that is
forward in flefh—to the graziers in autumn.

Befides thefe, fome of the larger breed of
oxen of South-Wales particularly of Glamor-
ganfhire; alfo of Wyefide of Glocefterfhire, as
well as round the foreft of Dean, and in the
over-Severn diftrict ; alfo fome Somerfetfhire,
and fome few Devonfhire oxen are fatted here ;
but thefe, collectively, are few in proportion
to thofe of the Herefordfhire breed ; which,
alone, I fhall confider as the objects of ftall-
fatting, in this diftrict.

The AGE at which thefe oxen are ufually
fatted is *fix years old !*

I do not mean to cenfure the workers of
thefe oxen, for throwing them up in their
prime as beafts of draught ; much lefs to
blame the graziers for fatting them, or the
butchers

butchers for ſlaughtering them in that uſeful ſtage of life ; but I cannot help expreſſing my regret, on ſeeing animals ſo ſingularly well adapted to the cultivation of the lands of theſe kingdoms, as are the principal part of the ſix-year-old oxen of Herefordſhire, proſcribed and cut off in the fulneſs of their ſtrength and uſe-fulneſs.

The graziers, indeed, conſidered merely as ſuch, do not, in this caſe, come within the reach of cenſure. They know from experi-ence that the cattle under obſervation gene-nerally leave them the moſt profit at that age. Some few individuals, however, will, it is ſaid, *grow* (that is, ſpread out in carcaſe) *as well as fat* (the two things deſireable to the grazier) at ſeven years old. But after thoſe ages, having ceaſed to *grow,* they pay for *fatting* only *.

It is, however, allowed that a full-aged ox *tallows* better than a young growing ox. But,

---

* I have met with an idea, in this diſtrict, that a gummy, thick-thighed, hard-fleſhed ox ſhould not only be kept to a greater age than one of the oppoſite deſcription ; but ſhould be worked down low in fleſh, previous to his being finally thrown up for fatting.

Vol. I.   R

But, on the other hand, it is argued that oxen which are hardly worked and hardly kept, become flat-sided, lose the laxity of their fibres, and do not, on being fatted, fill up so well in their points, as younger oxen, which have been less hardly used.

This, however, is not good argument against the general position: oxen, whether young or old, should never be worked down into a state of poverty of carcase: but ought, at all times, to be kept as full of flesh as their activity will permit. If horses pay for being kept up in carcase, while they are worked, how much more amply would oxen pay for a similar treatment.

But argument becomes superfluous where facts are produceable. There is one instance mentioned in this district, in which an ox was worked until he was FIFTEEN YEARS OLD, and then fatted " tolerably well".—And a still more valuable incident than this occurred in the practice of the first grazier within the district immediately under observation *; in which instance *three* oxen were *finished* in the usual time allowed for six-year-old oxen;
which

* Mr. DARKE of Bredon.

which three oxen were EIGHTEEN YEARS OLD;
a fact that I have fingular fatisfaction in regiftering. †

4. *Purchafe* and *points.* The *places of purchafe* are the fairs of Herefordfhire: held at the
different towns of the county, in almoft every
month of the year; and thofe who purfue this
fpecies of grazing, on a large fcale, may be faid
to purchafe the year round. But fpring and
autumn, as has been intimated, are the principal *times of purchafe.* Lean in the fpring,
for fummer grazing; and forward, in autumn,
for more immediate ftall fatting.

The *favorite points,* by which graziers
make choice of the individuals of this breed of
cattle, are *fimilar* to thofe which are obferved
in other diftricts; yet they are not altogether
the *fame.* In different diftricts I find graziers,
in their choice of cattle, not only particularly
obfervant of different points; but have, in
fome meafure, diftinct criterions to judge by:
and I am of opinion that different breeds or
varieties of cattle require fuch a difference of
judgement.

R 2   Every

---

† Thefe oxen were bred and kept to that age, by Mr.
Cook of the Moor, near Hereford.

Every variety of cattle has a tendency to degenerate; and each appears to have its peculiar propensity in degenerating. Thus the Glocestershire breed become, under neglect, narrow in the chest, light in the hind quarters, and long upon the legs. The Herefordshire breed,—get a lumpishness of carcase and a heaviness of the limbs. The long-horned breed, on the contrary become gaunt in the carcase, coarse in the forehand, and thick in the hide. While the Holderness breed tend to a gumminess of the hind-quarters and a hardness of flesh.

These observations, however, are, at present, offered incidentally; to endeavour to reconcile the jarring opinions of professional men on this subject. I perceive a captiousness, in every district, among men who stand high in their profession; arising from a partiality toward the particular breed they are most conversant with; and from a want of a more general knowledge of the several breeds of the island at large.

The profits of grazing rest, in a great measure, on the proper choice of the individuals to be fatted; be the species or the variety

what

what it may.   And although a quick and accurate judgement, in this cafe, as in almoſt every other, can be matured by practice, only ; yet the groundwork is certainly reduceable to ſcience.   If from men of experience, and ſuperior judgement, we can aſcertain the criterions of good and bad qualities of the ſeveral breeds of the animals to be ſatted, the ſtudent will be enabled to acquire the requiſite judgement much *ſooner* than he could without ſuch aſſiſtance.

From my own obſervations, corrected and made more full and perfect by thoſe whoſe experience has rendered them adequate judges of the ſubject, I am fully authorized, I truſt, to ſet down the following as deſireable qualities in the Herefordſhire breed of oxen.

QUALITIES *deſireable* in a Herefordſhire ox, intended for GRAZING.

The *general appearance* full of health and vigour ; and wearing the marks of ſufficient maturity ;—provincially "oxey"—not " ſteeriſh"—or ſtill in too *growing* a ſtate to *fat*:

The *countenance* pleaſant ; chearful ; open ; the forehead broad :

The *eye* full and lively:

R 3

The

The *horns* bright, taper, and spreading:

The *head* small, and the chap clean:

The *neck* long and tapering:

The *chest* deep; the bosom broad *, and projecting forward. †

The *shoulder-bone* thin, flat; no way protuberant, in bone; but full and mellow, in flesh.

The *chine* full.

The *loin* broad.

The *hips* standing wide; and level with the spine.

The *quarters* long; and wide at the nache.

The *rump* even with the general level of the back: not drooping; nor standing high and sharp above the quarters. The *tail* slender, and neatly haired.

The *barrel* round, and roomy: the carcase throughout being deep and well spread.

The *ribs* broad; standing close; and flat on the outer surface; forming a smooth even barrel: the hindmost large, and of full length.

The *round-bone* small; snug; not prominent.

The

---

* In a WORKING OX this is a most desireable point.

† This is, here, a very popular point, whether in a cow or an ox.

The *thigh* clean, and regularly tapering.

The *legs* upright and short. *

The *bone*, below the knee and hough, small. †

The *feet* of a middle size.

The *cod* and twist round and full.

The *flank* large.

The *flesh* every where mellow; soft; yielding pleasantly to the touch; especially on the chine, the shoulder, and the ribs.

The *hide* mellow; supple; of a middle thickness; and loose on the nache and huckle.

The *coat* neatly haired, bright, and silky; its colour a middle red—with a " bald face": the last being esteemed characteristic of the true Herefordshire breed.

QUALITIES

---

* It may be disputable whether the legs of a WORKING ox ought to be short or of a middle length. Cattle are naturally heavier, less active, than horses; whose legs are seldom found too short in harness. Nevertheless, oxen may require some length of leg, to assist them in travelling. It is observable, however, that the best working ox, I have known, had remarkably *short* legs.

† In a WORKING OX, the *sinew* should, nevertheless, be large.

R 4

QUALITIES *exceptionable* in a Herefordshire ox, for grazing.

The *general appearance* sluggish; spiritless; lumpish;—or aukward, through a deformity in make, or a want of sufficient maturity.

The *countenance* heavy, sullen,—" cloudy."

The *eye* hollow and dull.

The *horns* coarse and thick; provincially " goary."

The *head* large, thick; the chap coarse and leathery.

The *neck* short, thick, coarse; loaded with leather and dewlap; " throaty."

The *shoulder-points*—provincially the " elbows"—standing wide;—or projecting forward *.

The *chine*—" keen";—that is, rising sharp above the withers;—and hollow behind the shoulders.

The *loin* contracted; narrowing to a point at the chine.

The *hips* standing narrow; or placed below the general level.

The

---

* This is, here, spoken of as the most hateful point an ox can possess: while, in other districts, it passes, comparatively, unnoticed. In a WORKING OX, it is, especially in harness, a very great fault.

The *rump* drooping ;—" gooferumped ;"— or the tail fet on too high ; ftanding above the level of the fpine.

The *quarters* fhort, falling, and narrow at the nache.

The *barrel* contracted upward ; the ribs dropping flat from the chine—" flatfided ;"— forcing the intrails downward—" cowbellied."

The *ribs* narrow, and placed at a diftance from each other ; leaving vacancies between them ; throwing the furface of the barrel into ridge and furrow.

The *round-bones* large ; bulging out wide in proportion to the hips.

The *haunches* flefhy ;—" brawny."

The *limbs* in general large and unwieldy.

The *hind-legs* crooked inward at the gam-brels ; or the fore legs at the knees*.

The *fhank* long and thick.

The *feet large*, with the claws fpreading.

The *cod* flaccid ; with the point hard and knobby.

The *flank* thin, fingle.

The

* This is a defect, amounting, in fome cafes, to an in-firmity. I have obferved it, in an inferior degree, in other breeds ; efpecially in the fore legs. In a WORKING OX, it is an infurmountable objection.

The *flesh*, on the chine and ribs, hard.

The *bide* harsh, thick, and sticking to the carcase.

The *coat* staring, — " sett,"— not lying close; appearing dead; faded; not alive and glowing :— symptoms, these, of a diseased habit.

5. *Summer management.* The management of grazing, in this district, has been represented, aforegoing, as not being sufficiently interesting to require to be *detailed :* nor do I, in this department of it, find any *particulars* entitled to especial notice. In saying this, however, I do not mean to intimate, that it is more reprehensible, than that of other grazing districts. Indeed it is not, in this case, the main object of practice; being only used as a preparation to STALL FATTING.

6. *Winter management.* This, for reasons already given above, will require to be analyzed; and each part to be described in detail. And previous to this detail, it will be requisite to describe the building in use, here, for winter-fatting.

"OX-STALLS." What characterizes the bullock sheds of this district, and distinguishes them

them from thofe of every other, I have obferved in, is the circumftance of each bullock
having a *boufe* and a *yard* to himfelf; in which
he goes loofe; occupying them by turns, as
appetite or amufement directs him; having a
manger and a drinking trough to go to at
pleafure.   He, of courfe, eats when he is
hungry, and drinks when he is thirfty.   He
is alfo at liberty to rub, or to lick himfelf;
as well as to keep his body in a degree of
temperature, as to heat and cold.   Theory
could not readily fuggeft more rational principles.

The conftruction of thefe ftalls varies in
the minutiæ.   The water trough, for inftance,
is fometimes placed by the manger, in the
hovel or fhed:—fometimes in the open pen.
Other lefs noticeable variations may be feen
in different buildings.

The plan and dimenfions, which, at prefent, feem to ftand higheft in efteem; and on
which feveral erections of this nature have
been made within the laft fifteen or twenty
years; are the following.

The building fifteen to fifteen feet and a
half wide within, and of a length proportioned
to

to the number of stalls required. The height of the plates six feet to six feet four inches; supported on the side to the north or east by close walling; on that to the south or west by posts, set on stone pedestals. The gables walling. The covering plain tiles, on a single pitch-roof.

Against the back wall is a gangway, three and a half to four feet wide, formed by a length of mangers, three feet to three and a half feet wide, from out to out, at the top; narrowing to about fifteen inches within, at the bottom. The perpendicular depth fourteen or fifteen inches; the height of the top rail from the ground, about two feet nine inches. The materials two-inch plank; stayed and supported by posts and cross pieces; and stiffened by strong top-rails.

The dimensions of the area of the covered stalls, about eight feet three inches square; of the open pens, the same.

The partitions between the stalls are of broad rails, passing from the outer pillars to similar posts, rising on the inner or stall side of the manger; and steadied at the top by slender beams, reaching across the building;

each

each ſtall, or each partition, having a beam
and a pair of principals.

The partitions of the pens are gates, reaching from the pillars to the boundary wall;
and likewiſe from pillar to pillar.   When they
are fixed in *that* ſituation, each bullock has
his ſtall and his little yard.   When in *this*
each is ſhut up in his ſtall; the yards forming
a lane, or driftway, for taking in, or turning
out, any individual.

The boundary wall of the pens is about
four feet high; coped with blocks of copper-
droſs.   On the outer ſide of it is a receptacle
for manure.   On the inner a range of water
troughs; with a channel of communication
for the conveniency of filling them.   The
materials of the troughs, ſtone *; of the channel, gutter bricks, covered with ſlabs.

The

* STONE TROUGHS.   Theſe troughs, which are about
fourteen inches by two feet ſix inches within,—have a conveniency in their conſtruction, which is entitled to notice.
Inſtead of the ſides and the ends being all of them pecked
down to an angle, ſquare with the bottom, one of the ends
is left bevelling, ſloping, making a very obtuſe angle with
the bottom.   This ſimple variation renders them eaſy to
be cleaned; either with the ſhovel, or the broom.

The floor is paved with hard-burnt bricks, laid edge-way in mortar; being formed with a steep defcent from the wall to a channel, fome three or four feet from it; and with a gentle fall from the manger to the fame channel; which becomes the general drain for rain water and urine.

At one end of the pens is a pump (where a natural rill cannot be had) for fupplying the troughs with water; and, at the other, a ftack of ftubble for litter; which is ufed in the ftall only; the yard being left unlittered.

At one end of the building is a cake-houfe, at the other, the rickyard; with a door at each end of the gangway to receive the hay and the cake.

In one or more inftances, I have feen a double range of ftalls on this plan; the area between them being the common receptacle for the dung. When a number of ftalls, as twenty or thirty, are required, this arrangement brings them within a convenient compafs; and the two ranges, with a proper afpect, become fhelter to each other.

Befide thefe *loofe* ftalls, there are others, built nearly on the fame plan, but without

gates,

gates, and on a somewhat smaller scale, in which the cattle are *fastened* to the manger, or · the partition posts, with a long chain, which gives them liberty to rub and lick themselves, and move about in their stalls. In this case, a water trough is generally placed at the end of every second partition, level with the manger, with a general pipe of communication to fill them; each trough supplying two bullocks. This plan lessens the expence in some degree, and prevents the bullocks from souling their mangers.

There are individuals in the district, who have fifty, or more, of one or the other of these stalls, on their respective premises.

The number of oxen to a given quantity of hay.

The requisite attendance.

The season of stall farting.

The stated times of feeding.

The quantity of cake eaten in a day.

The manner of feeding with hay.

The progress of oxen at cakes, and

Putting them from dry meat to grass,—are subjects, which now require to be separately handled.

A. The

A. The NUMBER OF OXEN requisite to a certain quantity of hay laid up, depends on their size, on their state as to forwardness, and on the quantity of cake intended to be consumed with it. In places, where hay is a dear article, cake is the principal food; a small quantity of hay, cut with wheat straw, being given them between the meals of cake; by way of what is termed cleaning their mouths, as well as to correct the over-richness of the cake. On the contrary, in this district, where hay is generally plentiful and cheap, cake becomes, in most cases, secondary; hay being considered as the principal material of fatting. A man, whose practice is extensive; and whose character, as a grazier, is of the first cast; estimates a fullsized bullock to consume, in six months, two tons of hay; being allowed, in that time, fifteen hundred weight of oilcake.

B. The requisite quantity of ATTENDANCE depends, in some degree, on circumstances. The general calculation is one man to about twenty head of oxen:—cutting hay, breaking cake, feeding, watering, littering, and keeping clean, inclusive.

C. The

C. The SEASON of ſtall fatting laſts, in this diſtrict, from November to May; commencing when the aftergraſs is gone, or ſharp weather ſets in; and cloſing with the finiſhing of the bullocks; or when a full bite of ſpring graſs is formed.

D. The STATED MEALS vary with the proportion of hay and cake, and with other circumſtances. In the ordinary practice, three meals of hay; one in the morning,—one at noon, — one in the evening;— and two of cake, one in the forenoon,—the other in the afternoon; are the prevailing number of meals, and the uſual times of feeding.

E. The QUANTITY OF CAKE, which is uſually given each bullock at a meal, is about a quarter of a peck of broken cake;—giving, at the two meals, about half a peck a day.* When it is found requiſite to force them forward for a market, the quantity is ſometimes

encreaſed

---

* The cakes are broken in a large mortar; with a wooden lever-like peſtal, ſhod with iron; or with a beetle, or a ſmall ſledge hammer, in a wooden trough; or are ground in a cider mill; reducing them into fragments of two or three ſquare inches each, down to thoſe of a much ſmaller ſize.

Vol. I.   S

encreafed to near a peck of broken cake a-day. But in this cafe, it is given them at three or more meals; it being dangerous to cloy them with this fpecies of food; which is liable to make them fick;—and, in confequence, to loathe it, perhaps, for feveral days; and, in fome cafes, to perfevere in refufing it. In open yards, where cake is fometimes given to loofe bullocks, this accident not unfrequently happens; the mafter bullocks having an opportunity of eating more than their fhare; but in ftalls, where each ox has no more than the quantity which is affigned him, this in-conveniency can happen through imprudent management, only.

F. The METHOD of feeding with HAY appears in what has paffed: it is given to them, uncut, two or three times a-day, according to the number of meals of cake, which they have allowed them.

G. The PROGRESS of oxen, and the length of time requifite to FINISH them, in ftalls,—depend on the fpecific quality of the bullocks themfelves; on the ftate, as to forwardnefs, in which they are taken up; and to the quantity of cake they have allowed. In the

fpecies

species of grazing now under notice, a large ox, which is bought in lean, is expected to take from ten to twelve months to finish him for Smithfield market. If bought in May-June, for instance, he has the summer's grass, and lattermath, until, perhaps, the middle of November; when he is put to cake; and sent off to market at Candlemas, Ladyday, or Mayday, according to the progress he has made; or as the chance of a good market may direct.

They are seldom, however, kept the whole of the winter in STALLS; the head bullocks, only, being stalled at the beginning of the season; the rest having a smaller allowance of cake given them, in OPEN YARDS; or, perhaps, have an allowance of hay, only, in the FIELD. As the stalled bullocks go to market, their places are supplied by the forwardest of those, which are more at large.

H. If the last-stalled bullocks are not finished sufficiently for market, before spring grass is fit to receive them, they are sometimes TRANSFERRED FROM THE STALLS TO THE FIELD; and there have been instances, in which this was done with considerable advan-

tage

tage; though, in general, it does not seem to be considered as an eligible practice. It is sufficiently ascertained, however, that there is no danger in this expedient; and that the cattle, if they do not improve by it, may, at least, be kept from sinking.

If CAKE be continued to them at GRASS, there can be no doubt of the practice being frequently adviseable. The markets for fat cattle are generally low at the close of the winterfatting season. On the contrary, from that time, until grafs beef be ready, they are mostly favorable to the seller.

7. The MARKET for this species of fatting cattle is Smithfield; to which they are driven by occasional drovers, engaged for the purpose: there being no stationed drovers here, as in Norfolk (see NORF: ECON:). The usual time upon the road is eight days; the distance about a hundred miles. They are chiefly (or wholly from *this* diftrict) consigned to falesmen. The expence of drift, falesman, toll, &c. is generally about ten shillings the head.

8. The PRODUCE of oxen fatted in this manner, will, if valued according to the popular

lar

lar mode of eſtimation, appear to be very low.
They are not expected, during the ten or
twelve months fatting, to produce more than
two thirds of their firſt coſt; while there are
many breeds of cattle in this iſland, whoſe individuals would more than *double*, ſome of the
ſmaller kinds *treble*, their firſt coſt, in the ſame
time, with the ſame keep.

Leſt this fact ſhould be laid hold of, as an
argument againſt the Herefordſhire breed of
cattle, or the Gloceſterſhire method of fatting
them, it may be proper to intimate, that although large cattle conſume, on a par, more
food than thoſe of a ſmaller breed; yet it is
more than probable, that the diſparity does
not keep pace with the difference in their firſt
coſts.   Thus, it is not probable that an ox of
fifteen pounds coſt ſhould conſume as much
food as three cows of five pounds, or five
Welch heifers of three pounds, each.

The preſent price of this breed of oxen, in
working condition, immediately out of the
yoke, at ſix year old, is ten to ſixteen pounds
each.   In the ordinary eſtimation of the country it is expected that theſe oxen ſhould produce, *at graſs*, from three ſhillings to three

S 3

ſhillings

fhillings and fixpence a week; at *bay and cake*, from fix to feven fhillings; or, the largeft fize, at high keep, feven fhillings and fixpence a week: leaving at the end of ten to twelve months, a grofs produce of feven to nine or ten pounds. Twenty five pounds is not an uncommon price for a bullock of this breed in Smithfield market: there has been, I under-ftand, feveral inftances in which the Hereford-fhire breed of oxen, fatted in this diftrict, have fetched thirty pounds the ox.

32.

MANAGEMENT

OF THE

DAIRY.

THE OBJECTS of the dairy, in this di-ftrict, are

> Calves
> Milk butter
> Cheefe
> Whey butter
> Swine.

But

But previous to an account of the management of each object, individually, it will be proper to notice fome fubjects, which have a general relation to the whole.   Thefe are

1.   Dairy-women.
2.   Dairy-room.
3.   Utenfils.
4.   Milking.

1.   DAIRYWOMEN.   The management or immediate fuperintendance of a large dairy, efpecially one of which cheefe is the principal object, is not a light concern.   It requires much thought, and much labour. The whole of the former, and much of the latter, necef-farily falls on the immediate fuperintendant ; who, though fhe may have her affiftants, fees or ought to fee, herfelf, to every ftage of the bufinefs ; and performs, or ought to perform, the more difficult operations.

This arduous department is generally under-taken by the MISTRESS OF THE DAIRY ; efpeci-ally on middlefized and fmall farms. In fome cafes, an experienced DAIRY MAID is the often-fible manager.

S 4   There

There are three things principally requisite in the management of a dairy:

> Skill,
> Industry,
> Cleanliness.

Without the first, the two latter may be used in vain: and a want of the last implies a deficiency in the other two. Cleanliness may indeed be considered as the *first* qualification of a dairywoman; for, without it, she cannot have a fair claim to either skill or industry.

With respect to CLEANLINESS, the Glocestershire dairywomen stand unimpeachable. Judging from the dairies I have seen, they are much above par, *in reality*;—though not so to common *appearance*. A cheese dairy is a manufactory—a workshop—and is, in truth, a place of hard work. That studied *outward neatness* which is to be seen in the *show dairies* of different districts, and may be in character where *butter* is the only object, would be superfluous in a CHEESE DAIRY. If the room, the utensils, the dairywoman, and her assistants be sufficiently *clean* to give perfect SWEETNESS to the produce, no matter for the *colour*, or the *arrangement*. The *scouring wisp* gives an outward

ward fairnefs; but is frequently an enemy to real cleanlinefs. The *fcalding brufh*, only, can give the requifite SWEETNESS: and I have feen it no where more diligently ufed than in Glo-cefterfhire.

Cleanlinefs implies INDUSTRY. A Glocef-terfhire dairywoman is at hard work, from four o'clock in the morning, until bed time.

Her degree of SKILL requires not to be fpo-ken of here; as it will better appear in the fol-lowing detail, than in any general obfervations which can be made upon it.

2. The DAIRYROOM. The chief peculiarity obfervable in a Glocefterfhire dairyroom pro-vincially " dairyhoufe"—is that of its gene-rally having an OUTER DOOR, opening into a fmall yard or garden place; while the dairy of moft other diftricts is cooped up in a corner, with only a fmall window for the admiffion of air and light; every thing being dragged, in and out, through a number of inner doors, or perhaps rooms or paffages. But an outer door gives a freer and more general air; and a much better and a more commodious light; befides rendering the bufinefs of cleanlinefs more eafy. In the dairy yard there is, or ought to be, a well;

a well; with proper benches and other conveniences, for washing and drying utensils.

The room, too, is large and commodious: 15 feet by 18 may be considered as a middle-sized dairy. The cheese-making and churning are done in the "dairyhouse": so that the entire business is collected into as narrow a compass as may be: a circumstance of some importance, in a large dairy; and, in a small one, the advantage is proportional. The *floor* is generally laid with stone. The *shelves* are mostly of elm, or ash.

With respect to ASPECT, the outer door, when well placed, opens near the northeast or the northwest corner: the window on the north side: the inner door, on the south-side, opening into the kitchen.

A dairyroom on this plan is, perhaps, as commodious as art can render it.

3. UTENSILS. · A detail of the furniture of a dairy may appear uninteresting; and, by some readers, be thought unnecessary. It would be difficult, however, to give a minute account of the method of carrying on the *manufacture*, without describing the *tools* in use: a description of them is little more than a definition

tion of technical terms. Perfpicuity requires it.

1. *Milking pail.* The fhape nearly that of a bufhel. But formed of ftaves and hoops; with *one* " handle ftave" rifing three or four inches above the rim. (The Yorkfhire *fkeel* with one handel.) The diameter about fifteen inches; the depth about ten inches. Staves oak—hoops (broad and clofe) afh.

2. *Milk cooler;* provincially " cheefe cowl." —This is a large ftrong wooden veffel, proportioned in fize to the number of cows. From eighteen inches, to two feet deep:—and from two to three feet diameter. Two oppofite ftaves rife above the reft: the head of each having a hole in it, large enough to admit a pole; for the purpofe of moving it, or carrying it on men's fhoulders; anfwering the purpofe, occafionally, of what in fome diftricts is called a *bearing tub;* in others a *cawl.*

3. *Strainer; or milk fieve.* Made fieveform: twelve or fourteen inches diameter: five or fix inches deep: fome with hair bottoms: others have cloth bottoms; which are taken out every day to wafh. A frond or leaf of fern

is

is frequently placed at the bottom of the sieve to prevent the milk from flying over.

4. *Sieve bolder*; provincially " cheese ladder."—This is laid acrofs the cooler to place the *milk sieve* or ftrainer upon. It has here a valuable fingularity of conftruction: at one end are two crofs bars about three inches apart. This vacancy admitting one " ear" or handle of the cooler, the ladder is kept fecurely in its place. The wood, afh.

5. *Lading difh.* The ufual fhape but large ; near a foot diameter.

6. *Pail brufhes.* Common hard brufhes ; furnifhed with briftles at the end, to clean out the angles of the veffels more effectually. Utenfils, or rather tools, which no dairy ought to be without. Yet in many diftricts of the kingdom their ufes are unknown.

7. *Pail-ftake.* A fimple contrivance ; or rather a *thought*; which one would imagine, no perfon, having dairy utenfils to dry, could mifs: yet it appears to have been hit upon in this country only. In other diftricts I fee milking pails, &c. placed upon benches, or upon walls, to dry ; where they are liable to be blown down by the wind, or thrown down and

burft

burſt by other means. Here, a bough, furniſhed with many branchlets, is fixed with its
but-end in the ground, in the dairy yard.
The branchlets being lopped, of a due length,
each ſtump becomes a peg to hang a pail upon
or other utenſil.

8. " *Skeels.*"——Theſe are broad ſhallow
veſſels; principally for the purpoſe of ſetting
milk in, to ſtand for cream : made in the tub
manner, with ſtaves and hoops, and two
ſtave handles : of various ſizes, from eighteen
inches to two feet and a half diameter; and
from five to ſeven inches deep. Staves oak;
hoops (broad and cloſe) aſh.

9. *Skimming diſhes.* If of wood, very thin.
But chiefly of *tin.* About eight inches diameter; and five eights of an inch deep.

10. *Cream jars.* Cream is chiefly pre-
ſerved in earchen jars of a middle ſize.

11. " *Cream ſlice.*" A wooden knife ; ſome
what in the ſhape of a table knife. Length
12 or 14 inches.

12. *Churns.* Upright and barrel churns
are in uſe. The barrel churn with one fixt
and one looſe handle. Noway excellent in
their conſtruction. Butter is here a *ſecondary*
object

object. The Yorkſhire churn is preferable: but this might be expected: there butter is the *primary* object of the dairy.

13. *Butter board, and trowel.* A broad board and a wooden ſpatula, uſed in " printing" the butter.

14. *Butter prints.* The halfpound print four inches diameter.

15. *Cheeſe knife.* A wooden handle, four or five inches long,—furniſhed with two, or three iron blades, twelve inches long, and one inch broad, at the handle, down to about three quarters of an inch at the point; with two blunt edges, rounded at the point, like an ivory paper-knife. The diſtance between the blades, which are very thin, and ranged with their flat ſides toward each other, about an inch.

16. *Cheeſe vats.* From fifteen to fifteen and a half inches diameter; and from one and a half inch to two inches deep. The wood invariably elm. Some with, but many without holes.

17. *Cheeſe cloths.* Made of thin gauze-like linnen cloth. The ſize varies in different dairies.

18. *Cheeſe-*

18. *Cheese press.* The conſtruction various. Sometimes ſingle, but, in large dairies, generally double. The preſſure is moſtly given by a dead weight, raiſed by a roller, and falling perpendicularly on the cheeſe. In the upper vale, they are chiefly of ſtone. The dimenſions of one of a ſuperior weight are twenty two inches ſquare, by two feet two inches long; containing 12,584 cubical inches of freeſtone; weighing (on the ſuppoſition, that its ſpecific gravity is an ounce and a half to an inch) ſomewhat more than half a ton.

But, by an accurate experiment, I found, that a cubical inch of ſimilar ſtone (freeſtone of the Cotſwold cliffs) weighs only 500 grains. Therefore, calculating the pound averdupois at 7,000 grains troy, the ſtone under notice weighs eight hundredweight.

The dimenſions of other three (all of the ſame ſize and in the ſame dairy) are 20 inches wide, by 14 deep, and two feet four inches long: containing 7,840 cubical inches of Cotſwold freeſtone: conſequently, weigh no more than five hundredweight each.

Theſe are of the *old conſtruction*; which is *very* ſimple. In the center is fixt a wooden

ſcrew,

ſkrew, riſing three or four feet perpendicularly above the ſtone ; paſſing through a hole
in a croſs beam, reſting on the cheeks of the
preſs.   Above this croſs-piece is worked
a looſe nut, made out of a piece of wood,
eighteen inches to two feet long, and of a
diameter proportioned to the ſize of the worm.
Each end is reduced to the ſize of a handle,
and with this two-handled nut the ſtone is
raiſed and lowered.   The perpendicularity of
the ſkrew keeps the baſe of the ſtone hori-
zontal; and to keep it more ſteady in its place,
it is notched at each end about an inch deep,
to admit the cheeks, or ſlips nailed on the inner ſides of them, for that purpoſe.

4. MILKING.   The hours of milking are
here early: about five in the morning, and.
four in the evening; in order to give due
time for finiſhing the requiſite buſineſs of the
dairy, before bed-time.

Where a large dairy of cows are kept, the
whole family (excepting thoſe who have the
care of the teams) muſter to milking. An
indoor ſervant, by the name of a " milking
man" is generally kept, in the larger dairies,
for the purpoſe of milking, churning, and
                                        otherwiſe

otherwife affifting in the bufinefs of the dairy: he has the care of the cows and the cow-grounds; and is confidered as a principal fervant.

When the " COWGROUND" lies near the houfe, the cows are generally brought into the yard, or other fmall inclofure: if the paf-ture lie at a diftance, the pails are always carried to the cows. Alfo if the ground be very wet, and poach with the cows travelling over it, judicious dairymen have the pails carried to them. In more than one inftance, I have feen a horfe and barrel-cart employed, to take the milk from a diftant meadow or cowground to the dairyhoufe.

The practice is to milk the cows unfet-tered; and to ufe fquare-topped, four-legged ftools; refting one edge of the bottom of the large pail, here in ufe, againft two legs of the ftool. Hence the conveniency of its form.

The management of the particular OBJECTS of the dairy now require attention.

I. CALVES. Thefe, being the firft pro-duce, and as it were the origin of dairies, re-quire to be firft noticed.

The REARING OF CALVES has been already spoken of, in p. 255. The method of fatting them remains to be mentioned in this place.

The FATTING OF CALVES being, here, a *subordinate* object of the dairy, no very accurate ideas on the subject must be expected: the late-dropt calves are an encumbrance on cheesmaking, the primary object, and are of course got rid of as soon as possible. One singularity of management, however, requires to be noticed.

Calves, whether for rearing or fatting, are seldom suffered to *suck* more than two or three days; sometimes they are put to the *pail*, as soon as they are dropt; the milk being, I believe, pretty universally passed through the *kettle*; and given to the calves *warmer* than it comes from the cow. On the increased heat of the milk, the advantage of this *unnatural* mode of fatting is *here* thought principally to hinge. See YORK: ECON: ii, 295, on this subject.

II. MILK BUTTER. In the upper vale, milk butter forms a considerable object of the dairy: not only in the spring, while calves are rearing, before cheesmaking commences; but

but during fummer: owing to the species of cheese, which is univerfally made here; and which is, I believe, peculiar to the vale of Glocefter. It is called " two-meal cheefe." The evening's meal is fet for cream; and, being fkimmed in the morning, is added to the morning's meal, neat from the cow.

The method of making butter in this diftrict, therefore, merits a defcription in detail; efpecially as GLOCESTER BUTTER,—which is diftributed, by huckfters, to diftant parts of the country, bears a fuperior character. The ftages of the art are,—

1. Setting the milk.
2. Preferving the cream.
3. Churning.
4. Making up the butter.
5. Markets.

1. SETTING THE MILK. This I have feen done in different ways: every diftrict exhibits good and bad management,—in almoft every department of rural affairs. The beft method of fetting milk in this country, which I have feen, and which may, I believe, be called the beft practice of the diftrict, is this.

T 2

The

The milk having remained in the cooler, a time, proportioned to the heat of the weather; so as to lower it to about 80° of Farenheit's thermometer; it is parcelled out in " skeels:" or, if these are not sufficiently numerous to receive it, in any other dairy vessel;—leaving, perhaps, a part of it in the cooler*; dividing it in such a manner, as to leave it about an *inch deep*, in each vessel: the dairywoman measuring the depth, by the joint of her finger; and carefully placing the vessels level; so that one side be not left deeper than the other. The prevailing rule is *to set it as shallow as it can be conveniently skimmed*; under a conviction, that the shallower it is set, the more cream will rise, from a given quantity of milk. An inch and a half is the ordinary depth; but, in the practice I am more particularly registering, the dairywoman has dexterity of finger sufficient to skim it at an inch deep. This, however, could not be done without the assistance of a *tin skimming dish*; which being

thinner,

---

* MILK-LEADS are not common in this district. I have, nevertheless, seen some very old ones in use: a circumstantial evidence, that their use has been long *known* in this district.

thinner, gathers up the cream cleaner, than a wooden one; but requires a more steady hand to guide it.

2. PRESERVING THE CREAM. Earthern jars are the common receptacles of cream.—In thefe it is *ftirred* feveral times a day, with the " cream flice;" but feems to be *fhifted* lefs frequently, here, than in fome other dairy countries. Cream, here, has a peculiar propenfity to become " curdy;" lofing its liquid ftate; requiring fome ftrength of hand to ftir it; arifing probably, from its fuperior richnefs *.

3. CHURNING. In the practice, which I more particularly attended to, the bufinefs of churning is conducted in this manner:—If the weather be hot, the churn is previoufly cooled with cold water; and, if wanted, cold water is likewife put into the churn among the cream. On the contrary, if the weather be cold, the churn is warmed with fcalding

T 3

water;

---

* COLOURING BUTTER. In autumn, when butter generally becomes pale and tallow-like, the cream is not unfrequently *coloured*, before it be put into the churn. The material of colouring is the fame as that ufed in the colouring of cheefe; which will be fpoken of in the next article. The method of ufing it, however, is fomewhat different.

water; and, if wanted, hot water is put into the churn; which, perhaps, in severe weather, is placed near the fire, during the operation.

The cream of the vale is very liable to rise in the churn; owing, probably, to its peculiar richnefs. Under this circumftance, part of it is taken out; and, when that which is left in the churn is gone down again, the part taken out is re-added.

The mouth of the churn is fecured with butter, preffed plafterwife into the joints.—This is thought to be lefs troublefome than a cloth.

The *breaking* is here carefully attended to. It is confidered as very injurious to heat the butter in the churn.

4. MAKING UP BUTTER. In making up butter, the firft bufinefs is to prepare the feveral utenfils employed in the operation.—Here they confift of the " butter fkeel"—the " butter board"—the " print" and " trowell." The preparation required is to prevent the butter from hanging to the wood. It is here done with fcalding water, and *falt*, brufhed into the wood while moift and hot, with

with a foft thick-fet brufh: either putting the falt upon the brufh, or dufting it over the utenfil; which, being falted, is immediately plunged into cold water. The dairywoman's hands are prepared in·a fimilar manner.

I will give the minutiæ of this operation, as performed by a moft excellent dairywoman; whofe butter feldom fails of being of the firft quality. They differ from thofe, which I have already given;* and are, probably, the beft which I may have an opportunity of ob-ferving; and probably the laft, upon which I may beftow the tedioufnefs of regiftering.

The butter being taken out of the churn, and placed in the " fkeel," with a quantity of cold clear water,—the dairywoman breaks off a lump, (fomewhat more than a pound) and, with one hand, kneads it in the water, *with the fingers fpread widely abroad*; clofing them at intervals; thereby breaking the butter moft effectually; confequently giving the contained milk an opportunity of efcaping. Every time the fingers are clofed, the lump is rolled on the bottom of the fkeel; the hand fhifted,

taking

* See NORF: ECON: MIN: 109.

T 4

taking the lump the contrary way; and worked as before. This being several times repeated, the first roll is placed upon the butter board, and a fresh lump broken off.

The whole being gone over in this manner, the milky water is poured out (into the tub of buttermilk *) the skeel washed, and somewhat more than half the butter spread thinly and evenly, but *roughly*, over the bottom of it. Salt is then dusted upon this rough surface; the remaining lumps of butter spread over the salt; and over the whole another portion of salt is strewed.

The dairywoman now rolls the whole into one lump; which she immediately breaks down with the palm of her hand; the fingers expanded as before; forcing the butter from her; closing the fingers partially at every
stroke;

---

* Butter milk is here acidulated for the hogs; being mixed among the whey, which is also given to the hogs stale and sour: not, I believe, as a matter of choice, which is studied; but as a matter of conveniency.

In winter, when butter milk is sweet, it is sometimes run, among other milk, for " family cheese;" and affords a considerable quantity of curd; but it makes what is called a " bitter mess," and the running of it, is, I underderstand, considered as a mean species of economy.

ftroke; thereby leaving it at the bottom of the fkeel *exceedingly rough*.

Over this rugged furface frefh water is poured; the butter rolled up again into one large lump; again broken down in the manner laft-defcribed: and again formed into one large roll.—This is at length broken into pound lumps; and kneaded in the water, as in the firft inftance.

The butter is now a fecond time upon the butter board (over which water is always thrown before the lumps be placed upon it) and the fkeel being emptied of the briney water, the lumps are feparately kneaded (with one hand) on the bottom of it, *dry*; and fet in fhort rolls, againft the fide of the fkeel.

The butter fcales are then taken out of the falt water, which was poured out of the fkeel, and in which they have been immerfed during the laft operation, and evenly balanced with butter; the lumps divided; and weighed in *half-pound pieces*: which are again returned into the fkeel; or, for want of room, are placed upon the board.

This being effected, the lumps are prepared for printing; by kneading them, dry, at the

bottom

bottom of the skeel; and moulding each into a conical form; with the palm of the hand; and with the fingers joined, and set at right angle to the palm. The point of the cone-like lump thus formed, being placed in the center of the print, the base is pressed down, until the surface of the print be covered. What presses over, at the edges, is collected, (by running the finger round the print,) and put upon the intended bottom of the pat. The sides are finally smoothed with the trowel; the pat with the print set upon the butter board; and the print taken off: leaving the pat about 4 inches diameter and about 1½ inch thick. *

If

* BUTTER GAUGE. A cubical inch of well wrought butter weighed 230 grains; or somewhat more than half an ounce averdupois. Therefore a pound averdupois of well wrought butter contains somewhat more than thirty cubical inches (30. 4.) And the standard pound of this district (18 oz;) measures more than thirty four inches (34. 25.) The half pound somewhat more than seventeen inches. Hence a half pound print or pat of butter exactly four inches in diameter ought (if well worked and honestly weighed) to measure exactly 1. 3628 inches in depth.

A measure, of some regular figure, as a cube, accurately formed, on these principles, would be the best standard for a

market

If the print does not " loose" freely, the hand is placed, carefully and firmly, againſt the ſide of the pat; thereby gaining a degree of purchaſe to pull againſt. If the butter be found to adhere in any degree to the wood, the print is ſcalded, ſalted and bruſhed, until it looſen freely; without the indelicacy of *blowing* in the manner practiſed in moſt places. The pats remain ſome length of time, gene-rally one night, upon the board to ſtiffen; and, in the morning, are placed in cold water, previous to their being put into the baſkets, in which they are carried to market.

5. MARKETS. The butter markets of the upper vale are chiefly *Gloceſter*, *Chelten-ham*, *Tewkeſbury*, and *Eveſham*. That of Gloceſter is the largeſt and the *neateſt* butter-market I have anywhere obſerved. The but-ter is all brought in half-pound pats or prints, packed

---

market inqueſt; as it would not only check the weight; but the purity of the butter alſo: provided due care were obſer-ved in preſſing it cloſely into the gauge; thereby freeing it from the redundant moiſture, which dairy-women, who are ſkilfull and honeſt, extract before they take it to market; but which the ſlovenly and the deſigning ſell at the price of butter. See NORFOLK, MIN: 109.

packed up in square baskets, in a manner which merits description.

The baskets are invariably of one form: long-square; with a bow-handle across the middle; and with two lids, hingeing upon a cross piece under the bow. The dimensions of an ordinary basket are 18 by 14 inches within; and about 10 inches deep. This basket holds twelve prints (four by three) in one layer or tire. When the butter is firm, three layers or 18 lb. are put in each basket; when soft two tires or 12 lb. One of a larger size measures 18 by 23 inches within; carrying twenty half pounds in each tire; or 30 lb. in the three tires. The basket is put into a kind of open wallet; with generally a smaller basket or other counterpois at the opposite end of the wallet; which being strapt tightly to the saddle (judiciously made for this purpose) with the heavy end on the off side of the horse, the dairymaid mounts, and, with her own weight, preserves the balance. The basket being lashed on in such a manner as to ride perfectly level, the prints are preserved from bruising.

In

In fummer, the butter is invariably packed in green leaves: generally in what the dairy-women call "butter leaves": namely the leaves of the *Atriplex hortenfis*, or garden orach; which dairywomen in general fow in their gardens, annually, for this purpofe. They are fufficiently large; of a fine texture; and a delicate pale-green colour. For want of thefe, vine leaves, and thofe of kidney-beans &c. are ufed.

In packing a butter bafket, the bottom is bedded with a thick cloth, folded two or three times. On this is fpread a fine thin gauze-like cloth, which has been dipped in cold water; and on this is placed the prints; with a large leaf beneath, and a fmaller upon the center of each. The bottom tire adjufted, a fold of the cloth is fpread over it, and another tire fet in, in a fimilar manner. At market, the cloth is removed; and the prints, partially covered with leaves, fhown in all their neatnefs. The leaves are ufeful as well as pleafing to the eye. They ferve as guards to the prints. The butter is taken out of the bafket, as well as put in to it, without being touched, or the prints disfigured.

III. Cheese.

III. CHEESE. The art of making GLOCES-
TERSHIRE CHEESE was originally one of the
principal objects which induced me to make
choice of Glocesterfhire as a STATION. My
practice in Norfolk* had fhown me that, in the
quality of cheefe, although much may depend
upon SOIL and HERBAGE, much is certainly
due to MANAGEMENT.

GLOCESTERSHIRE has long been celebrated
for its excellency in this art: and where fhall
we ftudy an art with fo much propriety as in
the place where it excels? It may be proper to
add, that altho' my own experience had not
led me to perfection, it had fufficiendy enabled
me to make accurate obfervations on the practices of others. An ANALYTICAL ARRANGE-
MENT, of the.feveral departments and ftages
of the art, was a guard againft my fuffering
any material part to efcape my notice; and
the THERMOMETER a certain guide in thofe
difficult paffages, in which an accuracy of
judgement, is more peculiarly requifite.

* See RURAL ECONOMY OF NORFOLK. MIN: 108.

The

The objects of my attention have been

Soils	Management of the curd
Water	
Herbage	Management of the cheese
Cows	
Quality of milk	Defects and Excellencies
Colouring	
Rennets	Markets
Method of running	Produce.

The management of the two vales under survey differ in one most material article ;— the *quality* of the milk. In the lower vale, the milk is run neat from the cow (or nearly so). In the upper vale, it has been already said, the prevailing practice is to set the evening's meal for cream ; in the morning to skim it ; and then to add it to the new milk of the morning's meal. The cheese made from this mixture is termed " TWO-MEAL CHEESE": that from the neat milk, " one-meal cheese" or " BEST MAKING."

Besides this difference in produce, or SPE-CIES OF CHEESE, there are other differences in the practices of the two vales. It will therefore be proper to register them separately ; lest by mixing them, the perspicuity, which is

requisite

requifite in defcribing the minutiæ of an art fo complex and difficult as this under confideration, fhould be deftroyed.

Of the UPPER VALE the *foil*, the *berbage*, and the *cow* have been already mentioned: the fubjects which remain to be noticed in this place are

1. The feafon of making
2. The quality of the milk
3. Colouring
4. Rennets
5. Running
6. Management of the curd
7. Management of the cheefe
8. Markets.

1. THE SEASON OF MAKING. From the beginning of May to the latter end of October, including feven months, may be confidered as the feafon of cheefmaking, in this diftrict.

2. THE QUALITY OF THE MILK. The mixture for twomeal cheefe has been mentioned, in general terms, to be one part fkim milk (namely milk which has ftood *one* meal for cream) and one part new milk, *neat* from the cow. But *this* is feldom, I apprehend, ftrictly the cafe. A little *fraud* is, I am afraid,

generally

generally practised. A greater or less proportion of the morning's meal is set for cream, and returned the next morning to the cheese cowl,—*robbed* of its better part. This is a trick played upon the cheese factor: but he being aware of the practice, little advantage, probably, is got by it. However, where the soil is superiorly rich, a small proportion may be " kept out", and the cheese, nevertheless, be of a *fair* quality.

3. COLOURING. This is another *deception* which has long been practised by the Glocestershire dairywomen; and which, heretofore, probably, they practised · exclusively. The colouring of cheese, however, is now become a practice in other districts.

The practice has no doubt arisen from the Glocestershire dairywomen's having observed, that, on some soils, and in some seasons, cheese naturally acquires a yellow colour; and such cheese having been found to bear a better price, (either from its intrinsic quality, or because it pleased the eye better) than cheese of a paler colour, they set about *counterfeiting nature*; and in the outset, no doubt, found their end in it.

There is fome difficulty, however, in this as in other cafes, to copy nature exactly. Much depends on the material; and fomething on the method of ufing it. If the colouring material be improperly chofen, or injudicioufly ufed, the colour appears in ftreaks, and inftead of pleafing the eye, offends it. On the contrary, with a fuitable material, properly ufed, the artifice may be rendered undetectable.

The material which has at length obtained univerfal efteem; and which, I believe, is now, almoft invariably ufed; is a preparation of ANNOTTA; a drug, the produce of Spanifh America. It is brought to England (for the the ufe of the dyers principally I believe) under the appearance of an earthy clay-like fubftance; but is well known to be a vegetable production. †

It

---

† ANNOTTA is the produce of *Bixa Orellana* of Linneus. Miller defcribes the plant and its propagation. It is a tallifh fhrub, fomewhat refembling the lilac. The colouring material is the pulp of the fruit; among which the feeds are bedded, in a manner fomewhat fimilar to thofe of the rofe, in the pulp of the hep. It is a native of the Weft Indies, and the warmer parts of America: Annotta Bay in Jamaica

takes

It has been tried as a colouring of cheefe in its genuine ftate; but without fuccefs.   The PREPARATION, which is here ufed, is made by druggifts both in London and in the country; and is fold at the fhops in Glocefter, and other towns in the diftrict, in rolls or knobs of three or four ounces each.   In colour and contexture it is not unlike well burnt red brick.   But it varies in appearance and goodnefs: the hardeft and clofeft is efteemed the beft. *

The method of ufing it is this.   A piece of the preparation is rubbed againft a hard fmooth even-faced pebble, or other ftone; the pieces being previoufly wetted with milk, to forward the levigation, and to collect the particles as they are loofened.   For this purpofe a difh of milk is generally placed upon the

---

takes its name from this fhrub.   The pigment, it is faid, was formerly collected in Jamaica; but has of later years been brought there (in feroons, or bags made of undreffed hides) from the Spanifh fettlements.

* With refpect to the *crime* of colouring cheefe, I fay nothing in this place: as I fhall have a better opportunity of fpeaking of it, when the VALE OF BERKELEY becomes the fubject of notice.

the cheefe-ladder ; and as the ftone becomes loaded with levigated matter the pieces are dipped in the milk from time to time ; until the milk in the difh appear (from daily practice) to be fufficiently coloured. ·

The ftone and the " colouring" being wafhed clean in the milk, it is ftirred brifkly about in the difh ; and, having ftood a few minutes for the unfufpended particles of colouring to fettle, is returned into the cheefecowl ; pouring it off gently, fo as to leave any fediment which may have fallen down, in the bottom of the difh. The grounds are then rubbed with the finger on the bottom of the difh, and frefh milk added ; until all the finer particles be *fufpended*: and in this the fkill in colouring principally confifts. If any fragments have broken off in the operation, they remain at the bottom of the difh: hence the fuperiority of a hard clofely textured material, which will not break off or crumble in rubbing. ,

The price of annotta is about ten pence an ounce ; which will colour about twenty thin cheefes (10 or 12 pounds each). The colouring therefore cofts about a halfpenny a cheefe.

4, RENNETS.

4. RENNETS. Rennets are here learnedly spoken of,—by those who are superficially acquainted with their use. Experienced dairy-women, however, speak modestly on the sub-ject: what they principally expect from rennet is the *coagulation* of their milk ; having little faith in its being able to *correct* any evil qua-lity which the milk may be possessed of.

The universal *basis* is the stomach of a calf ; provincially a " vell" ; from which an extract is drawn, in various ways ; according to the judgement or *belief* of the dairywoman.

1. The PREPARATION OF THE VELL ;—namely the cleansing and pickling ; is gene-rally done to their hands. Besides the inter-nal supply, London and Ireland furnish this country with great numbers of vells ; which are brought in casks, in pickle, and sold by the grocers and other shopkeepers. The price of English vells about sixpence a piece, of Irish about fourpence ; these being compara-tively small. *

2. PREPARATION OF THE RENNET. In the dairy which I more particularly attended

U 3   ·to

* Some of them, it seems, are *suspected* to be "lambs vells."

to in the upper vale, the rennet underwent
no *eftablifhed* mode of preparation. The *prevailing* method is this: fome *whey*, being falted,
until it will bear an egg, is fuffered to ftand
all night to purge itfelf: in the morning it is
fkimmed and racked off clear: to this is added
an equal quantity of *water-brine*, and into this
briney mixture is put fome fweet briar, thyme,
hyffop, or other " fweet herbs"; alfo a little black pepper, falt petre &c.; tying the
herbs in bunches, and letting them remain in
the brine a few days. Into about fix quarts of
this liquor, four Englifh vells, or a propor-
tionate number of Irifh ones, are put; and
having lain in it three or four days, the rennet
is fit for ufe. No part of the preparation is
boiled, or even heated: and frequently no
other preparation whatever is ufed, than that
of fteeping the vells in cold falt and water.
Indeed, in another dairy, which I had an opportunity of obferving in the upper vale, no
other mode of preparation was ufed; and few,
if any, dairies make better cheefe: I fpeak
from my own knowledge.

Therefore, from the evidence which I have
collected in the upper vale it appears that,
provided

provided the *vells'* be duly *prepared*—be thoroughly cleanfed and cured—no fubfequent preparation of *rennet* is neceffary. Neverthelefs, were I to recommend a practice in this cafe, it would be that of doing away the natural *faint* flavor of the vells, by fome aromatic infufion. But I fhould prefer *fpices* to *herbs* for this purpofe.

5. Running. In this, as in every other ftage and department of cheefmaking there are *fhades of difference*, in the practices of different dairywomen. No two conduct the bufinefs exactly alike; nor is the practice of any individual uniform. There are, at prefent, no fixed principles to go by. Every thing is left to the decifion of the fenfes; uncertain guides. Neverthelefs, *practice*, carried on with attention, and affifted by good natural abilities, will do much; though it cannot, alone, attain that degree of perfection, which, when joined with *fcience*, it is capable of reaching.

The miftrefs of the dairy, whofe practice I am more particularly regiftering, has both natural and acquired advantages, which render her dairy, though not of the firft magnitude,

                a proper

a proper subject of study.' Her father was possessed of the best breed of cows in the vale, and was one of the largest dairy farmers in it. Her mother, the first among its dairy-women; and herself possessed of that *natural cleverness*, without which no woman, let her *education* be what it may, can conduct, with any degree of superiority, the business of a cheese dairy.

In giving a detail of my own practice in Norfolk, I mentioned some known principles of coagulation; as well as some received opinions of dairywomen, respecting the nature of this process. The same opinions are held in this district; in which some other received ideas prevail: namely, that the quantity of curd is in proportion to the length of time of coagulation: there being " the least curd when longest in coming."

That setting the milk hot, inclines the cheese to " heave": (a defect which will be spoken to hereafter.)

And that lowering the heat of the milk with cold water (when made too hot) has a similar effect.

To

To give fome idea of the practice of the upper vale, in this moft delicate ftage of the art, I will detail the obfervations made, during five fucceffive mornings, in the dairy which has been fpoken of.

Tuefday, 2 *September,* 1783. The quality of the milk, that which has been defcribed. Part of the fkim milk added cold; — part warmed in a kettle over the fire, to raife the whole to a due degree of heat. Coloured in the manner defcribed. An eftimated fufficiency of runnet added. The whole ftirred and mixed evenly together. The exact heat of the mixture 85° of Farenheit's thermometer. The morning clofe and warm, with fome thunder. The cheefe cowl covered,— but placed near an open door. The curd, neverthelefs, came in lefs than forty minutes: much fooner than expected: owing probably to the peculiar ftate of the air. The retained heat of the curd and whey, when broken up and mixed evenly together, 82°. The curd deemed too tough and hard; though much the tendereft curd I have obferved.

Wednefday, 3 *September.* The morning moderately cool. The heat of the milk when

set

set 83½°. The cowl partially covered, and expofed to the outward air as before. Came in an hour and a quarter. The heat of the curd and whey mixed evenly together 80°. But at the top, before mixing, only 77°· The curd extremely delicate, and efteemed of a good quality.

Thurfday, 4 *September.* The morning cool —a flight froft. The milk heated this morning to 88°. The cowl more clofely covered, and the door fhut part of the time. Set at half paft fix: began to come at half after feven: but not fufficiently hard, to be broken up, until eight o'clock:—an hour and a half. The whey, when mixt, exactly 80°! The curd exceedingly delicate.

Thus it fhould feem, that it is not the heat of the milk when it is run; but the heat of the whey, when the curd is fufficiently coagulated, which gives the quality of the curd. My own practice led me to the fame idea. And the Glocefterfhire dairywomen, by their practice, feem fully aware of the fact. As autumn advances, the heat of the milk is increafed. And accordingly as the given morn-

ing

ing happens to be warm or cool, the degree of warmth of the milk is varied.

Friday, 5 September. This morning, tho' mild, the curd came exactly at 80°! What an accuracy of judgement here appears to be displayed! Let the state of the air be what it will, we find the heat of the whey, when the curd is sufficiently coagulated, exactly 80°. and this, without the assistance of a thermometer, or any other artificial help. But what will not daily practice, natural good sense, and minute attention accomplish.

Saturday, 6 September. This morning the curd came too quick. The heat of the whey (after the curd had been broken and was settled) full 85°! The curd "much tougher and harder than it should be." Here we have a proof of the inaccuracy of the senses; and of the insufficiency of the natural judgement in the art under consideration: it may frequently *prove to be right*; but never can be *certain.* Some scientific helps are evidently necessary to UNIFORM SUCCESS.

6. THE

6. THE MANAGEMENT OF THE CURD.—
This ſtage of the proceſs has five diſtinct operations belonging to it.

   1. Breaking.
   2. Gathering.
   3. Scalding.
   4. Vatting.
   5. Preſerving ſpare curd.

1. *Breaking.* Here new ideas pour in.—
The curd, while ſuſpended in the whey, is
never touched with the hands*. The curd is
broken, or rather cut, with the triple " cheeſe
knife," which has been deſcribed. This
mode of ſeparating the curd and whey, tho'
not univerſal, appears to be highly eligible:
the intention of it is that of " keeping the fat
in the cheeſe:" a matter which, in the manufacture of two-meal cheeſe, is of the firſt
conſideration. The opera tion is performed
in this manner.

The knife is firſt drawn its full depth acroſs
cowl in two or three places; and likewiſe
round

* In another dairy, however, whoſe manager ranks high
among dairywomen, the curd is broken with the hands
alone; in the manner deſcribed in NOAF; ICON:

round by the fides; in order to give the whey an opportunity of efcaping as clear as may be. Having ftood five or ten minutes, the knife is more freely ufed: drawing it brifkly in every direction, until the upper part of the curd be cut into fmall checquers. The bottom is then ftirred up with the difh, in the left hand; and, while the lumps are fufpended in the whey, they are cut with the knife, in the right: thus continuing to ftir up the curd with the difh, and feparate the lumps with the knife, until not a lump larger than a bean is feen to rife to the furface.

2. *Gathering.* The curd having been allowed about half an hour to fettle in, the whey is laded off, with the difh; paffing it through a hair fieve into fome other veffel.

The principal part of the whey being laded off, the curd is drawn to one fide of the cowl, and preffed hard with the bottom of the difh: the fkirts and edges cut off with a common knife, and the cuttings laid upon the principal mafs; which is carried round the tub, among the remaining whey, to gather up the fcattered fragments that lie among it. The whole being collected, the whey is

all

all laded or poured off, and the curd left in one mafs, at the bottom of the cowl.

3. Scalding. It is, I believe, the invariable practice of the dairywomen of Glocefter-fhire, to *fcald the curd* *. This accounts for their running the milk fo comparatively cool. Were the delicate cool-run curd of this diftrict to be made into cheefe, without previoufly fcalding, the cheefes made from it would require an inconvenient length of time to fit them for market.

The method of fcalding the curd, here, varies from that mentioned in the Economy of Norfolk. There it was fcalded in the mafs; pouring hot water over the furface, as it lay at the bottom of the cheefe-tub: but, here, the mafs is broken; firft by cutting it into fquare pieces with a common knife; and then reducing it, with the triple knife, into fmall fragments; moftly as fmall as peas: none of them is left larger than a walnut: and among thefe fragments the "fcalding ftuff" is thrown; ftirring them brifkly about; thereby effectually mixing them together; and, of courfe,

fcalding

* See NORF: ECON:

scalding the whole as effectually, and as evenly, as this method of scalding will admit of.

The *liquid* made use of here, for scalding curd, varies in different dairies. Some dairywomen scald with *whey*; violently objecting to water; while others use *water*; objecting with equal obstinacy to whey: while dairywomen in general, I believe, mix the two together [*].

The *quantity* is in proportion to the quantity of curd: enough to float the curd; and make the mixture easy to be stirred about with the dish.

Part of it is heated to near boiling heat; and this lowered with cold liquid TO A HEAT PROPORTIONED TO THE STATE OF THE CURD: soft curd is scalded with hot; hard curd with cooler liquid.

In scalding, therefore, the dairywoman has a remedy for any misjudgement her sense of feeling may have led her into, in the stage of coagulation: let the curd come too soft or too hard, she can bring it to the desired texture, by the heat of the scalding liquid. And here

---

[*] It seems to be understood, that different grounds require different kinds of scalding liquor.

here feems to hinge, principally, the fuperior fkill of the Glocefterfhire dairywoman: by running the milk cool, fhe can, in fcalding, correct any error, which has been committed in running.

Saturday, 6 September. This morning, the curd being too tough, the *whey* was ufed cooler than it was yefterday morning, when the curd was fufficiently tender. (See page 299.) Yefterday morning 140°. this morning 125°.

Tuefday, 9 September. This morning the curd came at its proper heat 80°. and the heat of the fcalding whey was 142°.

The curd being thoroughly mixed and agitated among the whey, and having had a few minutes to fubfide in,—the dairymaid began immediately to lade off the whey. This, however, is not the univerfal practice: in fome dairies the curd is fuffered to remain among the fcalding ftuff half an hour: thus (as has been obferved) there are *fhades of difference* in every ftage of the procefs.

Wednefday, 24 Sept. This morning, the cur dcame too tender; and the morning being cool; the fcalding whey was heated to 161°.

and

and ftood upon the curd near ten minutes: this changed it from a ftate of jelly as to foft-nefs, to the fame tough hard mafs it is always left after fcalding.

4. *Vatting.* The fcalding liquor being moftly laded off, a vat is placed on the cheefe ladder, laid acrofs the tub, and the curd crumbled into it with the hands, fcrupuloufly breaking every lump; fqueezing out the whey as the handfuls are taken up; and again pref-fing it with the hands in the vat; which is every now-and-then fet on-edge to let the whey run off.

The vat being filled as full and firmly as the hand alone can fill it; and rounded up high in the middle; a cheefe cloth is fpread over it, and the curd turned out of the vat into the cloth: the vat wafhed or rather dipped in the whey; and the inverted mafs of curd with the cloth under it, returned into the vat. The angles, formed by the bottom of the vat, are pared off and crumbled upon the top, with which they are incorporated by partially break-ing the furface, and rounded up in the mid-dle as before; the cloth folded over and tucked in; and the vat with its contents placed in the prefs. *

5. *Spare curd.* Preferving the overflowings of the laft vat of today's curd, to be mixed up with that of tomorrow, is a common practice in this country; where cheefes, if they be intended for the factors, are obliged to be made of fome certain fize: the vats are all nearly of the fame bignefs; and cannot be proportioned to the curd, as they may when vats of various fizes are made ufe of.

In the neighbourhood of Glocefter, when the quantity of fpare curd is confiderable, as four or five pounds; it is frequently made into a fmall cheefe for the Glocefter market; in which it may be fold, in a recent ftate (namely at three weeks to two months old,) for 2d.¼ to 3d.½ a pound; according to its

age:

---

* It is obfervable, that only one CHEESEBOARD is ufed, in the Glocefterfhire dairies, let the number of vats be what they may. The bottoms of the vats being made fmooth and even, they anfwer the purpofe of cheefeboards to each other——the uppermoft only requiring a board. No " finking boards" are ever made ufe of here, as they are in other diftricts; the vats being rounded up with curd in fuch a manner, as, from experience it is known, will juft fill them when fufficiently preffed.

. age : three pence a pound is the ordinary price, for fuch little two-meal cheefes.

When the quantity of fpare curd is fmall, or where the making of little cheefes is not practifed, the whey is preffed out and drained off as dry as may be, and the curd preferved in different ways. In the upper vale I have feen it put into an earthen veffel and covered with cold water. The next morning it is refcalded thoroughly once or twice ; broken as fine as poffible ; and either mixt evenly with the frefh curd ; or, lefs eligibly, put into the middle of a cheefe. *This*, however, is, with good reafon, objected to by the factors. A harfh, crumbly, ill tafted feam is formed in the middle of the cheefe ; a difagreeable circumftance, which, in cutting a cheefe, is too frequently met with. Mixing the ftale curd more evenly among the frefh has an effect almoft equally difagreeable : the particles of ftale curd ripen fafter than the reft of the cheefe ; which is thereby rendered unfightly and ill flavored.

In a fmall dairy it is impoffible to make cheefes fufficiently *fizeable* for the Glocefterfhire factors, and at the fame time avoid having,

X 2

ving,

ving, frequently, fpare curd. But in a large
dairy, where three or four cheefes are made
from one running, it might, by a proper number and affortment of vats, be generally
avoided; and the cheefes be at the fame time
made within fize.

7. THE MANAGEMENT OF THE CHEESES.
This requires to be fubdivided agreeably to
the different ftages of management.

1.   The management in the prefs.
2.   The management while on the dairy
        fhelves.
3.   The operation of cleaning.
4.   The management in the cheefe cham-
        ber.

1. *The management while in the prefs.*
Having ftood fome two or three hours in the
prefs, the vat is taken out; the cloth pulled
off and wafhed; the cheefling turned into the
fame cloth and the fame vat, (the cloth being
fpread under and folded over as before,) and
replaced in the prefs.

In the evening, at five or fix o'clock, it is
taken out of the prefs again, and *falted* in this
manner: the angles being pared off, if wanted,
the cheefling is placed on the inverted vat;

. and

and a handful of falt rubbed hard round its
edge; leaving as much hanging to it as will
ftick.   Another handful is ftrewed on the upper fide, and rubbed over it pretty hard;
leaving as much upon the top as will hang on
in turning.   It is now turned into the bare
vat, without a cloth; and, a fimilar quantity
of falt being rubbed on the other fide, is again
put into the prefs.

Next morning it is turned in the bare vat;
in the evening the fame; and, the fucceeding
morning, taken finally out of the prefs, and
placed upon the dairy fhelf.

Each cheefe therefore ftands forty eight
hours in the prefs.   At the fecond or third, it
is turned in the cloth: at the tenth, the cloth is
taken off and the cheefling falted.   At the
the twenty fourth, it is turned in the bare vat.
At the thirty fourth, the fame.   And at the
forty eighth finally taken out. *

2.   The

* SAGE CHEESE. The method of making "green
cheefe", in this diftrict, is the following. For a cheefe of
10 or 12 lb. weight, about two handfuls of fage and one of
marigold leaves and parfley, are bruifed and fteeped one
night

X 3

2. *The management on the dairy shelves.*
Here the " young cheeses" are turned every
day, or every two or three days, according to
the state of the weather, or the fancy or judgement of the dairywoman.   If the air be harsh
and dry, the window and door are kept shut,
as much as may be: if close and moist, as
much fresh air as possible is admitted.

3.   *Cleaning.*   Having remained about ten
days in the dairy (more or less according to the
space of time between the " washings") they
are cleaned; that is washed and scraped;
in this manner: a large tub of cold whey being
placed

night in milk. Next morning the greened milk is strained
off, and mixed with about one third of the whole quantity
to be run. The green and the white milks are then run feparately; keeping the two curds apart until they be ready
for vatting. The method of mixing them depends on the
fancy of the maker. Some crumble the two together,
mixing them evenly and intimately. Others break the
green curd into irregular fragments, or cut it out in regular
figures with tins for this purpose. In vatting it the fragments, or figures, are placed on the outfides. The bottom
of the vat is first let with them; crumbling the white, or
yellowed, curd among them. As the vat fills, others are
placed at the edges; and the remainder buried flush with
the top. The after-treatment is the same as that of " plain
cheeses."

placed on the dairy floor, the cheefes are taken from the fhelves and immerged in it;
letting them lie perhaps, an hour or longer,
until the rind become fufficiently fupple.
They are then taken out, one by one, and
fcraped, with a common cafe-knife, fomewhat blunt; guiding it judicioufly with the
thumb placed hard againft its fide, to prevent
its injuring the yet tender rind: continuing
to ufe it, on every fide, until the cloth marks
and every other roughnefs be done away;
the edges, more particularly, being left with
a polifhed neatnefs. Having been rinced in the
whey and wiped with a cloth, they are formed
into an open pile (in the manner raw bricks are
ufually piled) in the dairy window, or other
airy place, to dry: and from thence are removed into the cheefe chamber.

4. *The management in the cheefe chamber.*—
The FLOOR is generally PREPARED, by rubbing it with bean-tops, potatoe halm, or other
green fucculent herbage, until it appear of a
black wet colour. If any dirt or roughnefs
appear upon the boards, it is fcraped off with
a knife; and the floor fwept clean with a hair
broom. The cheefes are then placed upon it,

X 4

regularly

regularly in rows: and kept turned, twice a
week; their edges wiped hard with a cloth,
once a week; and the floor cleaned, and rubbed with fresh herbs, once a fortnight.

The preparation of the floor is done with
the intention of encouraging the blue coat to
rise*.   To the same intent, the cheeses are
not turned too frequently; for the longer they
lie on one side without turning, the sooner
the blue coat will rise.   If, however, they be
suffered to lie too long without turning, they
are liable to stick to the floor, and thereby receive injury.   If, by accident or otherwise,
the coat come partially, it is scraped off.——
This, however, seldom happens in a rich-
soiled country, and all the care and labour
requisite, in this stage, is to turn them twice
a week; wipe their edges, once a week; and
to prepare the floor, afresh, once a fortnight.
If the cheese chamber be too small to admit
of the whole being placed singly.   The oldest
are "doubled:" sometimes put "three or
four double."

It is striking to see how well cheeses of this
district bear handling at an early age: even at
the

* See Norf: Econ:

the time of wafhing, the dairymaid will frequently fet the cheefe fhe is fcraping, on-
edge upon another, lying flat on the table,
without injury. At a month old, they may
be thrown about as old cheefes. Their rinds
appear as tough as leather. This muft be
owing to the fcalding. It cannot be owing
to their poverty. They are evidently richer
" fatter" than the new milk cheefes of many
diftricts.

8. MARKETS for CHEESE in the upper vale.
In large dairies, cheefe is here fold and deli-
vered three times a year, namely in July;—
again at Michaelmas; and finally in the fpring.
In fmall dairies, only twice: about the latter
end of September, and again in the fpring.

It is bought principally by cheefe factors,
who live in or near the diftrict. The fame
factor generally has the fame dairy, year after year; frequently without feeing it, and,
perhaps, without any bargain having been
made, previous to its being fent in. There
is, indeed, a degree of confidence on the part
of the buyer and feller, which we feldom
meet with among country dealers. Millers
and malfters buy by fample, and generally
take

take care to make a clofe bargain, before the corn be fent in.

In fummer and early autumn, the factors will take them down to fix weeks old; provided they be found firm marketable cheefes; that is neither broken nor " hove :" a defect, which even the beft dairywomen cannot always prevent. During winter, provided their coats be perforated to give the internal air an opportunity of efcaping, the fwoln cheefes will generally go down, and, in the fpring, become marketable.

The *confumption* of twomeal cheefe is chiefly, I believe, in the manufacturing diftricts of this and other counties. Some of it goes to the London market; where it is probably fold under the denomination of Warwickfhire cheefe: and fome is faid to go to foreign markets. The *fize* moftly " tens"—that is, ten to the hundred weight; or 11 to 12lb. each.

The *price* of twomeal cheefe varies with that of newmilk cheefe. At Barton fair, in 1783*, the " beft making" fold from 34s.

(to

* BARTON FAIR. A fair held annually on the 28th of September, in Barton-ftreet, Gloucefter. It has long been

the

(to the factors by the waggon load together) to 36s. (to families who bought by the hundredweight). " Two-meal," from 28s. to 29s. 6d. by the cwt. of 112lb. In 1788, " beſt making" 30s. down to 27s. " Two-meal" 25s. down to a guinea. Prices, which have not been heard of for many years paſt.

IV. WHEY BUTTER. It is the invariable practice of this diſtrict to ſet whey for cream. The lower claſs of People eat ſcarcely any other than whey butter. With due cleanlineſs and proper management, it may be made perfectly palatable; and, in every reſpect, preferable (while quite freſh) to the milk butter of ſome lean-ſoiled diſtricts.

The whey is, here, generally ſet in one large tub: not parcelled out, thin, like milk.

The

the principal cheeſe fair of the diſtrict. Formerly a principal part of the cheeſe, made in the two vales, was brought to this fair. At preſent, it is moſtly bought up by factors previous to the fair. In 1783, there were about twenty waggon loads (beſides a number of horſe loads) expoſed for ſale in the fair. Some bought by factors; but principally, I believe, by the houſe-keepers, and the retail dealers of the neighbourhood. In 1788, the quantity in the market was much greater; about forty loads; cheeſe being then a drug.

The management of whey butter is fimilar to that of milk butter. The price about two thirds of that of milk butter in the fame market.

33.

S W I N E.

I. BREED. The tall, long, *white* breed, which was formerly, perhaps, the prevailing breed of the ifland, is here ftill confidered as the " true Glocefterfhire breed."——- They grow to a great fize. At prefent, the *Berkfhire*, and a crofs between thefe two breeds, are the prevailing fpecies. The Berkfhire are thought to be " hardier ;" but are objected to, 'as being thicker-rinded, than the old white fort. A mixture of *oriental* blood, is likewife difcoverable in this diftrict ; but lefs, here, than in any other diftrict I have obferved in.

II. BREEDING,

II. Breeding, &c. Some are bred in the diftrict: others *purchafed* at Glocefter market; probably the beft fwine-market in the king-dom. Seldom lefs than three or four hun-dred in an ordinary market. Moft of them large grown hogs: many of them worth from fifty fhillings to three pounds a head. Brought by dealers from Herefordfhire, Shropfhire, &c. Some of the fmaller are bought by dai-rymen; the larger by dealers for the diftil-leries of Briftol and London.

.. III. The food of store fwine is princi-pally whey, mixt with buttermilk, and given to them in a ftale acidulated ftate.—This, however, is not invariably obferved: it is not unfrequently carried to them imme-diately from the dairy. While young, efpe-cially when recently weaned, they have fre-quently the " fweet whey" immediately from the cheefe cowl; without having been pre-vioufly fet for butter.

IV. The proportion of swine to a given number of cows varies in the upper vale, where dairying and tillage are mixed in various proportions.—The fubject is, indeed, in any cafe a vague one: the *number* depending on

the

the *size*. The only general rule observed is, to endeavour to have always such a *quantity* as the dairy will keep *well*: it being esteemed bad management to overstock a dairy farm with swine.

V. The materials of FATTING are whey, with beans crushed or whole; or with pea-beans; but seldom with peas alone.

VI. The MARKETS FOR BACON, are the manufactories of this and the neighbouring counties: the chief, I believe, is the "cloathing country,"—the woollen manufactory, in the Stroudwater district of this county.

LIST

LIST of RATES.

VALE OF GLOCESTER.

BUILDING MATERIALS, &c.

OAK TIMBER 1s. to 20d. a foot.
Elm ————— 7d. to 10d. ——.
Clamp-burnt bricks 15 to 16s. a thousand
Slag, (copper drofs*) 5 or 6s. a ton, on
the Kays.

Stone

---

* "SLAG." This, I underſtand, is the *ſcoria* thrown off
by copper, in the procefs of fmelting. Until of late years,
it was caſt away as waſte, or uſed as a material of roads,
only. Now, it is thrown, while hot, into moulds of different figures and dimenſions, and thus becomes an admirable building material. It is proof againſt all feafons,
in every ſituation; confequently becomes an excellent material for foundations; and ſtill more valuable for copings
of fence walls: for which ufe it is fometimes caſt of a ſimi-
elliptical form. It is alfo uſed as quoins, in brick buildings; in which cafe the blocks are run about nine inches

ſquare

Stone floors—(laid down) 4d. to 5d. a square foot.

Lime—6d. to 8d. a bushel.

Dimensions of bricks 9—4¼—2¼ inches.

——————— of plain-tiles 12 by 7¼ inches.

Journeymen carpenter's wages 22d. a-day.

——————— bricklayer's ——— 22d. a-day.

BLACKSMITH's WORK.

Common heavy work 4d. a lb.

Shoing 5d.—Remove 1d.

TEAM LABOUR.

Hire of a team (waggon, five horses, man and boy) 10s.

Price of plowing 6 to 9s. an acre.

——————— harrowing 2 to 3s. an acre.

YEARLY WAGES.

Head man 7 to 9 or 10l.

Second man 5 to 7l.

Boy 2 to 4l.

Dairymaid 3 to 5l.

Undermaid 50s. to 3l.

DAY

square, and eighteen inches long. It is of a dark copper colour; and has the appearance of a rich metal; but flies under the hammer as flint.

DAY WAGES.

In winter, 1s. a day and drink.

In hay harveft, 14d. to 18d.—mowers not lefs than 18d. fometimes more, with drink.

In corn harveft, 1s. a day, or 30s. for the harveft, with full board; or 2s. 6d. to 3s. a day, with drink, but no board.

Women, in autumn and fpring, 6d. a day; but are feldom employed by the day in thefe feafons; drefling grafslands being generally done by the job.

————, in hay harveft, 6d. to 8d. a day, and drink.

————, in corn harveft, 1s. a day, to thofe who will work : but women in this country, as in moft others, prefer " leafing" to reaping.   See YORK. ECON. i, 387.

TAKEN WORK.

Breaft plowing a pea ftubble, 6s. an acre.
Setting beans 16d. to 18d. a bufhel.
Hoing ———— about 6s. an acre.
Hoing wheat, 2s. to 4s. an acre.

VOL. I.   Y   Reaping

Reaping wheat about 5s. an acre and drink.

Mowing barley ; according to the crop.

Thrashing wheat, 3d. to 4d. a bushel (9$\frac{1}{2}$ gallons.)

———— barley, 2d. to 3d.

———— Beans about 1$\frac{1}{2}$d.

Mowing upgrounds 18d. and drink.

Mowing meadows 16d. to 18d.

Agistment price, in the hams, for one horse, or two cows, or six sheep, 25 to 30s. From Mayday to Michaelmas, or later. The hazard of floods is certainly an additional price: nevertheless, considering the superior quality of the land, it is low in the extreme.

P R O.

PROVINCIALISMS

OF THE

VALE of GLOCESTER.

THE VERBAL PROVINCIALISMS
of this diſtrict appear to be leſs numerous than
thoſe of many other provinces.   I have, however, had leſs converſation with mere provin-
cialiſts, in this, than in other diſtricts I have
reſided in. Beſides, it is obſervable, the lower
claſs of people, here, are leſs communicative
than they are, perhaps, in any other province:
poſſeſſing a ſingular reſervedneſs toward ſtran-
gers; accompanied with a guardedneſs of ex-
preſſion, bordering almoſt on duplicity: affording thoſe who are obſervant of men and
manners, in the lower walks of life, ſubject
for reflection.

WORDS, which relate immediately to RU-
RAL AFFAIRS, I have endeavoured to collect.

Y 2

But

But I find they are few in number, compared with thofe collected in Norfolk and Yorkſhire on the fame ſubject. Indeed, a liſt of technical terms require a length of time, or the immediate ſuperintendance of workmen, to render it complete.

Befide the deviations which are merely *verbal*, this quarter of the iſland affords, among others, one ſtriking deviation in GRAMMAR;—in the uſe, or abuſe, of the pronouns. The perſonal pronouns are ſeldom uſed in their accepted ſenfe: the nominative and the accuſative caſes being generally reverſed. Thus *her* is almoſt invariably uſed for *ſhe*;—as " her ſaid ſo"—" her would do it": ſometimes *he* for *ſhe*;—as " he was bulled"—" he calved"; and almoſt invariably for *it*;—all things inanimate being of the maſculine gender. Befide theſe and various other miſapplications (as *they* for *them*—*I* for *me*, *&c.*) an extra pronoun is here in uſe;—*ou*: a pronoun of the ſingular number;—analogous with the plural *they*;—being applied either in a maſculine, a feminine, or a neuter ſenfe. Thus " ou wull" expreſſes either *he* will, *ſhe* will, or *it* will.

This

This mifufe of the pronouns is common to the weſtern counties of England and to Wales; a circumſtantial evidence, that the inhabitants of the weſtern ſide of the iſland are deſcended from one common origin. But in another ſtriking deviation; the PRONOUNCIATION of the CONSONANTS; their propenſities of ſpeech are ſo diametrically oppoſite; and ſo different from any tendency of utterance, obſervable in the reſt of the iſland; one might almoſt declare them deſcendants of two diſtinct colonies.

In Glocefterſhire, Wiltſhire, Somerfetſhire &c, the ASPERATE conſonants are pronounced with VOCAL POSITIONS: thus ſ becomes z; f, v; t, d; p, b &c. On the contrary, in Wales, the conſonants, which, in the eſtabliſhed pronounciation, are accompanied with VOCAL POSITIONS, are there ASPERATED: hence z becomes ſ; b, p; d, t &c; —the mouth of the Severn being the boundary between theſe two remarkable propenſities of ſpeech.

In the PRONOUNCIATION of VOWELS this diſtrict, as Yorkſhire, has ſome *regular* deviation from the eſtabliſhed language; but differing

Y 3

ſering

fering, almoft totally, from thofe which are there obfervable: thus the *a* flender becomes *i* or *aoy*; as *bay*, " high" or " aoy"; *ftay*, " fty" or " zdoy"; *fair* " fire" or " voir"; *ftare* " ftire" or " zdoir" &c. The *e* long fometimes becomes *eea*; as *beans*, " beeans": the *i* long, *ey* (the *e* fhortened by the *y* confonant); as *I*, " ey"; *ride*, " reyd": the *o* long changes here, as in the middle dialect of Yorkfhire, into *ooa*; as *bome*, " hooam" or " worn";—the *u* long into *eeaw*; as *few*, " feeaw",—*dew*, " deeaw.

There are other deviations, both in grammar and pronounciation; as *be* is generally ufed for *is*; frequently *do* for *does*; and fometimes *bave* for *bas*. But thofe already mentioned are, I believe, the moft noticeable, and in the moft common ufe: I therefore, proceed to explain fuch PROVINCIAL TERMS IN HUSBANDRY as have occurred to my knowledge in this diftrict.

BLOWS

B.

BLOWS ; bloſſoms of beans &c.
  To BOLT ; to truſs ſtraw.
BOLTING ; a truſs of ſtraw.
BRAIDS ; pronounced " brides ;" ſee vol. ii. p. 283.
BROWN CROPS ; pulſe ; as beans, peas, &c.
BUTTER LEAVES ; ſee p. 285.

C.

CALFSTAGES ; ſee p. 225.
CARNATION GRASS ; *aira cæſpitoſa* ; haſſock
  or turfy air graſs ; tuſſock graſs.
CHARLOCK ; *ſinapis nigra* ; the common muſ-
  tard, in the character of a weed.
CHEESE LADDER ; ſee p. 268. .
CLAYSTONE ; a blue and white limeſtone, dug
  out of the ſubſoil of the vale.
COURT ; yard ; particularly the yards, in which
  cattle are penned in winter.
COWGROUND ; cow paſture.
COWL ; milk cooler ; cheeſe-tub.
CRAZEY ; the *ranunculus* or crowfoot tribe. See
  note p. 178.
CREAM SLICE ; ſee p. 269.
CUD ; a cattle crib.

D.

DAIRYHOUSE, or DEYHOUSE, pronounced
DYE-HOUSE; (from *dey* an old word for milk,
and *houfe*);—the milk houfe, or dairyroom.

DILL; *ervum birfutum*; two-feeded tare; which
has been cultivated (on the Cotfwold hills at leaft)
time immemorial! principally for hay.

E.

ELBOWS; the fhoulder points of cattle.

EVERS (that is heavers); opening fliles. See p. 41.

EVERY YEAR's LAND; fee p. 65.

F.

FALLOW FIELD; common field, which is occafionally fallowed: in diftinction to " every year's
land."

FODDERING GROUND; fee p. 230.

G.

GREEN; grafsland: " all green"—all grafs; no
plowland.

GROUND; a grafsland inclofure, lying out of the
way of floods; contradiftinct from " meadow."

HACKLES;

H

HACKLES; finglets of beans: fee page 151.

To HAIN; to fhut up grafsland from flock.

HAIRIF; *galium aparine*; cleavers.

HALLIER; fee to HAUL.

HAM; a flinted common pafture for cows, &c.

To HAUL; to convey upon a waggon or cart, as hay, corn, or fuel: proper, but provincial: hence HALLIER; one who hauls for hire.

To HELM; to cut the ears from the ftems of wheat, previous to thrafhing. The unthrafhed ftraw being called " helm". Not a common practice here.

HIT; a plentiful crop of fruit

HOVE; fwoln as cheefes.

K.

KNOT; polled; hornlefs; fpoken of fheep and cattle.

L.

To LANDMEND; to adjuft the furface, with a fpade or fhovel, after fowing wheat; chopping the clods, lowering the protuberances, and filling up the hollows.

To

To LEASE (pronounced leeze) to glean : a term, which is common to the weftern and fouthern provinces.

LODE ; this feems to be an old word for *Ford* ; hence Wain Lode——Upper Lode——Lower Lode St. Mary de Lode &c.

LUG or LOG ; a land meafure of fix yards ; that is, a *rod, pole,* or *perch* of fix yards ; a meafure, by which ditching &c. is done: alfo the flick, with which the work is meafured.

M.

MEADOW ; generally, common mowing ground, fubject to be overflowed ; or any low flat grafsland, which has not been plowed, and is ufually mown ; in contradiftinction to " ground" and " ham."

MINTS ; mites.

MISKIN ; the common term for a dunghill ; or a heap of compoft.

MOP ; a ftatute, or hiring day for farmer's fervants.

MOUNDS ; field fences of every kind.

N.

NAST ; foulnefs ; weeds in a fallow.

NESH ; —the common term, for tender or *wafhy*, as fpoken of a cow or horfe.

O.

OXEY ; ox-like ; of mature age ; not " fteerifh."

PAILSTAKE ;

P.

PAILSTAKE ; fee p. 268.

PEASIPOUSE : peas and beans grown together as a crop.

POLTING LUG (that is, perhaps, *pelting rod*) a long flender rod ufed in beating apples &c. off the trees.

Q.

QUAR ; the common term for quarry.

R.

RAMMELY ; tall and rank ; as beans.

RUNNING ; rennet ; the coagulum ufed in cheef-making.

S.

SEGS ; *carices*; fedges.

To SET ; to lett, as land &c.

SETTING PIN ; dibble ; fee p. 144.

SH (without a vowel) gee ; in the horfe language.

SHARD ; a gap in a hedge ; the common term.

SHEPPECK : the ordinary name of a prong, or hay fork.

SIDDOW ; vulgarly ZIDDOW ; peas, which become foft by boiling, are faid to be " fiddow"; a well founding term, which is much wanting in other diftricts. " Will you warrant them fiddow" ? is the ordinary queftion afked on buying peas for boiling.

SKEEL ; fee p. 269.

SLAG ;

SLAG ; copper-drofs. See p. 319.
STEERISH : fpoken of a young, raw, growing ox ;
   not " oxey."

T.

THREAVE ; twenty four boltings.
TUCKIN ; a fatchel ufed in fetting beans, fee 144.
TWO-MEAL CHEESE ; fee p. 287.

V.

VELL ; a calf's bag or ftomach, ufed in making
   " running."

W.

WAIN ; an ox cart, without fide rails.
WHITE CROPS ; corn : as wheat, barley &c,
WITHY ; *falix* ; the willow.
WUNT ; a mole ; hence
WUNT HILLOCKS ;—mole hills,

Y.

YAT or YATE ; a gate. This appears to have
   been once the univerfal name, and ftill remains
   the heraldic term, for a gate.

END OF THE FIRST VOLUME,

ALSO, *(in two Volumes Octavo,)*

THE

RURAL ECONOMY

OF

NORFOLK.

These volumes are published in pursuance of a
PLAN FOR PROMOTING AGRICULTURE, by collecting the ESTABLISHED PRACTICE OF SUPERIOR
HUSBANDMEN, in different districts of the island; a
plan, which is described in a preface to these volumes;
and which is farther explained in the advertisement
prefixed to the present volumes.

The MANAGEMENT OF ESTATES, including rent
and covenants, leases, buildings, fences, and planting: the ARABLE MANAGEMENT; particularly with
respect to marl, tillage, wheat, barley, turneps, and
buckweet. The MANAGEMENT OF STOCK; more
especially the method of fatting bullocks with turneps
abroad in the field, as practised in East Norfolk, are
severally treated of.

To this detail of the practice of the best-cultivated
district of the county is added, a series of MINUTES,
on various branches of rural knowledge.

ALSO, *(in two Volumes Octavo,)*

THE

RURAL ECONOMY

OF

YORKSHIRE.

These volumes are in continuation of the same
plan: including the three branches of rural economics; namely, the MANAGEMENT OF ESTATES,
PLANTING, and HUSBANDRY; as practised in the

more

more agricultural diftricts of this county. With a geographical defcription, of the county at large, and with a fhaded map, fhowing at fight its natural furface, as divided into mountain, upland, and vale.

The fubjects more particularly treated of in thefe volumes are—the inclofing of commonable property (an interefling and important fubject, whofe principles are here inveftigated and explained.) Drinking pools; roads; hedges; woodlands. Clearing rough grounds from the roots of trees and fhrubs, and fod-burning or breaft plowing fully explained, and rendered applicable to the improvement of the royal waftes: the draining and improvement of low grounds: lime, as a manure, amply treated of: corn weeds and their extirpation: vermin and their deftruction. The dog confidered as a fpecies of vermin, and an object of taxation: the probable evils of paper money, and the impropriety of its being fuffered to be *coined* by country bankers. Raifing frefh varieties or forts of wheat. The cultivation of rape or cole feed. Raifing frefh varieties or forts of potatoes, and their cultivation with the plow. The cultivation of raygrafs and faintfoin; and the ancient and modern methods of laying land down to grafs: The management of grafsland; particularly the management of pafture grounds and aftergrafs. The breeding, &c. of horfes. The breeds and points of different defcriptions of cattle and fheep. The rabbit warrens of the Wolds.— The improvements of the Morelands. With a copious gloffary, and prefatory obfervations concerning the provincial language of Eaft Yorkfhire.

547029